PRAISE FOR

Born of No Woman

"*Born of No Woman* is a dazzling, heart-wrenching tale of cruelty and mercy, secrets and horrors. The novel is deeply immersive, gothic, and taut with dread; the prose sings and the characters burn in the heart. Easily my favorite book of the year. Not to be missed."
            —Kim Taylor Blakemore, bestselling author of *After Alice Fell*

"One of the most disturbing yet lyrically exquisite novels I've read in a long time. The poetic and pastoral beauty of the nineteenth-century French countryside is vividly contrasted with the often-brutal treatment of breeding livestock on the farms—which in its turn mirrors the treatment of the fourteen-year-old Rose when she is sold by her poor father to the master of a manor. Once enslaved in her new home, Rose is tormented and abused, soon forced to contemplate the horrors concealed within some hidden chambers where she discovers the true fate of her master's absent wife. Brave, sometimes horrific, *Born of No Woman* is one of the most compelling novels I have read in many years. Infused with lurid elements of the most gothic fairy tales, it explores the darkest realms of human sexuality."   —Essie Fox, author of *The Last Days of Leda Grey*

"A haunting, suspenseful gothic tale set in nineteenth-century France that weaves many layers, from the plight of women in that era to class distinctions that lead to oppression of the vulnerable. The story also challenges ethical and religious boundaries of what might be considered justifiable responses from those who suffer relentless cruelty. The tragic Rose arrives at the home of a wealthy man and his mother. Immediately, their cruel welcome is ominously coupled with the mysterious, sickly wife who is locked in a room that Rose is forbidden to ever enter. Betrayed at every turn by her father, her employer, and her lover, Rose endures a string of abuses. She finds the strength to fight back and retain her sanity. Ultimately, this is a book of hope and the resilience of the human spirit to overcome tragedy. The narrative is elegant, and the viewpoint of every character is compelling and credible. Highly recommended!"

—Debbie Herbert, *USA Today* and *Washington Post* bestselling author of *Not One of Us* and *Cold Waters*

"Here, everything is epiphanic, essential, surprising, whether it be the revelation of a secret or the painting of a detail…At once classic and phantasmagoric, *Born of No Woman* proves that fiction…can still amaze."
—*Le Monde des livres*

"A vivid, mesmerizing tale."
—*L'Express*

"Rare are those who, like Franck Bouysse, manage to write the indescribable, to touch the unspeakable, with so much subtlety and intensity. In spite of the severity and darkness of certain pages, *Born of No Woman* is a deeply moving and luminous book."

—*La Libre*

BORN OF NO WOMAN

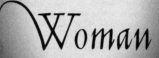

Born
OF NO
Woman

FRANCK BOUYSSE

Translated from the French by Lara Vergnaud

Other Press
NEW YORK

Originally published in 2019 as *Né d'aucune femme* by La Manufacture de livres, Paris
Copyright © Franck Bouysse, La Manufacture de livres, 2019
Published by arrangement with Marie-Pacifique Zeltner, Agence Bibemus
English translation copyright © Lara Vergnaud, 2021

Production editor: Yvonne E. Cárdenas
Text designer: Jennifer Daddio / Bookmark Design & Media Inc.
This book was set in Centaur and Tagliente
by Alpha Design & Composition of Pittsfield, NH.

1 3 5 7 9 10 8 6 4 2

Library of Congress Cataloging-in-Publication Data
Names: Bouysse, Franck, 1965- author. | Vergnaud, Lara, translator.
Title: Born of no woman / Franck Bouysse ; translated from the
French by Lara Vergnaud.
Other titles: Né d'aucune femme. English
Description: New York : Other Press, [2021] | Originally published in 2019 as
Né d'aucune femme by La Manufacture de livres, Paris.
Identifiers: LCCN 2021009435 (print) | LCCN 2021009436 (ebook) |
ISBN 9781635420227 (paperback) | ISBN 9781635420234 (ebook)
Classification: LCC PQ2702.O9845 N413 2021 (print) |
LCC PQ2702.O9845 (ebook) | DDC 843/.92—dc23
LC record available at https://lccn.loc.gov/2021009435
LC ebook record available at https://lccn.loc.gov/2021009436

"Nature never rhymes her children."

RALPH WALDO EMERSON

*"If it were a question of words, if it were sufficient to set down
one word and one could turn away in the calm consciousness of
having entirely filled this word with oneself."*

FRANZ KAFKA

*"I was not bowing to you,
I was bowing to all human suffering."*

FYODOR DOSTOEVSKY

The Man

He was somewhere far away, farther than the hands of my watch could reach.

It hasn't happened yet. He knows nothing of the confusion. The smells of spring hang in the cool morning air, the smells first, always, smells stained with color, in shades of green, floral anarchy on the verge of explosion. Then come the sounds, noises, cries, the telling, revealing, disrupting, the falling apart. There's blue in the sky and shadows on the ground, they stretch the forest and extend the horizon. And it's not much at all, because there's also everything that can't be named, expressed, not without the risk of leaving behind the core of an emotion, a feeling in all its grace. Words are nothing against this, they're everyday garments, fancier on occasion, donned to mask the skin's deep and intimate landscape; words, an invention by man to measure the world.

At the time, I was no longer expecting anything else in my life.

Quiet the words. Let things come. All that remains then is naked skin, smells, colors, noises, and silences.

I'd stopped making up stories long before.

The stories we tell, the ones we tell ourselves. Stories are just houses with paper walls, and the wolf is prowling.

I had given up on ever leaving… After all, where would I go?

Returns are never peaceful, always fed by the reasons for departing. Both the leaving and the coming back, whether willing or by force, weigh heavy.

The sun was chasing away the white frost.

The monstrous sun seeps, duplicating the forms it strikes and betrays, outlining large shadow cathedrals empty of substance. It's the season.

I never saw it. How could I have guessed?

He knows this place as more than a memory. Something speaks beneath his skin, a language he doesn't yet understand.

How could I have imagined who he was?

It's high time that the shadows confessed.

The Child

He moves across the grounds, feet bare, arms slightly apart from his body, hunching over, hesitation in his step; advancing straight ahead, as if in a corridor so narrow it's impossible for him to deviate from an imaginary line. He's not yet five, his birthday is in seven days. The date is underlined in a calendar in the large sitting room.

A frail figure warmed by the rays of a sun that's always been forbidden him, "to protect your skin," the old lady repeats without further explanation; but aren't interdictions made to be broken, and even ransacked, trampled, destroyed, so that others may emerge, more unbreakable still and above all more tempting? He proves himself no exception as he walks down the path. At first he winces when gravel encrusts itself in the tender soles of his feet, then he stops feeling anything, too absorbed by this freedom he's been dreaming of, day in, day out, usually planted behind the large closed windows with their perfectly transparent panes, playing innocent, holding a picture book or some object intended to stave off boredom.

The shade of the trees doesn't reach him. This makes him happy, the feel of his skin shivering at contact with the unfiltered light. The women didn't see him leave the vast manor that resembles a castle. It's the first time he's escaped their vigilance; he's long been preparing for this, so as not to miss his chance. He doesn't turn around, fearful of seeing someone running toward him, face draped in panic, someone who will give him a lecture and bring him back at once to that suffocating womb of stones. Her, the old lady. So he doesn't look back, appeals to some childhood version of God to keep them away, long enough for him to attain his heart's most fervent desire. Of course, he's too young to understand space and time; he only understands freedom and this thing opening up before him: an immense door, without panels or fittings or hinges or locks, or even the shadow of a door.

He's almost made it, just needs to extend his arm. This time it's a real door, made of solid wood. "Dear Lord, if you let me reach him, I'll belong to you forever"; he makes this vow out loud. And, as he prepares to open the door, his heart

stops beating. A noise from above, amplified by fear. Cooing.
It's just a pigeon moving back and forth across a roof tile in
search of debris amassed by the night's rain. His heart once
again pumps blood and sends it back out fortified. Time and
all that's happening inside take on meaning, even the disor-
der has meaning.

He lifts the handle and pulls the door toward him with
all his strength, using both his small hands with groomed
nails, to create a small opening just wide enough to slip his
body through sideways. He enters a long corridor divided into
stalls that are shingled below and barred with thick iron rails
above; he counts eight stalls in total. Emerging from dimness
bleared by the outside light, the horses nicker as they haugh-
tily watch the child, begging for some feed for form's sake by
moving their heads, more curious about the apparition than
about what they might obtain from it, not truly believing
that such a small creature could satisfy their demands. The
child observes the animals, seeks the one that, more than any
other, excites his young heart each time he sees it through
the windowpanes, parading beneath an expert rider, the man
that he is also forbidden to approach; two wedded silhouettes
on their nuptial march across the grounds, one beloved and
the other envied. Here it is. The revered animal. The child
lets time pass, he wants the horse to recognize him as he
recognized it at that first glance, which sent his heart galloping until exhaustion, until the very moment of their meeting.
Janus, he knows its name because he heard the old lady say
it; her son's favorite, she had told him one day while wiping

away a venomous tear. The child waits another few seconds. A gentle fear shudders beneath his skin, one of those delicate fears that lead to the unknown. He opens the stall door, enters, closes it, and stops there. The horse snorts, retreats, calms somewhat, motionless against the back wall; it looks like a jade stone buried in ordinary rock, a demonic sheath filled with burning fire. The child is nothing before the animal; he knows this, and yet he walks toward it, his bare feet treading on straw packed countless times by the prodigious creature, which proudly lifts its head and never completely lowers it. Now standing beneath its throat, the child lifts an arm, holds it as high as he can, and the tips of his fingers barely skim the base of the animal's chest.

Janus, known for its spirit and untamable character, the legacy of wild ancestors, raises one hoof, sets it down, and raises it again, higher each time, harder each time, ardently observing the child; and the pounding devours the space that just barely separates them. This isn't an expression of true rage but rather the hint of a bestial power. At this instant, the child should be terrified. He isn't. His eyes shine with pride in a proclamation of silent joy; then he lowers his head, closes his eyes. Waits. Waits for the inconceivable link to finally emerge, the time to give the animal the opportunity to spare him or send him into nothingness. Whatever happens next doesn't matter. This must be.

Gabriel

I aged, moved through time as an obedient and attentive voyager. I find myself still in the hands of the Lord, swathed in confusion. In truth, I never left his grasp, even if it seems to me that on many occasions he didn't know what to do with me. In my actions at least, I never betrayed him.

I remember the day I was granted the distinguished honor of serving the Church, under the aegis of Canon D. in the cathedral of T., soothed by the *veni creator* in the background of my profession of faith; in thoughts and in words, a hand on the Gospels as my signature: *So help me God and his holy saints.* I then kissed the altar's cold stone, offering my heart to the Passion of Christ. A kiss whose taste still returns when I feel the desire to remember, like any man pained by the present.

My parents would have liked me to ascend higher in the Church hierarchy, in any case higher than a simple pastoral mission. They are no longer around to give me grief about it, or to encourage more ambition than I have; gone too soon, as they say in such circumstances. I imagine that, since they named me Gabriel, they had the idea of charting a course from the beginning that would lead me directly to the priesthood. I still think of them often, differently than when they were alive, of course. Our conversations are calmer now, and I have to admit that they weren't wrong about everything, or right either.

I don't believe that I ever doubted the holy word. This isn't a question of God, but of the men and women with whom I have interacted throughout my life. Perhaps I should have become a monk, and thus been less obliged to endure their contact, the torments of their souls. I would have immersed myself in silence, occupied with praying, meditating, reading sacred texts, examining my conscience in the depths of the great mystery. A form of freedom far superior, in my mind, to a freedom that today strikes me as subjugated to my faith. The divine tax that I have paid day after day has never seemed so heavy as it does now, in this convergence where the human world and God's don't want to mix.

If I hadn't grown old, would I have felt this rising doubt that I ever lived up to my mission?

Is aging the only way to truly test one's faith?

I'm not an angel; even the most virtuous of men is only a man and cannot claim to be more. I have nothing in common with the blistered paintings of cherubs that adorn the church arches. They are not my idea of children. Those little angels who lose their wings as they grow up, with their opulent locks, too mature bodies, and indecent nudity, don't resemble mine. Every day I wait for the paint to crumble a little more and fall to pieces. I won't do anything to stop it. I never wanted to trouble these waters.

I am an echo, nothing more. I need to hear the words come out of my mouth; as if, through speech, I am hoping to discern a sign, or some buried symbol that will lead me back to God. This from a man who keeps silent, a man who silences even the abominable, because I swore, yes, swore to cast away this earthly body in order to purge my soul of all the wrongs confided in me, without ever absolving myself of the suffering of others, like the terrible story that I keep inside and that has been gnawing at me for so many years, that I could never share with anyone, because for that I would have needed a great friend, and also not to be a priest. My dedication to God stifles those feelings in which other, kindred people drape themselves. When you're bound by faith, you can't offer something you're unable to receive in return. I've seen many a man not survive that.

You have given me for a life a mere handbreadth. My time is nothing before you...Every man is but a breath, an image destined to disappear, a quivering shadow. I learned that only questions matter, that answers are nothing but certitudes weakened by the time that passes, that questions are the soul's domain and answers that of perishable flesh. I learned that every story feeds on its own mystery, especially when it hurts, and that we will suffer less when we are near to God, he promised us that. I wanted to repel my own pain to better shoulder that of others. The suffering of a single woman proved all I could bear.

My renunciation came willingly. It was never an effort to reserve myself for God through a life of prayer, meditation, spiritual readings, visits, and retreats. I was prepared for it. I wanted to deliver the holy word, relay it, make it comprehensible, be its interpreter in some way. The true effort, the immense difficulty, has always been to listen to my parishioners, to simply listen to them. Before I heard them give confession, I couldn't imagine the mission would be so difficult to carry out well. I didn't shy away from the sins and admitted lies, the betrayals and the intimate suffering. I absorbed them without ever betraying my vows, and never took any action of a kind to influence someone's destiny. Or nearly.

"Forgive me, Father, for I have sinned…" Words heard countless times, and just as many gentle pronouncements to utter in return. I sometimes dreamt of judging my parishioners more harshly, I admit, just as swiftly remembering that it is not my remit to pardon in my name, that only God has the power to forgive all sins. I merely listen to small secrets translated into individual transgressions that each day pile up in the common grave, with the other sins of the world. Then I recite my lesson.

"Forgive me, Father, for I have sinned...," an injunction that carries an apology. I recognize all their voices now. And so when I walk through the village and I encounter such and such a person with face averted in shame upon reading, or thinking they're reading, in me what I know of them and force myself to hide, I see them lower their head, as if they were asking my forgiveness once again, by no means certain that a single confession was enough to absolve them of their great sins. Did I say every voice? No, that's not true, there was one exception, one terrible exception.

I remember the "my Father...," but for the first time, there was no "forgive me"; there was nothing for a while, apart from shaky breathing. "I'm listening," I said. Another "my Father...," and that was it. For all that I had strained my memory, this thin voice was unknown to me. A woman, clearly. She then repeated, more distinctly, "my Father," as if she were flinging a jet of acid that could eat into stone and thus immortalize a scene; and in that way her "my Father" etched itself into an inaccessible place in my mind. She swallowed, her breathing quickened. I could sense emotion in her voice, physical exhaustion, or some spiritual burden about which I still knew nothing. Eyes fixed on the perforated partition, I waited for her to release the tension, in a silence disproportionate to the tiny space in which I was trying to sketch a profile amid the carved-out diamonds, making out an eyelid blinking at irregular intervals, the bridge of a nose pitched in shadow, a chin iridescent with specks of light, trembling lips that I imagined were being prodded by too many words to sort, in order to say the essential, drowning the useless ones to save the rest. "My Father…" again, in a calmer voice, not like a stranger driving new nails into the partition that separated us, but rather like someone trying to remove some. I looked away, to concentrate on the voice just barely veiled by the desire to be heard only by me, or perhaps and surely by him who would soon speak through my lips. I was wrong. "My Father, soon you will be asked to bless the body of a woman at the asylum." Then she stopped. I heard her catch her breath. I was afraid she would leave and moved closer to the partition.

"And what's so extraordinary about that?" I asked, not understanding why such a confession appeared to be demanding so much effort.

"It's not…"

She broke off. I squinted to better penetrate the darkness. Her skin looked extinguished, as if the pale light coming from the church had slid off the soft slopes of her face, a river that had abruptly dried up.

"Under her dress. That's where I hid them," she managed to say.

"What are you talking about?"

"The notebooks…"

"What notebooks?"

"Rose's," she added, as if it was obvious.

"Who is Rose?"

She wasn't listening to me.

"I don't want to be the only one who knows."

"And why not bring me these notebooks if they're so important to you?"

"They search us every time we leave. With you, they wouldn't dare..."

A footstep echoed on the stone floor. The woman froze. Several seconds went by in palpable tension.

"You'll do what I ask?" she said in a choked voice.

"Wait!"

"You'll do it?"

"Don't go yet."

"Tell me you'll do it."

"I will."

The curtain opened slightly, she cast a glance into the church, then left in all haste. Face glued to the partition, I barely had time between two rustles of cloth to glimpse a hooded silhouette walk briskly away without turning around. I exited the confessional as quickly as I could. No trace of her. Angèle was kneeling on a prie-dieu, head buried in her hands, like a shell intended to protect her from any distraction. I felt as if I was emerging from a dream. I turned back to sit in the confessional, futilely seeking proof that the woman had been here, wondering if the conversation had truly taken place. Future events would very quickly bring me a definitive answer.

I WAS TWENTY-EIGHT YEARS OLD at the time. I was readying myself to bless animals, fruit trees, unharvested crops, and not a single human. It was the day after the unknown woman's visit, three days before Ascension, and the first of the Rogations. I had left on foot at daybreak, with my sacristan Charles and a few children from Bible study.

We covered the whole parish, going from farm to farm, invoking divine protection for future harvests, reciting countless litanies, and invariably receiving in return an appropriate *ora pro nobis*: pray for us. These brave people of the earth always had something to offer us, food or drink, and some even that which they didn't have. During this period of rural prayers, it wasn't a question of being presumptuous enough to imagine liberating the world of misfortune but simply of communion; so that if a catastrophe were to occur in the future, it was always possible in retrospect to imagine worse. The suffering placed on our path is made to be endured, a way to test our grazed souls. I've always known that. The Fathers taught me that you can't gloss and shine a soul, that it's healed from the inside, that it's far more charitable to pardon a man buffeted by misfortune than to court one protected by birth and fortune. Virtue without merit is nothing more than a carnival disguise.

I spread the Good Word in this way, never faltering. When we were done that day, we went back to the village. The children returned to school chirping like chicks let out of the coop. It was time to prepare Low Mass with my sacristan. Charles and I had known each other for one year, since he'd entered my service. He was a young, intelligent man, enigmatic in many respects, of irreproachable loyalty, an orphan, and on top of that a mute. He had learned to read lips and communicated using a slate stuffed inside a haversack he

always had with him. Shortly after his arrival, he had confided in me that his parents had died of tuberculosis when he
was a child, and that he had then been placed with the Jesuits.
I wanted to ask him other questions about his background,
but seeing him withdraw, I quickly decided against it. I used
to surprise him sometimes, lost in his thoughts, absent from
the world surrounding him, meditating perhaps, leaving me
nothing to see but a sad exterior.

We hadn't yet finished our preparations when a man arrived at the church, in the gray uniform worn by the employees of the asylum located at the limits of my parish. He asked
me if I would come bless a body. The night and morning
gone by had nearly made me forget the unknown woman's
visit the previous day; the man abruptly revived my memory.
After a moment of hesitation, I told him that I would come
to the asylum as soon as was possible that afternoon.

Low Mass having concluded, I lunched on some walnuts
and a piece of fresh bread with cheese. Shortly after, Charles
came to alert me that the horse and cart were hitched and
that we could get on the road as soon as I wanted.

We left the presbytery at the sun's zenith. Normally I
would take advantage of the ride to admire the landscape,
but this time, thinking back to the woman's words, I wasn't
inclined for contemplation. Soon, the slate spire of the large
chapel appeared around a bend, emerging from abundant
vegetation, planted in a clear sky.

The asylum was a former monastery, converted thirty years
prior into a secular establishment for the mentally ill, lost

within a vast forest, surrounded by the high walls of an enclosure that gave it the appearance of a fortress. Everything began in the thirteenth century, during the reign of Philip Augustus and the papacy of Gregory IX. An unscrupulous lord in the region, who lived in a castle overlooking the Vézère Gorge, killed a priest from the neighboring abbey in cold blood. The clergyman had had the impudence to oppose the election of one of the lord's nephews as abbot. Shortly thereafter, the pope, hearing of the troubling matter, ordered the nobleman to atone for his crime in "a dazzling manner." The nobleman graciously complied by erecting a Carthusian monastery in the middle of the forest, as proof of both his redemption and his omnipotence. He first had a church built, which was extended by a large cloister connecting twelve identical cells intended to house monks. The pope, satisfied, granted his forgiveness. The matter was settled. The monastery prospered and grew for a little over a century, welcoming ever greater numbers of monks, who found there a perfect setting for meditation. However, the murderous folly of men would soon spread to this haven. War followed war. The monastery was destroyed and rebuilt on multiple occasions. Warned by the local farmers of imminent attacks, the monks would quickly take refuge in the many tunnels dug over the years, which led into the heart of the forest, and some even to the outskirts of the neighboring villages. Taking flight, they would carry their most precious relics with them. Then, once the pillaging was over and the warfarers at last gone, the monks would return to the ruined monastery, tirelessly re-erecting it. Their fate for five centuries.

At the beginning of the nineteenth century, with the order unable to maintain the monastery, the last monks left, hearts heavy. A rich benefactor who had become aware of deviant behaviors, owing to the severe mental problems afflicting one of his children, soon purchased the monastery to create a research facility to develop this then-burgeoning branch of medicine.

Having always been keen on history, I became fascinated, as soon as I arrived, with this region and the monastery's fate. I was able to gather numerous documents during my many trips to the diocese archives and the nearby towns. That year, my sacristan and I even succeeded in mapping the complex network of unused tunnels, which allowed us to eventually visualize the monastery and its surroundings as they were in their heyday.

The watchman had been told we were coming. He opened the heavy double gate for us, then we entered the grounds. On each previous visit, I had felt minuscule, a particle of something that no longer existed, as if crushed by some great buried mystery. Charles drove the horse and cart down the main pathway, past the chapel and the old monk cells, stopping before a large building. By then I knew perfectly the protocol to be followed. I descended alone and climbed the flight of narrow steps dipping in the middle up to the treatment building, which housed the office of the psychiatric doctor who ran the asylum. I turned down a corridor that smelled of waxed wood, then knocked at the door of the man in charge. I heard the barely audible sound of a voice. I entered. The man rose swiftly from his armchair.

"Hello, Father."

"Hello, Doctor," I said, approaching a desk littered with piles of folders.

"You came quickly."

"As always."

He gave a faint smile and placed his hands behind his back. He didn't offer me a seat, remaining standing as well. He was a portly man, in his forties, squeezed into an impeccably tailored three-piece suit. He was also wearing a blindingly white shirt buttoned to the collar, topped with a scarf that failed to cover, on the right, the tip of an ugly scar that resembled a hawk's talon. From a face hollowed by deep-set features emerged two small, bright eyes of a very pale, nearly transparent, blue, that seemed to grant no respite from the moment they landed on you. Despite his short stature, the man's confidence made for an imposing presence.

"May I see the deceased?" I asked.

"Of course. Wait for me here. I'll be back."

The doctor walked to the door, opened it, and disappeared without closing it. He returned a few seconds later, accompanied by a nurse. She greeted me with a curtsy, then led me to a small room adjoining the infirmary, which served as an occasional morgue. A coffin rested on a table. I went closer, making the sign of the cross, and saw the body of a tall, white-haired woman wearing a black dress. She didn't seem all that old. It was like her hair had prematurely whitened, as if, it would appear, provoked by intense emotion or else great fright. The dress went down to her ankles and her scrawny feet emerged like two small, incongruous growths. She looked to be in a peaceful slumber. As I observed her, the nurse stood across from me, on the other side of the coffin.

"Would you leave me alone with her for a moment?" I asked.

She took a long breath before answering me. "Of course, Father."

The voice ran me through. It was the one from the previous day in the confessional, I was sure of it. I contained my distress as best I could, eyes fixed on the dead woman.

"Is everything all right?"

I quickly turned around and found the asylum director in the doorway. I had forgotten he was there.

"Yes, everything's fine."

He cast an unequivocal glance at the nurse. "You're dismissed," he said curtly.

She came around the coffin, head down. The doctor entered the room to let her pass.

"I'd like to be alone with her," I said.

He hesitated for a moment, lightly touching his scar.

"Certainly," he said a few seconds later.

He exited grudgingly, leaving the door open. I waited for him to walk away. There was no time for indecision. I circled the coffin. Now on my guard, facing the door, I wouldn't be surprised again should the doctor reappear. I delicately grasped the bottom of the dress, careful not to touch the body. I slowly lifted the fabric, exposing the dead woman's legs. I felt as though I was committing sacrilege, but my desire to know was stronger. Then the notebooks appeared, as if birthed, folded in two and wedged between her knees. Not even opening them, I grabbed them and hurriedly hid them beneath my alb, secured with my belt. I immediately put the dress back in place and then wiped my forehead with the back of my sleeve.

I tried to concentrate on a prayer, despite the many conjectures blooming inside my poor mind, the result of the unlikely events that had unfolded in barely twenty-four hours' time. After this pause, which also allowed me to collect myself, I left the room, casting a final glance at the mysterious woman. A ray of light brightened her peaceful face, as if she was thanking me with a smile.

The doctor was waiting in the adjoining room. Seeing me approach, he brushed his scar again, several times, with his index finger, and placed his weight on his heels, then on the balls of his feet, in a rocking motion, before returning to neutral.

"When do you want to transport the body for burial?" I asked.

He opened the folds of his jacket and buried his thumbs in the side pockets of his vest, now watching me with a saddened look that read false.

"I don't think that there will be a religious funeral," he said. He shook his head, mouth pursed, before solemnly continuing: "She killed her child."

For a few seconds, I remained speechless at this declaration. I knew that human nature could sometimes reveal itself to be merciless, but I had never before been confronted with infanticide.

"Why not tell me that right away?"

"To respect a last wish made before a witness."

"How did it happen?" I asked.

"All I know is that she killed the child with her own hands, and after that madness never left her."

The doctor's attitude irked me. I didn't want to let him off so lightly after the way he had manipulated me.

"We have a burial plot for that kind of case," I said.

The doctor placed his hands behind his back, staring at me curiously.

"Are you sure?"

"When can you have the body transported?"

He reflected for a moment, as if he was expecting me to change my mind.

"As you like. Tomorrow morning."

"I need a name to engrave on the tombstone."

He sighed, lowered his head.

"There may be no point in giving her a name."

"What do you mean?"

"Who are we, either of us, to deprive a soul of its anonymity? A person who loses her reason, or self-awareness, is already on the path of souls, and it's not in my power to divert it in any way. Science can't do everything, contrary to your God."

He was clearly enjoying himself, trying to interpret my reactions with his small shining eyes.

"It would appear we're on the same side, then," I said.

"I'm not so sure. God's failings aren't held against him. It's only those of man that remain visible."

"To be sure, but I fear we're straying from the subject."

The lines of his face loosened like taut ropes giving way.

"She has no family left. Wouldn't it be laudable, charitable even, to do away with the thing linking her to her sin…meaning her name?"

The doctor was terribly quick-witted, always sidestepping to get out of a predicament.

"I won't leave without it."

"Rose. Her name was Rose, that's all I know," he finally, bitterly, admitted.

"Why so much mystery over a simple name?"

"I'm afraid you're confusing mystery and reticence, Father."

In one quick motion, he grabbed a watch from his vest pocket and checked the time.

"Professional imperatives, if you'll please excuse me," he said before guiding me to the door.

A breath of fresh air greeted me outside. Charles was waiting for me, caressing the horse. I signaled that we should get on the road straightaway. He let me climb up first, watching me insistently with his somber gaze, then sat next to me. We headed toward the exit. Crossing the monastery, I had the uncomfortable sensation of being a thief carrying his spoils right under everyone's noses. Spoils of whose value I was unaware.

We had advanced almost a full league before I was finally able to relax a little. Charles had sensed my distress and was casting frequent questioning glances at me, which I hastened to avoid.

At the village entrance, I asked Charles to leave me there, adding that I would return on foot. I stopped at the gravedigger's to tell him to ready a grave as soon as possible. Back at the presbytery, I shut myself in my room, sat on my bed, and removed the notebooks from their hiding place. They were numbered 1 and 2. I waited several minutes before opening the first one, as if I still needed some time to convince myself they were real, and thereby delay the considerable upset that would shatter lives. Then I finally read the first words written on the yellowing paper. I remember them by heart: "Everything's quiet. There's no more time to lose. This is it. Time to jump into the cold water. My name is Rose. That's how I'm called…" I kept reading until nausea and fatigue plunged me into a sleep full of faceless demons. To think that before then I had considered good and evil to be reassuring concepts for which I had forged several weapons; soon I would have to slide other irons into the fire.

When I awoke, the notebooks were still beside me. Something alive inside them was calling on me, beseeching me even, to continue immediately, but I hesitated once again, seized by uncontrollable fear. I heard the squeaking of an axle. I set aside Rose's story, torn between impatience to know the rest and the relief of abandoning, for a few hours, the unspeakable truth taking shape before my eyes.

A hearse wagon was waiting in front of the presbytery, with two men in the jump seat. Charles was already there. We accompanied the convoy to the cemetery gate, our steps in rhythm with the sound of hooves and metal-rimmed

wheels. Next we helped the men unload the casket and carry
it into the cemetery.

When he saw us, the gravedigger hurried to relieve me
of my load, claiming that it was not upon me to do *that*. I
then followed the bearers to the freshly dug grave. They
rested the coffin on two planks placed across the hole, amid
identical graves, each marked by a simple bulge of earth
and a stone in the shape of a boundary marker. Without
a word, the gravedigger slipped two large straps under the
coffin, then he looked at me, clasping his hands to invite me
to say my prayer.

At this point, I only knew one part of this woman's life,
the terrifying destiny underway. My words were lost in the
milky morning sky, words about the passing of the body and
the invisibility of the soul. When I was done, I took a step
back. The gravedigger gripped one of the straps with both
hands, signaling the men from the asylum to take hold of the
free ends. They lowered the coffin into the hole, each with
one leg bolstering the other, their whole bodies creating resistance. I watched the light wood disappear slowly, swallowed
by a dark and silent mouth. Apart from us, there was no one
to accompany the deceased. Not one person was mourning
her, as the doctor had claimed. A feeling of despondency
overwhelmed me. Whatever she had done in the past, whatever the circumstances that had pushed her to commit a terrible act, there had to have been someone who cherished her
at one point in her life. Someone had to have at least one
sincere tear to shed, I told myself, otherwise none of it had

any meaning. And yet, in this cemetery where the immobility of stones contrasted with the volubility of souls, no one had known her, much less loved her enough to feel legitimate grief. A few solemn presences did not suffice.

As soon as the coffin touched the bottom with a doleful creak, the gravedigger retrieved the straps, rolled them between his shoulder and forearm, and placed them on the ground. Then he spat in his hands, looking in the distance, as if to make us understand that it was time to go and leave him alone to his work. He grabbed a shovel and began to throw in earth, which hit the wood in a clip-clop.

The asylum employees left. As the wagon set off, I remained a moment longer at the grave. Charles was across from me, hands crossed, praying. With the cortege now in the distance, a squeaking of metal was easily heard. We raised our heads in concert and discovered that a large man who had just opened the gate was advancing in our direction, a peeled stick the color of ancient bone in his hand. He walked slowly down the grassy path, without hesitation, entirely unconcerned with our presence. He turned down an intersecting row. After a few steps, he slowed, but didn't stop, and returned to the main path. I expected him to leave the cemetery, but he came closer and stopped before the half-filled grave, still without a glance at anyone. He took off his hat. Various lines crisscrossed his tanned face, and a few whiskers, overlooked during a shave, projected like straw from a bale. Ample corduroy trousers trembled lightly along his legs. He placed his free hand on the one holding the hat, breathing with difficulty, as if his lungs only worked in a single direction, visibly the intake, and that the air was then too foul for him to expel without straining.

I resisted the urge to disturb him in his prayer. In that instant, his eyes seemed filled with a kind of weariness having nothing to do with the pain of such circumstances, or the scars that usually accompany them. Something akin to a painful relinquishment. His moment of contemplation concluded, he turned, still without paying us any mind, and set off. I let him gain several feet before following, abandoning the gravedigger to his task and Charles to his astonishment. I called out to the man over the gate.

"Did you know her?" I asked loudly.

He stopped and turned around, eyes on the stick he was navigating in front of him.

"No, I don't think I did," he said after a moment.

"Why are you here then?"

He quickly lifted his chin. He indicated the cemetery entrance with his stick.

"Well you're here too, aren't you?!"

"This is my role."

"What do you know of mine?"

"There's no need to be suspicious of me."

He lowered his stick, waited a beat, and gravely said, "All my life, I've needed to be suspicious of others."

"Who are you?"

He gave me a look in which I detected not suspicion, but rather fierce determination.

"Someone you're not about to catch in your nets," he said.

Without waiting for an eventual response, he resumed walking. I didn't follow this time, watching him move with surprising agility, not bending over or leaning to one side, advancing resolutely, firmly planted on his legs, and the stick serving no purpose. At the bottom of the slope leading to the road, he once again lifted his stick in the air, lingered in that position, visibly designating some crucial spot in the sky, and without turning around, he added: "You strike me as rather softhearted, Father. Watch out for his machinations. He has more than one trick up his sleeve."

I had no doubt as to whom he was talking about. He quickened his pace, now wielding the stick in front of him, as if clearing brush to make his way through.

"You knew this woman, didn't you?"

He slowed, as if fighting against the wind.

"I have nothing more to say to you."

I watched him slowly move away, then disappear. I had only one wish at that point—to continue reading the notebooks.

THAT WAS FORTY-FOUR YEARS AGO and I remember everything.

The flame is flickering at the end of a twisted candle. It resembles a small ballerina trapped in wax. Her locks of smoke blow a powder of letters clumped into words around the axis of the story, this confession for which I now find myself the guardian. As my breathing quickens, then slows, I'm able to modify the passage of lethal shadows across the faded paper, and an unknown face appears to me, like scrollwork on a tomb. This woman whom I never met in my life, but whom I nonetheless feel I know, whom I have yet to leave on her long path, whom I will never leave. And I resolve to lower my gaze to the first page, so that the deceptive shadows disappear, making way for new ones, which I steel myself to discover at the risk of casting them in even greater darkness. A darkness that spares nothing and no one, except on that most perfect of nights that is death, before the final judgment.

I patiently copied Rose's story, only correcting a few mistakes, nothing more. The original notebooks are no longer in my possession. I gave them to their rightful owner, years ago. Though I know what they contain, I feel compelled to return one final time to the vile truth whose poison I can already feel welling up inside me, as if I was living a life other than my own, as if I was fated to relive it indefinitely, possessed by the mad illusion of giving new words time to fill the paper.

I let myself be flooded by the sounds that veil the silence, music composed of the frantic racing of rodents on the worn floor, the creaking of wood, the distant voices of nocturnal animals. I find myself as obedient as a dog summoned by its master. It's the moment for Rose to speak to me one last time; she has so many things to tell me, from which I can't escape. So much still to teach me, now that I'm at the threshold of the eternal dwelling place.

Rose

Everything's quiet. There's no more time to lose. This is it. Time to jump into the cold water.

My name is Rose. That's how I'm called, just Rose, the rest's got nothing to do with what I've become, and anyway, it's been a while since anyone's even called me Rose. Sometimes, when I'm alone, when everyone is asleep, I repeat my name out loud, but not too loud, just so I can hear myself, faster and faster. After a while, there's no beginning or end anymore, so I stop and it keeps going in my head, like I've started some devilish machine. If anyone heard me, I'd surely merit some special treatment and everything would come to naught.

I thought this writing would be more difficult. I've spent so many years waiting for this moment, dreaming about it. Every day I readied myself to put things in order, to sort my ideas, hoping for when I could finally set down my story on actual paper. And now the big night's arrived. I've decided to throw myself into this grand business of words. Most likely no one will read this. That's not the important bit. What matters is that for once I'll get to the end of something without anyone stopping me. I won't back down. This wasn't possible until I met Génie, a kind soul. I'll talk about her later. I've thought a lot about what I would write first, which part I should start with, obviously not the true beginning of my life, but another beginning, the moment I understood that I was leaving one world for another, without anyone asking me.

I HAD JUST TURNED fourteen. I lived on a farm with my father, my mother, and my three sisters. In the Landes, as it was called. For that matter it must still be called that, seeing as places don't change names easily, even when people leave. We were four daughters, born one year apart. I was the eldest. Girls aren't worth much to farmers, in any case they're not what parents hope for to make a farm run, you need arms and something between the legs to give your name to the time that passes, and me and my sisters don't have anything of the kind between our legs. If I heard my father say that girls were the ruin of a house once, I heard him say it a thousand times. He didn't even hide it from the four of us but said it loud and clear, as though we were the only ones to blame for the misfortune weighing on him, us, his own daughters made of his own blood and my mother's blood, and her listening, frowning, but never saying anything, never contradicting him, or else, if she did one day, I wasn't there.

At least we got along well, my sisters and me. We stuck together and didn't balk at the work. Despite everything we got done, my father made us understand that it wasn't enough, it would never be enough. The more we did, the better we did, it didn't change anything. So we found ways to create moments to amuse ourselves, in secret. We laughed often. We were only children with no concern for tomorrow. I never saw my mother laugh, or really smile either, and my father just the once, the day after my fourteenth birthday, at the fair in L., he had insisted I go with him, but for sure it wasn't a look that prompted joy, more like a grimace. Yes, he had an odd smile that day, quaffing drinks in the inn with that man who was paying for them, and him never. With years of hindsight, I know that it wasn't a true smile, or a true grimace, but his way of convincing himself that he had to become someone else to see through what he had started.

They were sitting at a table in the middle of a room full of customers. I was standing at the entrance, where I'd been told to wait, watching them talk, unable to hear what they were saying. The man was drinking less than my father and from time to time, he gave me a look that chilled me like a wind in winter. He was big and fat, clearly a little younger than my father, wearing clothes not like ours, not cut the same and not made from the same cloth, the kind that cost a lot more. I wondered how it was that my father knew someone like him. As the conversation went on, I could see it taking an odd turn. My father's face was tightening, and it eventually became as serious as the man's. I understood later that they were haggling, and that it wasn't easy to reach a deal, seeing as how nobody wanted to give in. I didn't know it yet, but they were haggling over me.

The fat man got annoyed. He tried to get up and leave, but my father grabbed his arm, though he didn't seem to like that and my father let go right away. The man sat back down anyway. My father nodded, they shook, and a purse changed hands on the sly, and a bindle too, in the opposite direction. The man seemed in a rush to be done with it, he grabbed the bindle with disgust and my father stuffed the purse in his jacket. It didn't seem all that full to me. My father gave me a hard look. I couldn't tell if he was mad at me for something, or if he wanted to say sorry for something else. I didn't understand what was in that rotten look which I hadn't recognized on him anymore than I had the smile from before. Now I know it. And then he dropped his gaze. The man approached me holding out the bindle. His fat belly, swollen like the belly of a cow ready to calve, spilled over his pants. In an unkind voice, he whispered in my ear to follow him, that he had something to show me, that my father and he had just agreed on it. I asked what they could have agreed on, what it had to do with me. He didn't answer. I looked at my father, who made a head gesture that meant obey. He poured a big glass of wine into his mouth, then refilled it just as quick. He didn't look at me after that. And so, turning around several times, I followed the man, because I had always been taught to obey men without discussion. Nobody paid us any mind. Once we reached a covered cart harnessed to a beautiful black horse glistening all over, he explained to me that we were going to his home, that he had work for me. When he spoke, I got the impression someone was pulling sharp splinters out of his mouth. I was frightened. I didn't understand why my father hadn't told me anything. I didn't want to follow the stranger. I didn't even know yet that he had just bought me.

I need to say goodbye to Papa, I said, eyes welling with tears. I started to turn around, but the man straightaway grabbed my shoulder, pulling me back. That's not a good idea, he said in a voice that had nothing friendly in it. He pushed me against a wheel and lifted me to force me into the buggy. I wasn't capable of fighting back. I stepped onto the footboard and fell onto the seat. The man got up next and I truly thought the buggy would tip over with his weight, then he sat next to me, put an arm around my waist, and took the reins. My heart was dancing a jig in my chest. Let me at least tell him goodbye, I beg of you, Mister, I'll come back after, I said trembling. The man didn't react, he cracked the reins hard on the horse's back, and we set off. I couldn't stop trembling like a leaf. I couldn't even cry. All I could think about was jumping, but I couldn't do it. Where are we going? I asked. He didn't answer.

We left the village at a trot and I began to imagine all manner of things that would never be as bad as what I was to endure. It was the start of spring. The sun was out. The roads had been battered by the winter snow and the rains that followed. The man still didn't say a word, he just glanced at me from time to time, an odd, sick look on his fat face, and it certainly wasn't to check that I was safely seated. At one point, the road narrowed. We entered a forest. The trees were coming together above us, making a dark green sky that nearly covered all of the real sky. I could only see the sun on the side, between the tree trunks. It was as if it were chasing after us, playing at scaring me, and it was working pretty well, seeing as how I'd never seen the sun like that, or at that speed. It's true that on foot or in a cart pulled by a cow, you don't see things go by the same way. The forest was getting denser and denser. I'd have liked to get away from the sun, but it always found a way to sneak back through. I really believe that if it could have devoured me, I would have let it.

I can't say how long the trip lasted, but it felt endless. I had relaxed just a little when the man reined in the horse at a difficult pass. I smelled acacia flowers, which my mother used to pick once a year to make fritters for my sisters and me, nice greasy fritters that we loved. I felt like crying again, but the tears didn't come. Next, we crossed a bridge over a river, then we turned onto a small road. The ditches were well maintained. We came to a wide-open gate attached to two columns at least twelve feet high and linked by a kind of iron railing, like two lines in a notebook, and between them you could read LES FORGES. I automatically lowered my head as we passed underneath onto a gravel path. We circled around a large bed of bushes with flowers of every color, and stopped in front of a kind of castle surrounded by lots of smaller structures.

Then the fat man turned toward me with an odd smile. From now on, you will call me Master, and you will obey everything we say, he said in a cold voice. I didn't know what that we meant yet. He got down first and I stayed sitting. What are you waiting for? he asked. I obeyed. One of my clogs slid on the footboard and I landed on my bottom. You don't seem too smart to me, don't forget your things on the seat. I stood up. I grabbed my bindle. My bottom was aching and my legs trembling.

When I turned around, an old lady, thin as a rake, was standing on the stairs to the castle. She was wearing a long black dress that the sun made shine in spots and her gray hair was up in a bun held by a black lace net. She was staring at me with a superior air but also curiosity, it seemed to me. I said hello. She nodded at the master. He went up the stairs, and I stayed below, seeing as nobody had told me to do anything. Once he was all the way up, he looked at me, and then the old lady, sighing, like I was nothing.

We really have to tell you everything, are you perhaps waiting for the flood to come up here?

35

I obeyed. The woman entered the house first, the master behind, and then me. We came to a large high-ceilinged room with enormous beams with a single base, and in the back a fireplace where you could have roasted a whole cow. A long wooden table filled the room, big enough for at least thirty to eat without bumping elbows. The old lady said that I was under the blacksmith's roof now, that he owned Les Forges, and that therefore I belonged to him from here on. She looked at the master. He nodded his fat head. Then she laid out what was expected of me. I would be responsible for keeping house and cooking, she wouldn't tolerate any dereliction, which would be punished, and she'd be keeping an eye out every God-given day. I marked her words. Then she asked me my name. Just so I know, she said, seeing as she'd been calling me my child, though in her mouth there wasn't anything kind about it.

If you have questions, ask them now, she added. So I asked her if it was just me taking care of the castle.

The old lady chortled. The castle, she repeated. The girl before you got along just fine without help. Then they exchanged a look of understanding that I didn't care for. They turned toward me, like the same engine was driving them. I'm going to show you your bedroom, said the old lady. The master didn't move. She walked to the other end of the room and opened a door to the right of the fireplace. I hurried to follow her. Then we went up a staircase, passed two landings, before finding ourselves just beneath the roof. She opened a small door to a bedroom, with a bed pushed against one wall, a dresser with three drawers, a straw-bottomed chair, and barely any space to move between them, though it's not like you could say I've ever been terribly round. On the bed was laid out a black dress, a white apron, and a white headpiece.

Here's your uniform, it ought to fit you, said the old lady, who had stayed in the doorway, one hand in the other. She glanced at the bindle I was holding at my side, then she looked me right in the eyes with a crooked smile that changed nothing on her withered face but her lipless mouth, and that said plenty about the way she thought of me. I'll expect you downstairs in ten minutes, that should suffice to unpack your things and put on your uniform. Then you'll need to prepare the meal, she said, before turning on her heels.

I was alone, frozen in the room, listening to the footsteps on the stairs. A door slammed and I came back to myself. At that moment I wasn't thinking of my family, I was only thinking of these strangers whom I would now have to serve. They wouldn't do me any favors, I was sure of that. I quick unknotted my bindle on the bed. Inside was a chunk of rye bread wrapped in newspaper, a wool cardigan, two pairs of underwear, three pairs of socks, a winter dress, and the small rag doll that my mother had made when I was a baby. Everything I owned plus what I was wearing fit in that sorry bindle. One drawer was more than enough to hold everything. Time was slipping by, and as I didn't want to get yelled at the first day, I pulled on the dress and the apron over it, placed the bonnet on my head, and I went downstairs.

The master was no longer there. The old lady was waiting for me, impatient as anything. You took your time getting ready, she said coldly.

I went as quick as I could.

Don't talk back when someone tells you something.

Yes, ma'am.

She showed me the kitchen first. I will decide the menus for the next day the night before and you will follow them to the letter. Every morning someone will bring you everything you need to prepare the meals, she said. I stopped myself from asking who was this new someone she had mentioned. It couldn't mean her, or her son, so who else, seeing as she had told me that there was no one else at the house to help me. I'd find out soon enough.

You can read at least? she asked.

Read and write, more or less, I answered looking up.

You will ask me, if there's something you don't understand.

Yes, ma'am.

On the table was a basket filled with carrots, potatoes, and one cabbage, and also a big piece of salt pork soaking in a basin.

Salt pork and vegetables, that'll be your baptism by fire.

Nothing too complicated, I thought, looking at the vegetables.

We eat at seven-thirty sharp, she added, pointing to a clock hanging on the wall. We take our meals in the dining room, just the two of us. She marked a beat before continuing, like she was trying to force herself to seem sad. You should know that the master's wife has been unwell for some weeks now. I am the only one who brings her her meals, she said, emphasizing the only. The silverware and all the utensils you will need are in the large sideboard in the back. But don't break anything. If you have questions, it's now.

I bit my lip but I couldn't stop myself. And my wages? I asked. Her eyes opened wide as an owl's. I quick understood that I had made a blunder that I'd regret.

Content yourself with doing what we ask of you for now and meriting your pittance and bed, we'll discuss your wages again when it's time, she said with a chortle. She didn't look anything like an owl anymore, more like an old mean turkey. With that she left.

Once I was alone in the kitchen, I went directly to the large sideboard to go through what was inside. For utensils, I wouldn't lack anything. I picked one of the copper pots hanging on the wall and I set it on the range. I lit the stove with a fagot and fed it with the logs kept to the side. I straightaway poured the water from the basin into the pot, and I set to peeling the vegetables, which I dumped into the water as I went. That was when it hit me without warning. My family came back, and the tears started falling all at once as I realized what I would become without them, far from my freedom, because, even poor, there had still been freedom in my life in the Landes. I was angry at my father, and also my mother. I cursed them for having brought me into the world, seeing as all they had had to offer me was to be a slave to people who were nothing to me and who looked an awful lot like they wanted me to have a hard time of it. I kept crying as I peeled the vegetables, and I trembled, from not being able to get the sadness out of my head. Bubbles were coming up from the bottom of the pot, as if they were preparing to leap into the air, and I would have liked for them to crash into my tears, instead of bursting for nothing at the surface. I calmed down after a while, but the bad thoughts kept coming all the same.

Everything was ready when they arrived. They sat at the table without a word and I served them. The master began eating immediately. The old lady took her time eyeing her plate before taking a bite. Based on their faces, it seemed the food was good, though they still didn't pay me any compliments. But I knew I'd done a fine job, seeing as I'd been doing the cooking with my mother for ages. The master served himself seconds while the old lady pecked like a bird. Then she placed her silverware on each side of her plate as if they were relics. She raised a glass and examined it from every angle with a nasty expression.

These glasses aren't transparent. You'll need to wipe them with a cloth before each meal. In the future, I will not tolerate drinking from glasses that aren't completely clean, she said.

I'm sorry, it won't happen again, ma'am. I quick understood that in reality, she would always find fault with something.

They didn't say a word the whole meal. The old lady left the table without finishing her plate. She bid the master good night. Then, without looking at me, she said that breakfast should be ready by seven. The master didn't take his eyes off me while she spoke, as though I'd always been there and it surprised him that his mother was reminding me of breakfast time. Breakfast, lunch, dinner, words I had never used before, seeing as how on the farm we suppered and sometimes broke bread, and the point was always to fill your stomach as best you could with what was on hand.

The master went to bed not long after the old lady, and I found myself alone. Their manner, on top of the night falling, chilled me through and through. The thing that struck me was the sadness that seemed to be coming from the castle, a great sadness, and also something else, that was making me uneasy even before I knew anything else about this family. I tried to swallow a mouthful of cold vegetables, but I was so tense that I spat it out. Instead, I cleaned the dishes and put everything away, hoping to have memorized where the silverware and utensils went. Then I sat on a chair. I was emptied. I started to cry again. I went up to my room still crying, and I cried some more on my bed thinking that I would never stop crying, even when the tears stopped flowing, and at the same time I repeated, my name is Rose, that's how I'm called, Rose.

Onésime

He walked along the rocky path. An attentive observer would have noticed the hesitation in his steps, ever since he left the village. This had little to do with the alcohol he had drunk, whose effects had since diminished. It was as though he were trying to stop himself with every stride and, failing to do so, continued to ascend the gentle slope leading to his farm in the cradle of the pale evening glow. He was impervious to the sound made by his wooden shoes. Everything was silent in his head, a silence that persisted despite himself, a silence hated more than anything, and far heavier than the thin purse weighing down his pocket. The price of his daughter's life.

He reached the farm, crossed the deserted courtyard, hearing as he passed the voices of his three other daughters busy at this hour milking the cows in the barn. Before entering the house, he hoped that he wouldn't find his wife there. Then he saw her standing, erect as a dead tree, in the sole room. He went as far as the table, set his hat on the back of a chair; his steps quieted. The silence that followed ebbed and flowed in an echo of his betrayal. He didn't look at her and she stared at him as she dried her hands on her apron, rubbing one side then the other against the stiff fabric.

"What did you do?" she said.

Still he didn't look at her, staring at his hands, as if wishing they would help him see through a mission he himself couldn't accomplish with any dignity; then he tossed out these few words: "What I had to, you simple woman."

He stuck one hand in his pocket, took out the purse, briefly hefted it before setting it on the table with a sound of trinkets clinking under the moiré cloth. There wasn't the slightest trace of pride on his face, just an immeasurable mark of guilt. She leaned over the purse, not even dreaming of touching it.

"Where'd you get that money?"

"That there will tide us over for a while."

"That's not what I'm asking."

He looked up at her, but said nothing. Then: "We had no choice."

"Who exactly are you talking about?"

"About us, for Christ's sake!"

She thrust her chest forward and her heels didn't move an inch.

"Tell me that you sold one of our animals. Tell me something I can stand to hear."

"We got nothing like that to sell, you know that."

She paused, swallowed, and began to frenetically wipe her hands on the front of her apron again. He lifted one arm and pushed the purse a little farther across the table.

"She'll be better off where she is now," he added.

"Better where?"

"I can't say. I signed a paper."

"I'm your wife."

"I know who you are."

She flung one hand into the air with a flourish, like she was scattering seeds in a field.

"Some damned piece of paper is worth more than your own daughter, that's what you're trying to tell me?"

"Without it we could have lost everything."

"And what do I care!"

At that moment, in that house battered by inconceivable winds, as if he had just remembered something definitive that would rally his wife to his side, and without taking the time to reflect, he said: "We have to think of our family now."

She let her arm drop, and unbounded anger seemed to set her eyes afire. "Which family are you talking about?"

He pushed the purse again, lightly, with the back of his hand. "He gave me double what was promised."

"You'd have just needed to work more to get us out of this misery."

He took this, knowing that anything he might say in his defense would be of no use. Silence settled in. She tried to gather her thoughts, not caring about her unfair words, or the pain they caused her husband, simply wanting to find a note of hope, at least one.

"When can we go see her?"

He moved his hand from the purse.

"Not as long as he doesn't want us to. That's what we agreed."

She came closer, fists clenched, and hit him violently in the chest, shouting, "Damn you!"

"We didn't have anything better to offer him," he said, not even trying to avoid the blows.

She stopped hitting him and stepped back. Her arms fell alongside her body, like flags on a mast abruptly deprived of wind.

"And the others, you plan on selling them too?" she asked, challenging the closed door.

"Of course not."

"Well, how would I know you're not gonna sell every last one of 'em?"

"You have my word."

"Rose...I carried her in my belly. What could you understand of that?"

She tilted her head slightly to force Onésime to make eye contact, to trap his gaze, not to find any comfort there or even an answer, but to transmit all the hatred contained in her own.

"Shouldn't have given 'em to me," she said.

Rose

It was six o'clock. Day was just breaking. I smelled tobacco as I went down the stairs. I figured that the master had risen earlier than usual and I would surely be reprimanded for being late. When I entered the great room, nobody was there. My heart quickened when I noticed light around the closed door to the kitchen. I moved forward real quiet. I was anxious as I opened it.

A lamp had been set on the table. He was sitting on a chair near the stove, one leg over the other, watching the end of his cigarette burn.

It wasn't the master, it was another man, not old or young, between the two, for sure the one tasked with bringing me vegetables and meat for the meals. I was still clinging to the door handle, watching him, fearful as anything. He didn't move, he didn't talk, and me, well, I kept my eyes on him. I was waiting for him to speak at least, but he didn't right away. What surprised me most about his face were his eyelids, they almost never blinked. He reminded me of a lizard sitting on a wall out in the sun.

So you're the new girl. Don't just stand there, you'll take root, he said after a minute, without looking up.

I went into the kitchen and stayed next to the draining board, at a respectable distance. Mister, who are you? I asked, uneasy.

The gardener and the horse groomer, among others, that's who I am. He raised his eyes at me and lowered them right away. You seem awful young, he said.

I wondered how he could say such a thing, seeing as he'd barely looked at me. Not that young, I replied perking up.

He turned toward me. A smile lit up his face but immediately went out, like someone had thrown a bucket of water on it. You don't have parents?

Of course I have parents, I said boldly.

His face grew serious, which made the skin on his forehead crinkle. Well, you shouldn't be here if you have parents.

I guess you think they asked my opinion, they're the ones who sent me here.

If I were you, I'd go back where I came from, quick.

Maybe it's not much better where I'm from.

I doubt it. First off what do you know about it, that you can doubt it? He changed position, the leg that was on top went underneath. He nudged his elbows onto his thighs. The cigarette was still burning between his fingers. The ash grew into a curve without falling and it fascinated me that it didn't fall. You ought to listen to me, little girl.

I shrugged. I don't get it, so you tell people what's best for them, on top of everything else, is that it?

Looks like you're the one who doesn't get it. It isn't too late yet, he said, hushing his voice.

Are you trying to scare me? Say what you have to say.

You're already scared, is what he snorted, peeling his back from the chair.

Not at all, takes more than that, I was raised to be tough, I said, not really confident.

It's not about that.

What about you then, why are you here if it's so terrible?

It's not the same for me.

And the maid who was here before, what happened to her?

He raised one finger, smoke twisted around it, then he cupped his other hand to tip the ash inside, looking at it for a good while before closing his fist. She left, he said. His voice almost went out at the end of his sentence.

I guess she listened to you then, I mocked.

His lips moved, but the words struggled to get out of his mouth, like they were costing him an awful lot. I don't think she did, he finally said.

Maybe you didn't tell *her* to leave.

He sighed. His eyes came back to me and mine didn't budge. How old are you, girl?

Sixteen, I lied.

He squinted. What do you know at sixteen?

Surely more than you think.

And surely less than you seem to believe.

A door slammed upstairs. The man stood up like the chair beneath him had just caught fire. He was a good two heads taller than me. He pointed, with his chin, to the sideboard. I put eggs for the master's omelet, with the paper. I have to head off now.

They don't call you Groom, I imagine, I asked before he went out the door. That prompted a sad smile, but this smile didn't stay long on his face either.

Edmond, he said.

Edmond, I'm Rose.

That's when I saw his face break down. What did you say?

Rose, I repeated, why, don't you like it? He didn't answer, he looked at me with what I could have taken for disgust if I had never seen fear in someone's eyes before, then he left, with the ash and cigarette butt clasped inside his fist.

I waited for a moment with thoughts tangled in my head, not knowing where to begin my work. The smell of cigarettes swept through the kitchen, and my eyes kept returning to the empty chair and the large shadow still seated there. A second door slammed. I quick collected myself when I heard the master's heavy steps above my head, and then on the stairs. Next the legs of a chair slid across the floor in the dining room. I immediately brought the master the newspaper. He took it without saying a word, and I went back to prepare his omelet.

The master was eating and reading the newspaper when the old lady arrived. She sat across from him. As I served her, she observed my every gesture with her mouth pursed. The master began commenting aloud about the news and the old lady nodded at the same time. I don't think she was listening. She just barely tasted the omelet, nose wrinkling. There's not enough salt, she said raising her voice. I didn't know how much I should use, I answered. Don't argue, just bring the saltshaker. I ran to get the saltshaker. I held it out to her and she grabbed it from my hand. It's easier to add than take out, I said without thinking. She started yelling at me to keep quiet, that I'd better not talk back again, that I was nothing but an incompetent, an insolent brat, and I'm leaving out the ones I don't know how to write. The master lifted his nose from his newspaper to look at us in amusement, not at all angry with me, it seemed. When the old lady had calmed down, he asked me to bring him the bread and cheese. He'd found nothing bad to say about my omelet, judging from his scraped-clean plate. Walking by the old lady, I was dying to ask her if I should salt the cheese too, but I'd had enough. I thought about what Edmond had told me earlier in the kitchen. Maybe I'd ended up with a mad family, with the master who looked like an ogre, his ailing wife, who I had yet to see, and the old lady who seemed an awful lot like a devil. Back in the kitchen, the silence hit me like a stick against the back of the head. I realized there were no children in the house, and without knowing why, it made my blood run cold not to see or hear at least one in the background.

That morning the old lady showed me around the castle to explain in detail how to do the cleaning. I'd never seen a house with so many rooms. She'd set up a specific order for cleaning them all, with a clock to dust and hang back up in every one. On the second story, she stopped in front of a door, telling me that I must never seek to enter the bedroom where the master's wife was resting, until she had recovered. I figured that'd be one less thing to take care of. Before setting me on my own, the old lady thought it worth adding that she would verify every day whether I had done my work correctly. After the business with the glasses and the salt, I knew that no matter what I did, she would find a reason to reprimand me. Later, as I polished the furniture, I wondered what could be the point of having such a large house for only three people, plus me, seeing as Edmond didn't seem to live there.

I spent the day cleaning, cooking, and washing dishes. At least while I worked I wasn't thinking about anything else.

It was only once I returned to my room that night, the second spent at the castle, that I realized what had happened to me, that my own father had sold me to a stranger, that my mother had to have known, and that she had done nothing to stop it. Sitting on my bed, I burst into tears again, but they weren't the same tears as the night before, these ones burned my eyes. I pictured my sisters and all the moments of happiness I'd shared with them, and only those moments, as though I had no other choice but to lean into my misfortune. And yet we'd had our lot of misfortune at the farm, but that past misfortune was nothing next to this great pain twisting me up. I closed my eyes, and my sisters began to spin around me in the bedroom, laughing. It was only an image of them, just that, and yet it was everything, all at once. I was still crying, but an image of me was laughing with them, as if I was split in two, and as if the bad piece was forcing the good one underwater to drown it, and as if that piece was struggling not to die, and I didn't even know if it was good or not that it die. The hard work at the farm was a lot more desirable than obeying these people, so far from my family.

When I opened my eyes, I felt as if my life before had stopped, on this night, at the age of fourteen, in a big strange house, with strangers, that the tears that had fallen would be the last, that I would never again shed tears for anything or anyone that was dear to me. And I swore to myself that I would never return to the farm. Even if I had the chance one day, I wouldn't go back, because everybody was dying inside my heart, and the image of my sisters would eventually disappear too, since that was the only way to make it through, to survive all this. Because I didn't want to die of despair so young, and because, in order not to die, I needed to destroy the fourteen-year-old girl, to kill her one way or another, not knowing yet who was on the other side of those fourteen years. Because it couldn't end for me in this way. And so, within this great torrent of emotion, I called upon Our

Lord Jesus Christ. I prayed that he would come to my aid, for an explanation for the hardships he was forcing on me. I felt a current of air, and the lamp flame dimmed. I wanted to believe that it was his way of telling me that I would have to count on myself first, that he would only be at my side if I decided to fight. I would fight, I promised myself, protecting the flame with my hand to revive it.

Through the night I fell deeper into listless despair. By the early hours, I was completely exhausted. I had cried so much, cried all that I had in tears, that I had touched the bottom, and in touching it, I had felt something solid beneath me. As day approached, my despair transformed into cold, hard anger, something I could put my weight on. I didn't yet know what there was beyond anger, or where it would lead me. If I had known, I imagine that I would have tried to sink a little deeper still.

Onésime

Rachel was picking up branches abandoned in the undergrowth by winter. She gathered them on the ground in small fagots that her father would then knot with a twist of wicker, and afterward load in a cart hitched to a knock-kneed cow. The girl was wearing a dress of unbleached woolen cloth that rustled against her clogs. She had on a cotton bonnet held in place under her chin by two over-stitched straps. Her father's clothing was also made of worn fabric: brown pants, coat, and vest, and a yellowed white shirt extending from his coat sleeves like wrist cuffs stained by moss and lichen. In the trees, curious chickadees twitched their soot-colored heads as they observed the scene below, which evoked a canvas by one of those Dutch painters, masters of light and shadow capable of immortalizing motion in a melancholy aura.

It was still cool. The sun was clearing the forest with difficulty, laboring to dent the fog and open a path between the branches and budding leaves. Onésime climbed up the spokes of one wheel, set a final fagot in place, then assessed the load. The cow was peacefully chewing on fog. Rachel was now leaning against the animal's flank, watching her father up close, as you'd contemplate a winter sunset. It was morning, and winter was over. Onésime descended from his perch, avoiding his daughter's gaze, busying himself at first so as not to confront it. He'd known that the questions would come sooner or later and that he'd have to face them, but he thought that by working he could control the moment.

"Papa!"

He replied, testing a cart shaft, "What?"

"Where's Rose?"

He skirted round the cart, so that the unmoving cow's bony mass separated him from his daughter. He started to check the other shaft, pulling on the bridle, then knelt down for no real reason and got back up.

"Left," he finally said.

"Where to?"

Onésime was now standing up straight, as still as the animal, no longer avoiding his daughter's gaze, which he knew he couldn't escape. New grooves had formed around his eyes, deeper than those that usually marked his face. This time, it was Rachel who couldn't bear this lost gaze she didn't recognize. So she looked down at her clogs, anything would have done, so long as it wasn't her father's eyes. Both their desires unmet. Onésime was breathing hard, trying to spit out as much foul air as possible with each exhalation, and if he could have he would have expelled everything that remained in his lungs, so there'd be nothing left of the vileness they carried, like those words he had yet to utter. He would have given his life to protect his daughter from a pain that would never be his alone.

"What is it you think?"

Rachel looked up, slowly, like taking a dirty bandage off a wound.

"I saw the both of you leave together. How is it that she wasn't with you when you came back?"

"You saw that, huh?"

"Couldn't help it."

"I found her work somewhere else. She's old enough."

Rachel wrapped her two small arms around herself.

"Plenty of work here."

"Not any that brings money."

"You can't eat money is what you always said."

"'Course you can't eat it but you can't live without it, these days."

At all of twelve, Rachel knew enough of life to imagine absence, but not yet loss. She wanted to hear her father's voice, hear it push away something unthinkable, but also wanted to convince herself of the rest; everything that he would never tell her and which she would cover over with the little bit of childhood remaining in her.

"When is she coming back?"

"I can't say yet."

She looked imploringly at him, dropping her arms to her sides.

"I won't tell anyone, you know."

"I know you won't tell anyone, but I don't know."

"The people she's with, they don't want us to bother her, is that it?"

"That's it. If your sisters ask about her, you don't tell 'em anything different, all right?"

She hesitated. Then, as if suddenly realizing all the trust her father was placing in her, she said, grudgingly almost, "All right."

The fog had lifted by then. The sunlight was reflecting off the tree trunks, and the forest floor looked like a cemetery full of scattered monuments erected for the glory of a pagan god.

"Let's go," he said.

She didn't move straightaway, eyes fixed on this father who let nothing show on the outside. This father who until now she had only ever known by one name, and who, henceforth, would be less than that, less than that father from before, whenever she thought of her missing sister.

"Papa."

"What now?"

"I'm going to miss Rose."

Onésime didn't say anything else. He grabbed the hazel tree stick lying across the cart shafts and tapped the cow, who immediately bent one foreleg, then the other. The wheels began to move, and the cart advanced in a moan of metal and wood. He thought: *I miss her too.* The words swelled in his mind, taking up all the room, but he couldn't let them out, incapable of liberating himself of such a weight for fear he would be judged weak by his ancestors, and also by this twelve-year-old girl he had engendered.

Edmond

He brought back a girl, yesterday.

Her name is Rose.

Good God, it can't be chance.

Rose.

She's as beautiful as a sunny day.

She says she's sixteen.

I think she's lying, though she's already developed and she seems to do her work well enough.

She has black eyes ringed with gold.

When she looks at you, it's impossible to turn away.

I know that kind of gaze, that can read a person like an open book.

For God's sake, I know.

She doesn't smell of moss.

She smells of freshly turned-up earth.

It suits her.

As long as it's not the smell of moss.

I don't know where he found her.

She didn't want to tell me.

They're going to make her life hard, him and the queen mother, that's for sure.

There's not much that can stop them, I'm well placed to know that.

There're bad things here, hidden everywhere.

I told the girl that she'd do best to leave.

I don't think she'll listen to me without proof.

She seems clever, but at the same time too proud for it to do her any good.

Good Lord almighty.

It's not my business.

This Rose is nothing to me.

I need to stop fretting over her.

When I left her, I went into the forest.

When my mind's gone astray, that's the only thing that calms me, being alone in the middle of the woods.

I walked for a long time.

And then I stopped and closed my eyes.

I smelled moss first.

And then the smell of earth covered it up.

I quick opened my eyes in panic.

Mustn't mix the smells.

Good Lord, mustn't mix everything up.

Rose is her name.

Rose, for God's sake.

Rose

One week had gone by. And goodness I had to be quick on my feet. Not one day changed from the next. The old lady organized them like clockwork from sunrise to sunset. At the slightest slip, she'd be on me, and that happened at least once a day, always for a trifle, invented as needed.

Every morning, Edmond brought in vegetables, a chicken or a rabbit, and the paper. He'd already been by when I came downstairs. In one week, I only saw him one other time in the kitchen, and again, he'd seemed in an awful hurry to go. I tried to talk to him before he left, like we had talked the first time. He nodded without answering me, without even looking at me, as if he had said all he had to say and seen all he had to see. It was as if my presence truly bothered him. I didn't insist. I let him walk out. I tried to guess why he was acting like I wasn't there. Maybe he was mad at me for not doing as he told me. Who does he think he is? is what I thought. He hadn't even been able to tell me what I would have gained by leaving. If pretending that the other didn't exist was a game, he was going to realize that I could play too.

I was starting to get a clear picture of this little world. At first, I had thought that the master and his mother behaved like strangers, and then I quick caught on that they didn't need to talk much to understand each other. Seen from the outside, it didn't look much like a family, more like people set one next to the other, with Edmond who'd suddenly gone mute and the master's wife who I still hadn't seen, and in fact I even wondered whether she was a ghost they'd made up.

The night of the eighth day after I arrived at the castle, they said nothing during supper, like usual, but they kept slipping glances at each other. From time to time, the old lady would look at me, real hard, like she was waiting for something she was sure would happen. I felt uneasy, because I could almost see longing in her eyes, something like that. I didn't think it was normal for someone like her, to give that kind of look to someone like me. I thought I must have seen wrong and that soon she would go back to her usual self.

After the meal, they went to bed within a few minutes of each other, except this time it was the old lady who went up last. I rushed to clean up, keen to get some rest. Now that I knew where everything was kept, I went a lot quicker, which stretched out my nights. I took off my shoes so as not to make any noise going up the stairs. The silence was suffocating. At the first landing, I approached the door to the forbidden room, holding the candle in one hand and my shoes in the other. I was dying to know what the master's wife looked like, if she was like them, if I might find an ally in her. Then a shiver swept through my body for no reason and I didn't dawdle any further. Once all the way upstairs, I opened my door. I jumped when I saw a figure sitting in the chair. I dropped the candle and the figure almost completely disappeared.

Hurry and pick that up before you set fire to the house, said the old lady. I got on my knees. I grabbed the candle, burning myself on the wax. The fright I'd had kept me from feeling any pain. I held out the still-lit candle in front of me to spread as much light as possible. The old lady hadn't moved, glued to her tall sickly shadow on the wall. The edges floated around her, like she was burning with a black fire, also because my hand was trembling. I couldn't ask her what she was doing there. In the moment, I didn't even really believe in her presence, so I closed my eyes, and when I opened them she was still sitting in the chair, but leaning forward now, patting the quilt with the flat of her hand.

Sit down, don't be frightened, I don't mean you any harm, she said in a honeyed voice that I'd never heard from her before.

It's just I didn't expect to find you in my room, I said. My feet were heavy as anvils.

Sit down, she repeated, a little annoyed this time. I obeyed. You don't feel welcome here with us.

I didn't understand why that mattered to her all of a sudden, that I feel welcome. I hesitated before answering as convincing as I could.

No, ma'am, I do feel welcome, I eat my fill and I have a roof above my head, what more could I ask for?

You don't miss your family too much.

I gritted my teeth. Sometimes, I said.

That's normal, it will fade with time. How old are you?

Sixteen.

You've surely already been told that you're very pretty.

No, ma'am, never.

Pretty and already quite shapely. Her voice grated when she spoke, like a door that hadn't been opened in a long time. There was for sure no more honey in her mouth.

You have everything you need, otherwise you should tell us.

I don't need anything.

Good, good. If you continue like this, we can talk about your wages soon. She started smiling and I didn't like the smile. May I ask you a more personal question?

You don't need to ask my permission, ma'am.

Perhaps, but we're talking equal to equal right now, she said furrowing her brows and letting the smile slip away.

Equal to equal, I couldn't help repeating, with a nervous impulse to burst out laughing. She looked at me, as if she was surprised by my reaction. I couldn't see what she was getting at. I just wanted her to finish soon enough and leave. It wouldn't take me long to understand that she'd prepared everything so as to lull me, by making me believe things that weren't true.

Have you ever been with a boy? is what she asked me.

I only have sisters, I answered like it came to me.

A lover, I mean.

I felt the heat rise to my cheeks along with an unpleasant feeling of embarrassment. No, ma'am, of course not.

You wouldn't lie to me.

Never, ma'am.

And yet it's at about this age, boys. I must have been red as a beet, but she couldn't tell, seeing as there was so little candlelight. She rose just enough to scoot the chair forward and come closer. She looked up at me. It was as though she wanted to carve out my eyes and stare straight down into me. Seeing me resist, she touched my knee, the weight of her hand like a big stone bearing down to crush it. Unless you're lying to me about your age, she said.

What good would it do me to lie to you? I said, staring at her hand that I'd have liked to destroy.

That's very true, my dear, it would do you no good. She stood up. Her hand left my knee and she raised her arm in the air. I thought she wanted to touch my head, but she stopped midway, the kind of motion a priest would make to bless someone. She seemed to think for a moment. Well, I'll let you sleep now, she said with a sigh.

She rose to leave. Her shadow followed her, and they both disappeared. As she went down the stairs, I heard her dress rustling against the steps but not the sound of her shoes. I hadn't noticed what she was wearing on her feet. Maybe she wasn't wearing anything at all, I thought. I couldn't get rid of the image of the old lady barefoot in the house. And even later in my bed, once I'd shut my eyes, she was still there, sitting in the chair, staring at me with her vicious little eyes probing me, making me feel like less than a person, with her words too, turning in my head, tying more and more complicated knots, impossible to untangle.

In the morning, when I entered the kitchen, the eggs were already on the sideboard, beside a skinned rabbit. I smelled tobacco, but I didn't recognize it. I heard coughing in the dining room. Without thinking, I rushed in assuming Edmond was still there. Despite what I had promised myself about him, I wanted to talk to him, to tell him about the old lady's visit to my room, to know what he thought about it. I figured he wouldn't be able to sneak off. I stopped short when I saw the master smoking a pipe and reading the newspaper, standing next to the fireplace. I had to catch my breath before I spoke.

I'm sorry, I'd have gotten up earlier if I'd known.

He smiled. It's fine, I couldn't sleep.

I'll make your omelet right away.

Wait, he said, raising his voice. He came closer. He was breathing heavy, and a nasty smile was glued on his fat red face. You feel welcome here? His question rooted me to the spot. It couldn't be chance that the old lady had asked me the same. I didn't understand what it meant, or where the two of them were going with it. Why were they worried about me feeling welcome?

You're not answering.

I can't complain, I said avoiding his gaze.

We don't mean you any harm. We want you to feel a little like you're part of a family. A family, I had just the one and he deserved some of the blame for me leaving it. And what he was pretending to offer me surely wasn't the family I was dreaming of. The words rang false in his mouth. I knew that you can't have two families in a single life, that dreams are nothing more than dreams, and that any dreams people sell you without you dreaming them yourself should be avoided at all costs.

I'm just your maid, I said.

Of course, you're in our employ, but things can change, it's simply a matter of mutual trust.

I felt like if I didn't speak I would faint. What do you expect from me?

He waited a beat. He was ogling me. I didn't need to look at him to feel his eyes planted on me. Do you know how much your father sold you for?

I needed a second to take this in before I answered. I lifted my head. You mean how much you paid for me?

His smile broadened. If you like, is what he said.

I'd prefer not to know, if you don't mind.

Then he took on a kind air that rang false, like everything else. You're angry at him.

We've always been poor, and there aren't all that many ways to get out from under it.

You didn't answer my question.

No, I think I did.

You see, myself, even if I was the poorest of men, I don't think I would sell my own daughter, he said, with a face meant to appear sad. He wasn't a good actor, not for sadness, or seriousness, or else he was acting bad on purpose. I was lost, I admit.

You've never been poor, I said.

No, that's true. You know, I, we, simply want you to be happy, Rose. It was the first time that I'd heard him call me by my name. His lips disappeared into his mouth and they came out all wet. You understand what that means, your happiness? he added.

Happiness, I repeated with a shrug, that's no doubt not a word that concerns me.

Everyone has the right to it, for all that we don't know how to seize it.

If you say so, I said to end it. I wanted him to finish quickly, like the old lady the night before. Since the beginning of the conversation, I'd had the feeling he was talking to someone else about someone else.

Then he held out his hand, like the old lady had before leaving my room. I didn't know what he wanted to do with it, and I don't think he did either, since he let it drop with a sigh, like the old lady. Go on, now, he said.

I ran to the kitchen straightaway. When I came back to serve the omelet, the master was sitting down. I couldn't see him behind the unfolded newspaper. It was as if the conversation had never happened, or maybe it had never happened the way I had remembered, I thought to reassure myself. I slid the omelet from the pan to his plate. I looked at him. In truth, it wasn't him I was looking at. It was the newspaper that fascinated me, with words of different sizes dancing across it and that seemed to be calling me, columns of letters rising from the page like air bubbles. I don't know what went through my head, why at that moment I had a craving that had nothing to do with the kind that twists the belly, no, another hunger that just grows and grows. A hunger for words.

Onésime

Nothing for it, not any effort on his part or the stench of the pigsty he had set about cleaning so it could house a litter of four soon-to-be-weaned piglets. Remorse was in his veins and pulsing at his temples, like a hammer striking from inside his skull. The misery he had thought to remedy a little, thanks to the contents of a purse that no one had unknotted yet, or even touched, was nothing compared to this remorse judging him at every moment for having committed the unforgivable. Since the day he received the cursed money, it, misery, had dogged him relentlessly—it was the human kind, and human alone.

Even in the worst of moments, he would often hear the chirping of his daughters, but now he didn't hear them anymore, would never hear them as before. Though there were three remaining beside him, he was missing one, and that made all the difference; Rose subtracted, because of him, from the family tally. And his wife, who wasn't even speaking to him anymore, wasn't even looking at him anymore, absent and yet present, as if she were merely sitting on the edge of this world in which she had opened eyes the day of her birth, into which she had brought four daughters and birthed six times in all; four surviving females, small cloven beings, connected by nothing, excepting the heart. The heart, a paltry metaphor for a vague, uncomfortable feeling, because, however you interpret it, the heart isn't made of gold, it doesn't serve for much, if anything. In the best of cases, it parades around on holidays, the duration of a first kiss; but after, dearth sets in, spreads, encrusts itself in the sickly flanks of fate, and then all that matters, all that pours out, is blood. Bad blood.

With great raging motions, Onésime scraped off the dry shit of two pigs slaughtered the previous winter, rage extending to a face contorted by grimaces, oblivious to the effort, to the pain exaggeratedly sought. He heard the squeals of the piglets in the neighboring stall, gathered around the sow. A mother with teats wounded from the cutting teeth of the mob, observing her small, shit-soiled combatants; torn between the desire to be rid of them and for the maternal interlude to last a little longer, before becoming the female again, before once more feeling the boar's mass weigh down on her, rubbing against her hindquarters, penetrating her, then spurting forth to spread his seed in her womb.

After he scraped off the hardened manure, Onésime piled it by the door. He would transport it later in a cart drawn by his cow, not even an ox, all the way to Espalion, where, making broad arcs with his dented shovel, he would scatter it with little faith onto dirt that he would then turn over, to plant hayseeds intended to keep weeds from sprouting.

The sow recoiled when he came to get the piglets, grunted, swinging her large head at him for form's sake. Onésime didn't back down, provoking her simply to get a little closer, just to see how far she was willing to go in their confrontation, and him too. The animal lowered her head, retreated to a corner, back curved, as if she wanted to offer this man a greater surface to strike, as if submission was her lot and the only way to submit was through violence, as if she needed violence to resign herself, and needed resignation too.

Onésime carried the piglets one by one to the cleaned sty, holding them like babies, unbothered by the smell or the piercing cries or even the wriggling and headbutting against his chest. Each time he grabbed a new piglet, he would look at the sow with rage: *Go on and try it, don't hold back*, he seemed to be telling her. The animal didn't move.

Little Suzanne, eleven years old, Onésime's youngest daughter, his favorite, had offered to come help him. He hadn't wanted her to, pretexting the stench, grime, and danger, but in reality to avoid the questions she might ask him, as Rachel had in the forest. Fleeting solitude didn't heal him of anything, but he still preferred it to any other presence, even a silent one, and this so he wouldn't spew out his rage against someone other than himself, for the animals held back from provoking him.

With the last piglet in the sty, Onésime watched the sow across the divider as the creatures sparred, nudging his legs with their hard snouts in search of the missing teats. Their mother lifted her absurd head one last time, then began to slowly circle in place, like a top at the end of its spin, finally stopped moving, and lay down heavily with a wheeze. A few feet away, the boar grunted, pushing his nose against the wood partition, restless from the constant urge to rut, the only role expected of him, the only one for which he had ever been created in the eyes of man. Instinct impeded by absence, which always made him a little more crazed.

Onésime kicked away the hungry piglets and left. The sky was lightening, projecting an azure blue at high altitude, empty of birds. With a dirty sleeve, he wiped his damp forehead, allowed a little sun into his eyes, then walked the length of the pig stalls, then the barn, until he reached the door to the house. After a brief pause, he entered its sole room, which served for eating, sleeping, and sometimes the mixing of flesh in quiet gasps, with suppressed pleasure. For love would have been too great a word to express that hunger, and what it always cost to satisfy it.

Rose

efore going up to bed, I took the newspaper, hidden beneath my dress in case I
ran into the master or the old lady. Every
time I opened the door to my bedroom, I expected to find her sitting in the chair, but she
hadn't come back. I figured she'd gotten all the
answers she was looking for. I wanted to believe
that. Sometimes she would smile at me, not that
I understood why, smiles that left me far more
uneasy than her angry outbursts and which
made me look away. I tried hard to understand
what could have happened to make her attitude

change, even only from time to time, but I couldn't. It wasn't like her to simper. At least, I told myself, she wasn't on my back reproaching me, that was something.

I spent part of the night deciphering the newspaper. I'd never been to school, but my mother had given us a few lessons, making us read and copy passages from the Gospels. Which hadn't bothered me, unlike my sisters. I had always wanted to learn. I got by pretty well. When I didn't know a word, I would ask my mother, except the days she was out of sorts, which happened more and more often at the end. Then the meaning of the words would often come on its own and, if it didn't come, I would make it up, cobbling together as best I could to get it right.

Those evenings reading the newspaper became moments of joy I wouldn't have thought I could have in the castle. Nothing else existed. The outside world would invite itself into my little bedroom under the roof, and I let it grow. In the end, that world belonged to me. My only possession on this earth.

And then, that morning happened. I had come downstairs first, put the newspaper back on the pile of old ones, so nobody would notice that I had taken it, as usual. Next, I prepared breakfast. The master arrived at seven o'clock. He sat at the table without a word. I served him. He wasn't done eating yet when a man entered without knocking, like it was his home. Not too tall, wearing a nice suit, clean and well ironed, with a scarf around his neck. Clearly surprised to find me there, he observed me for a while from behind his round glasses. Then he placed a leather satchel on the table. He looked at the master like he was asking him something and he sat at the table too. The master told me to serve him a coffee. I felt their eyes pressing on my back as I walked to the kitchen. When I returned with a cup, they were discussing the master's wife's health, unbothered by my presence. I soon caught on that the man was the family doctor. He drank his coffee in one gulp, rose, took his case. I'm going up to see her, he said. I stayed where I was, watching the master finish his meal, a burning question on the tip of my tongue. He looked up after a moment. I was still musing.

What are you waiting for, you have something you want to say to me?

What's wrong with your wife, exactly? I said, as if I had the right to ask such a question.

He glared at me, and clenched his fingers. I thought he was going to make me pay for my brazenness by hitting me, but he didn't; to the contrary, he released his fingers, relaxed. I could see he was making an effort to answer me. She has a fragile constitution, the doctor calls it extreme fatigue, there's not much to be done other than monitor her and wait for the fits to pass, he said, like he was reading a lesson. Fits, that's the word he used. But I didn't see what that meant, as I had never heard the woman cry out, and for me, a fit went along with cries.

I hope to see her in good form soon, I said, still hoping she wasn't like them.

That's what we all hope, said the master not too convincingly.

When the doctor returned, he and the master shut themselves in the office for a long while. Then they came out. Next, the master walked the doctor to his buggy. I watched them discreetly from the kitchen window. From the look on his face and the way he was moving his arms, the doctor didn't seem pleased at all. They continued to talk once they reached the buggy. The doctor kept scratching his neck, as if something was bothering him beneath his scarf. It looked to me like the master wasn't done talking when the doctor got onto the seat and set his horse off at a gallop. The master returned to the house. The old lady arrived just after. He told her that the doctor had been by. She asked how he had found her that morning. The master answered that it was following its course, nothing more. I heard everything from the kitchen. The old lady joined me next. She shook her head, without a word, like she knew there'd be nothing joyful about the future, then she walked out. The master left. I found myself alone, more than happy to return to my business.

Later that morning, I set to the cleaning. Once I reached the second story, I checked that the old lady wasn't nearby before approaching the forbidden bedroom. I stuck my ear against the door, but I didn't hear anything, not even a noise, breathing, something. Then I carefully turned the doorknob. Locked, of course. I found it odd that they would lock a sick woman's door. That had to mean the doctor had a key, since he'd gone up alone to see her. I thought that maybe the master's wife was afflicted with a contagious disease and that's why they shut her away. The people in this house seemed to be such good liars. Why all the mystery?

When I'd finished the cleaning, I knew that the master was at the forge and the old lady in her chambers, as she would say. She wouldn't come out before the noon meal. The desire to know was madness, a madness out of my control. I circled around the house to find the window that looked out from the forbidden room. Easy as there was just one with closed shutters. I knew where to find a ladder hanging beneath a lean-to used to store gardening tools. I checked again that no one was around, then I took down the ladder and carried it to the wall. I was scared stiff that someone would catch me, but my curiosity was stronger than everything else. I leaned the ladder against the wall, right under the window, and I went up, turning round at every rung. At the top, I peeked between the two shutters, through a slit no wider than a knife blade. Of course, it was black inside, surely not the best way for a person to feel better, constantly cloaked like that in darkness, I thought. As I was waiting for my eyes to get accustomed, I heard odd muffled noises quite close. I pressed myself to the ladder, clutching the rails, taking myself for one of those bugs that start to resemble stone when they're on stone or something else when they're on something else. A line of sweat dripped down my back before I realized that it was my heart pounding in my chest making that terrible racket. Relieved, I pressed my eye back against the slit. I could just make out a bed, and a human form in it.

Get down from there, you wretch.

My heart skipped a beat when I heard a voice someone was trying to keep low. Fear grabbed me in my gut. I almost fell backward. Gripping the rails, I didn't dare look right away to see who was talking to me.

I'm telling you, get down. I peeked my head between two rungs. Edmond was standing at the foot of the ladder, making big hand motions. Get down for Christ's sake, get down, he kept saying. I climbed down slowly. My legs were jelly. When I reached the ground, Edmond grabbed the ladder and hurried to put it back in its place, while I stayed against the wall, unable to move. Then he came back. He took me by the shoulders, shaking me. His hands were so big that I felt like they were holding the whole of me. The oddest thing was that it didn't bother me that he was holding me like that, to the contrary, even. I felt protected. If I'd listened to myself, I'd have let myself fall against him and lay my head down without doing anything but not thinking, but I didn't. I stiffened to resist the temptation. He wouldn't have understood what I didn't understand myself.

Have you lost your mind, child? That child didn't sound at all the same in his mouth, as the my child in the old lady's.

I'm sorry, I don't know what got into me, you won't tell them, right? I said in a trembling voice. He let me go and looked up at the window.

What'd you see up there?

Nothing, I saw nothing at all, it was too dark.

But you know it's forbidden.

Yes, I know, I'm sorry, I don't know what got into me, I won't do it again, I swear on Jesus's body dead on the cross, I answered like it came to me, seeing as I couldn't find better to make Edmond believe I was being sincere.

Good God, why didn't you listen to me when I told you to run away, why didn't you listen, you damned pigheaded girl? Now there was anger in his voice.

I told myself I didn't deserve that and that he had no right to lecture me on anything other than getting up on a ladder. What about you, what do you have against them, why are you still here?

He gave me a long look. His mouth moved like a bellows, before the words formed inside. I can't tell you, he said softening. I didn't quite know which question he was answering, both no doubt.

We have that in common, then, because I can't leave either, and anyways where would I go?

He held his arms out toward me, like he wanted to touch me, but there was still one invisible handbreadth between us. The edges of his eyes gave way, like the rim of a hat taking on rain. You could go back to your family, and pick up your life from before, I'll help you, if you want, he continued.

I clenched my jaws as hard as I could when he mentioned my family, and then it came out all on its own. My father sold me for a purse that didn't seem all too full, why would I go back to a family like that?

He thought before answering. You could find work somewhere else.

I don't understand why you want me to go so bad, mightn't it be more that it's you I'm really bothering?

Shut up, you don't know what you're talking about, he said, annoyed again but trying to hold it in.

Well then better give me a good reason to listen to you, why won't you give me one? I have a roof here, I eat my fill, and they're not as hard on me as in the beginning, what better could I hope for elsewhere?

He gave me a hard stare from the two tiny black slits where his eyes had been a second earlier. Don't trust them, especially the queen mother, she's the worst.

Why would I take you at your word, who's to say it's not you I shouldn't trust? He nodded in defeat, taking a second to better control his breathing, which had quickened as he talked about the old lady. Then he stuck a hand in one of his coat pockets and took out a knife. He grabbed my wrist, unfolded my fingers one by one. Then he placed the knife in my hand, folded my fingers over it, all at once this time. I let him do it. He let go of my wrist. I didn't know what to say. I didn't understand what this gift was meant to be, it wasn't a tool, more like a weapon to defend myself, which made my throat knot up even more.

It's not me you need to be wary of, little girl, it's not me, he repeated before turning around. I watched him disappear into the shadows of the path that led to the garden, in that same slow rhythm. And then he was gone.

Suddenly I felt a chill grab me by the shoulders, an unease that came from somewhere other than the conversation that had just ended, a weight that had nothing to do with the knife I was holding in my hand. By instinct I turned around to see where it was coming from. My gaze mechanically climbed up the wall and stopped above the master's wife's window, on the round dormer in the attic, where the old lady was standing like a wildfowl on watch. She stepped back as soon as she saw I was looking at her. Her face disappeared. It was as though someone had been flipping a locket over, and on the other side was always her face, which would remain etched for eternity in the dormer window. I was terrified at the idea that she had seen what I'd done. I tried to reassure myself a little by thinking that at least she couldn't have heard what Edmond and I had said to each other. I felt the knife I was clenching in my hand. The three rivets that extended a little from the horn handle were digging into my flesh. For the first time since arriving at Les Forges, I felt real terror running through my body.

When I entered the house, there wasn't a sound inside. I'd expected to see the old lady hurtling downstairs to yell at me. I would much rather have known what she had really seen, in all, over that deathly silence. I needed to busy myself to get it off my mind. I went into the kitchen clanging pots so that she'd know I was working. I was ready to confess the truth, if ever she asked me, to tell her that I had been worried about the master's wife, that it was the only reason that had driven me to disobey, that I truly hadn't meant to spy, and that I wouldn't do it again. Back then, I didn't know yet that I would decide nothing, that the only time I could have done so, I hadn't wanted to listen to Edmond. It was already too late. I could make as much noise as I wanted for the rest of my life, the silence would always win. It was too late.

At noon, I served the master and the old lady. She didn't have a word to say about me and that made me even more uneasy than if she had spit it out. I was certain she'd seen everything, I read it in her face. They had a brief, serious discussion about a matter of money. The old lady quietly said, more than once, that they didn't have the means anymore, but the master didn't at all agree. The doctor was mentioned. I was too far to hear the why. If I hadn't been around, I'm fairly certain it would have gotten heated. The master cut the conversation short and it ended there.

Several days had gone by since my escapade on the ladder. After loading the wheelbarrow with dirty laundry, I went down to the river, to the spot that the old lady had told me about and that she called the washing place. I felt relief once I was far from the castle. When I reached the riverbank, the big and flat white boulder was there, the one that sloped softly toward the water. I tipped the wheelbarrow and dumped the laundry out. I grabbed the soap I'd brought with me. I got on my knees. I picked up a sheet, and I bent over to soak it in the water. That was when it hit me, without warning, a torrent of emotion, shivers wrinkling my skin, as if this spot was enveloping me, protecting me. The flowing water, the birdsong, the buzzing of insects, and the sun too, not the one that had chased me through the forest several days earlier, but an unmoving sun that was boring small tunnels between the tree branches to show me secret places full of treasures that I had never taken for treasures in the past, without me needing to look for them. I was dying to take off my clothes and go for a swim, for the rest of my body to join the sheet and the hand that was holding it. I bent over again, slipping my entire arm underwater, and my face breached the surface. I kept my eyes open. At the river bottom, I could see a bed of shining stones. Twigs were following the current and small bugs went past, using their legs as oars. I held on as long as I could without breathing. Then I straightened up, hair dripping liquid light. The motions came back on their own. I pulled the sheet toward me, out of the water, and I began to soap it on the flat boulder, dunking it again, soaping it again, beating it, rinsing it, wringing it, before spreading it out on a rock in the sun. I did the same with the rest of the laundry, without flagging. When I was done, the muscles in my arm were as hard as stone and the sun had crossed to the other side of the river. I dipped my hands in the cool water. I splashed my face so the river would remember me. I drank several gulps, as good as if they'd come from a spring. I finally stood up holding my lower back. I grabbed all the laundry that had begun to dry and I carefully piled it in the wheelbarrow, starting with the least dry, and then I returned to Les Forges, leaving the world of the river for a time. At least I knew it wouldn't move, that we'd find each other again at the first opportunity.

Back at the house, I rushed to spread the sheets on the back wall that faced due south, while the sun was still out and a soft breeze was blowing. I had almost finished unloading the laundry when I heard steps behind me on the path. I recognized them right away but I didn't turn around. The steps stopped close by. That left nothing but the breeze whistling at eye level. I spread out the last sheet acting like I hadn't noticed anything, then I swiveled round, I couldn't resist anymore. The old lady was standing up straight, head slightly tilted, as if it was too heavy on one side, or like she was trying to figure something out, or avoid it, I didn't really know. Her eyes were cold as old ashes.

You'll prepare a vegetable soup for tonight, she said calmly.

Yes, ma'am, I answered, regretting that there was nothing else to spread out, as I didn't know what to do with my hands anymore.

The missus feels better. She's regained her appetite. It would seem the doctor's treatment is finally paying off.

I'm very happy for her, I said.

She sighed, staring into space. Someone who didn't know her might have taken her for a saint. Our dear doctor is so devoted. You met him the other morning during his visit, isn't that right?

Yes, ma'am. She looked back over at me. There was nothing saintlike about her then.

After all this time, he's almost become a member of the family. She went toward the wall. She began to inspect the laid-out laundry. She paused in front of one of the sheets. I was waiting for her to find fault with something. A smile split her lips, but she didn't speak. It was by following her gaze that I understood why she had stopped at exactly that sheet.

The first time I bled was not long before All Saints' Day. I had woken up one morning and discovered the sheets stained and dry blood on my thighs. My sisters, who slept with me, jumped from the bed when they heard me shout. Mama came running. I got up. I lifted my nightshift to show her my soiled thighs saying that I was bleeding out, that I was surely dying, that she had to save me. She looked at me, not panicked at all. She took my hands in hers and made me sit calmly on the bed. She looked from my sisters to me, both kindly and concerned. I saw the lines of her face jostling, like she was looking for the right words to say the least possible.

I have the devil inside me, that's it, isn't it? I said in tears.

She tried to smile. The devil has nothing to do with what's happening to you, my dear.

What's happening to me then? Tell me.

Don't worry, it's normal. The blood will come back every month, now that you're not a little girl anymore.

Not a little girl anymore, that doesn't mean anything. And anyway, I want to be a little girl forever, I had said, unable to stop blubbering. She placed one hand on my head, very gently, something she always did when I was sick. I took from that that I had a serious illness, and that she didn't want to admit it. She began to stroke my hair sadly, like it was the last time she would do such a thing, but not for the reason I thought. Then she sighed before speaking again. I sensed she had finally found her words, and that the ones she had chosen cost her a great deal.

This is what happens when you become a woman, she said.

I don't understand what you're saying. I had stopped crying.

From now on, you can have children. The good Lord also created us, us meaning women, for this, to make children and then stay in the shadows. Blood is the sign that the moment's arrived, she said without taking her hand off my tangle of hair.

But I don't want children.

That time, she really did smile at my silliness. Well of course you're not going to have any yet. It's just that it's possible, a kind of signal from nature, you see.

Why didn't you tell me about it before?

It's not an easy thing for a mother to say.

I want to remain your little girl.

Don't worry, you'll always be my little girl, but now, like I told you, you're more than that. You know, my mother didn't tell me about it before it happened either, I guess it's something you have to discover on your own first.

I still wasn't reassured. It's nothing serious, you promise?

I promise, I'll explain what you'll need to do so you soil your clothes and sheets as little as possible, and then you'll have to listen to your stomach in the future, it'll warn you when the time is coming.

I'm still a little afraid.

It's the first time, it'll pass, dear, it'll pass. As she spoke, she wasn't looking at me like I possessed a new power, but like I had just lost one in her eyes, one that I would never get back.

Mama?

Yes?

Do you bleed too? Of course, otherwise I never could have had you.

Do we bleed our whole lives? I asked.

No, at one point we stop bleeding there, but that doesn't mean we don't have any more to give, in some other way, she said, talking at her clenched hands. My sisters hadn't moved since the beginning, glued to the wooden bed, listening in silence. But my mother couldn't explain to me how the blood flowed, or where it came from, just why. I think that she didn't actually know how the blood came to be or from where. I stopped asking questions, at the risk of the fear coming back. My shame was plenty to deal with already. Then she took her hand off my hair and filled a big basin of water so I could wash myself. We never talked about it again. The whole time, my father stayed outside.

The old lady had noticed the dark mark on the sheet, the bloodstain I'd been unable to completely remove, even by scrubbing hard. She'd begun stroking the fabric, where the stain was.

It won't take long to dry, with this light wind, she said.

I worked as fast as I could.

I must admit that you get along rather well.

Thank you, ma'am—

—In your work in general. But you still have things to learn, you know, she added in that brittle voice of hers. I should have guessed the compliment hid something else.

Yes, I know, I said.

Do you know what they mean by a person's condition, my dear?

Condition, yes, I think I do, ma'am.

Go on, then.

I thought for a good while before answering. It's the life you're meant to live until the end, that depends on your birth and nothing else.

One of her lips rose on a single side. My word, that's nicely said, with the vocabulary at your disposal. Everyone must stay in their place, oil always floats above water, that's how the world is, you see.

Of course, ma'am, oil stays on top, we can't change that.

So you'll agree with me that it's not us poor humans who decide our own condition, it's a divine decision, predetermined.

Certainly, ma'am, I take no issue with that.

Then you'll also agree that anyone who dreams of upsetting that divine order would be terribly presumptuous.

They would be, ma'am, terribly, I repeated mechanically, using the same word, even though I didn't know what it was being used for. The old lady lifted her head set atop the white, wrinkled neck that had just emerged from the buttoned collar of her gray dress. You'd have thought she'd tried to swallow something stuck in her throat, and that she really didn't want to let it come back up. In truth, it was the opposite.

In that case, how do you explain that there are people presumptuous enough to think that water can mix with oil?

I could see where she was going, the thing I could no longer escape, but I pretended not to understand. I don't know, ma'am.

For example, mad enough to climb on a ladder for God knows what reason, she said sharply.

I felt my legs giving out. I grabbed onto the wheelbarrow frame so as not to fall. I could find nothing better to say than that I was sorry, that I wouldn't do it again.

Shut your mouth, I thought I was very clear, that I could trust you, and I realize that's not the case, it's a great disappointment, believe me.

I promise you that it won't happen again, I don't know what went through my mind, I meant no harm.

And Edmond, I saw you two talking, what did he say to you?

He yelled at me.

That's all? she asked squinting.

Yes, I swear to you.

I'm obliged to pass this on to the master, we'll have to decide on an appropriate punishment together.

I put on a resigned air. You do what strikes you as fair, I take no issue with that.

Very happy to hear you take no issue again, go on, finish up this laundry quickly and then go take care of the house, there's an unspeakable mess inside and dust to be wiped off all the furniture.

Yes, ma'am. I felt humiliated. I would have liked to disappear into a hole and never come out again, to not exist at all, because it wasn't worth it to exist, if it was only to live like this. The idea of ending it came into my head for the first time, and I wasn't yet fifteen. The old lady looked at the stained sheet one more time. Her lips trembled, like she was fighting not to smile again, surely satisfied to see me in that state, then she left.

Of course, it wasn't true about the mess and the dust. Thinking about it later in my room, what struck me as strange was that the whole time she'd been talking to me, I hadn't gotten the impression she was really angry, more as if she was forcing herself to seem angry for some specific aim. I'd soon find out that the promised punishment didn't depend on my mistake, that it had been decided once I'd set foot in the castle, and probably even before my father sold me. In this, for one's condition, the business with oil and water, the old lady had been right.

Onésime

Eight weeks Rose had been gone. He went over to the chimney mantel, grabbed a dented tinplate box set on the lintel, pried at the lid with his fingers; one side, then the other, never applying force to open it. He took out the still-full purse, the string not even untied. The money now in his hand, Onésime gazed at his wife, who was crushing garlic cloves in a boxwood bowl. Without any apparent concern for his presence, she sniffed loudly, wiped her nose with the back of her sleeve, raised the pestle in the air, then brought it down, allowing her hand to resume its circular dance. Tiny cracks quivered in the corner of her mouth.

"This can't go on," he said, hefting the purse as if it was burning and he wished it would burn him, that it would catch fire and nothing would remain, not the money any more than the reason he possessed it.

She slowed the movement of her wrist but didn't look up. Then she stopped pounding the garlic, still looking down, holding the pestle like a dagger buried in the wood. She remained silent.

"I'm going to return the money so we can get our daughter back."

She continued to stare at the bowl, at the off-white pulp in the bottom, whose heady odor was filling the room.

"Maybe there won't be enough," she said.

"We didn't touch it."

"You signed a paper, you said."

"They'll quick find someone else to sign a new one, I reckon. People like them."

She leaned her head against a beam black with soot, a good third of it eaten away by a fire that had broken out one evening, and that the two of them had contained using the bedsheets.

"I won't come back without her," he added.

She put down the pestle, lowered eyes emptied of all compassion for him, eyes emptied of all kindness.

"No point coming home if not," she said, not even raising her voice.

But despite her doubts, the lines on the woman's face gradually softened as she observed her husband, rediscovered in his mantle of misery that, though still befitting, he now wore like a fine cloak in relation to the bag of riches weighing in his hand, which had made of him for a time the betrayer of an entire family's soul. He came closer. One step, one single hesitant step, no more. There remained at least five before he could hope to touch her by extending his arm. She rubbed her lips together, quickly coating them in saliva, because it was the only way that came to her to make this man understand that he was regaining a little of her trust along with his dignity. She would prove it to him upon his return, but if he betrayed her a second time he wouldn't get another chance.

Onésime had no intention of waiting any longer, already in a hurry to leave his wife, to be far from her and her unbending judgment. He didn't feel like he was there anymore, in fact he wasn't really there, in that house, on that farm; the place, then, where he would have to fight again in the future, as much as before and even more than before, but at least with a lighter heart from having in part remedied his error, though not in any way at peace. For that, he would need time, waiting for the forgiveness that would perhaps one day emerge from two female mouths.

He sliced two pieces of corn bread, stuffed them into one jacket pocket, the purse in the other, then grabbed the stick leaning on the doorframe. He froze for a moment before the door and looked back at his wife. "Say nothing to the girls. It'll be a surprise. It's best like that." He tried to appear lighter, like a child asking another to count before starting a game of hide-and-seek.

She went back to pounding the garlic mush. He left. She didn't look at him, would look later at the door closed behind him.

Rose

It took a long time to get a clear idea of my surroundings. The estate was tucked away in the forest, a true den of boars and wild-fowl. The forge was on higher ground, farther to the south. From the house, I would hear clank-ing noises when the wind came as it must, and I would see smoke rising above the trees, except on Sundays. I could only imagine what went on there, seeing as the old lady had made it clear that the river on one side and the gate on the other were boundaries to be crossed under no circumstances. I wondered how many workers there were at the forge. They never came to our side. They must not have been allowed to cross the river either, though in the opposite direction. I often itched to go past the gate, but since the business with the ladder, I hadn't ventured out, afraid of getting caught and stirring up something everybody seemed to have forgotten.

In the center of the grounds, there was a large cluster of small trees, which the horses always skirted on the right, and never the left. That habit had to have some importance. I couldn't imagine what at the time, and I still can't imagine. The stable was filled with horses. I couldn't have said how many. Edmond took awful good care of them, judging from how handsome and nicely groomed they looked. More than once, I'd envied the master for being able to ride around on one of those creatures. I thought the world must look differently from up there, seeing as how not just anybody was allowed.

That day I'd needed a few carrots for the evening soup. I quick ran out to gather some from the garden. The sun had already struck every window in the castle. Come noon, after being drenched in orange all morning, they had taken on a greenish tint, before sinking into shadow. There was no time to waste. I hurried down the path.

I was about to open the garden gate when I noticed Edmond on his knees, weeding, it looked to me. I couldn't see his head, nothing but his back and shoulders, which were sticking to his shirt, shoulders as broad as a stere of wood, or nearly. You'd have thought that the plants in the garden were all part of him and certainly not the contrary. He hadn't heard me arrive. I didn't move. I watched the knots of muscle moving up and down his sweating back. I didn't understand what was happening to me, why I couldn't look away from his back, and why I didn't just go gather the carrots I needed for my soup, as if nothing was wrong, without bothering him. But my feet didn't want to leave the ground and my eyes didn't want to leave this man either, who was now nothing but a back and shoulders. And the why, the why couldn't even find its place yet in my poor girl brain. It was stronger than me, stronger than that poor girl, spinning on and on inside my head. These weren't reasonable kinds of thoughts, but still all I wanted was for the arms on either side of that back to hold me tight, like at the bottom of the ladder, and tighter than that even, certainly not like how a father would hold his own daughter. The thing turning me inside out was something other than a father's arms, especially mine. I felt little jabs in my stomach, which was twisting in a way so as to let the heat rise, the better to trap it. I knew I shouldn't imagine what it would be like to touch those shoulders, but I would have done it, if only I could have convinced myself that they had been abandoned just so I could touch them and nothing else, just to know how it felt to place my hands there, and perhaps even take hold of them, steal them, hide them to bring out whenever I felt the need. Not just any shoulders. There was a real reason I felt like touching these ones and no others, but I for sure didn't want to admit it to myself at that moment.

I leaned against the gate to try to compose myself. I had come with a purpose, but I didn't know what it was anymore. In truth, I didn't care. All I knew was the madness it was to stay rooted there, to let myself sink into a strange mire that the sight of those shoulders had piled around me.

After that everything happened very quickly. Edmond stiffened, no doubt sensing my presence, but he didn't move for several seconds. Then he finally straightened up and turned around. He didn't speak right away when he saw me tarrying at the gate. He gave me a strange look, and I let him, not moving either, not able to, not wanting to, like the not so poor girl that I could tell I was in his eyes.

What do you want? he asked after a moment, in a way that made it seem like he was pretending he wasn't happy to see me. I tried to answer, but the words got stuck in my mouth that had turned to clay, full of that same mire I'd had at my feet. Looks like you lost your tongue.

I breathed out, and the words came at the same time. I need carrots, but don't mind me, I'll manage on my own.

Nobody touches my garden or what's growing in it, he said, not annoyed, but like it went without saying. He stood up. It was beautiful to see a person stand up like that, without visible effort, or maybe with the pleasure of making an effort that didn't look to be one. I gripped the slats of the gate even harder. How many do you need?

Four or five should do it.

He smiled. Four or five?

Five.

He went to pull the carrots out, taking his time. Next he tapped them against his leg to knock off the dirt, then he came closer and held them over the gate. I couldn't even lift an arm to grab them by the green bits. You sure you're all right? he asked. I must have smiled dumbly.

I'm fine.

Doesn't look like it. You want these carrots or not?

Yes, I'm a bit dizzy, too much sun pounding on my back, I guess.

He scratched his head with his free hand. It's in front of you, the sun is, he said, concerned.

Maybe it is, I said without thinking.

Don't tell me you walked all the way here backward. Then he started to laugh. That was the first time I'd ever seen him laugh, showing his nice, straight teeth, a little yellowed from tobacco. He held out his arm again shaking the carrots. I had to force myself to take them. I raised my hand and closed my fingers around the tops. He didn't let go right away. He didn't let go until a few seconds had passed, and then all at once. He wasn't laughing anymore, just smiling. I was holding the carrots up in the air. I really think that if there hadn't been a gate between us, I would have fallen into his arms. I looked at the carrots, as if they'd arrived in my hand by miracle, then I turned around and began slowly walking back.

Careful of the sun, now that you're facing the right direction, he said.

I felt foolish, but I still wanted to go back to the gate to smile with him, and most of all go back in time a little, to return to the shoulders, the swelling beneath his shirt. But I also knew that bringing the past back didn't mean you could stop yourself from wanting to change it, to something better, and that changing it wouldn't be possible that day. It was better that I keep the image in a corner of my mind, an image that I could easily find again when I needed to, a little like the river. It was as I got closer to the castle that I understood that no other kind of shoulders could ever have that effect on me, even if I lived to be a hundred years old.

All night long I thought about Edmond, about his shoulders, about his eyes when they had ambled over me, like they were looking for something that they'd been amused not to find easily. A moment came back to me, when I instinctively tightened the top of my calico dress with one hand and my breasts rose. It wasn't embarrassment, more a way like any other to show what I could become for him without knowing it myself. He had furrowed his brows. He seemed to have found what he'd been looking for. The whole time, I didn't feel like the girl I used to be before I started bleeding, but the one that came after.

EVERY SUNDAY, I had to get up even earlier than usual because the master went hunting. He would leave with his pack of hounds, sometimes on horseback, sometimes on foot, it must have depended on his mood. He would free the howling dogs from their kennel and let them jump around him before setting out. I never saw him return empty-handed, even when he left without a rifle. I still wonder how he managed, his fat body weighing him down, to run game to exhaustion. Just the thought of him tracking his prey and never letting it go sent shivers down my spine. He always brought back at least a hare or a rabbit. Edmond would wait for him at the kennel to take care of the game, which he would bring to me, skinned and gutted, ready to cook. The master loved rabbit stew. The old lady never ate any though. Once, the master returned with a boar on his back. He bled it with a large hunting knife. He didn't leave the butchering to anyone else.

That was my favorite day, Sunday. Once the master left for the hunt, the old lady would go to Mass driving the buggy herself. I'd have a few hours of solitude, without her on my back ordering me to do this or that. That Sunday, the ninth one, Edmond had joined me in the kitchen. He began to smoke, watching me toil away, a little preoccupied, without saying a word. I figured he was under orders to watch me after the ladder business, but I didn't dare ask him for fear of finding out for sure. The master had never said anything about it, though the old lady certainly must have told him. I was even starting to forget about the punishment she'd promised me. I thought about Edmond often, without knowing the reason, I didn't want to know it. After my visit to the garden, I felt like something had changed between us. I couldn't have said whether it made us closer or more distant, if it was the same for him as it was for me. At least he wasn't asking me to go away anymore. His being there reassured me, and it sure seemed like he was looking at me every time I sneaked a glance his way. Then he turned all the way around so as not to see me. He wasn't planning on leaving, something was holding him back. The silence didn't bother me, it felt good, like silence can be a place to hide when you don't feel right with someone, or maybe too right. He put out his cigarette, though it wasn't quite done, and right away began to prepare a new one. I tried to observe his face, all innocent like, as he rolled the cigarette between his fingers. His skin was colored by the sun, a little cracked around the eyes. It reminded me of the ground in August. Though I didn't have time to linger on every detail, I guessed he was around thirty, twice my age at most. One day I had heard my mother say that at the same age, women were in fact much older in their heads than any fellow, that it was a truth to take into consideration. I'm not sure about the word older, but fellow yes. Maybe it was mature and not older that she said. What I remember with certainty is that she had said this very seriously in front of my father, who didn't seem to understand what she was talking about, or who either.

Do you want a match? I said to break the silence and prove my mother right a little. Edmond didn't answer me, he stared at the cigarette in his hand. It was as if he'd just realized he was holding it, like someone had slipped it between his fingers without him noticing. Then he looked at me dazed, at me and also through me to the truth I'd just been thinking. He took his lighter from his pocket, and he lit the cigarette, taking a long drag. Little furrows dug themselves on either side of his eyes, before getting themselves lost beneath a mess of hair. He swallowed down the smoke, then blew it out in front of him. I could have sworn he was trying to make me disappear behind that smoke by puffing harder and harder. It didn't seem to be working all that well, trying hard as he was to forget that I was in the same room as him, seeing as how he started talking.

You won't do anything foolish if I leave now. I felt a prick in the small of my back.

Why do you want to go so soon? It's Sunday, I asked, trying not to show that he had said exactly what I didn't want to hear.

Things to do that can't wait anymore, he said with nerves in his voice.

It won't bother me, if you stay a little longer.

I'm no use here.

You're meant to watch me so I don't do anything foolish, aren't you? I said, again so that he wouldn't go.

He shook his head, then rose from the chair. I trust you.

Maybe you shouldn't.

Shouldn't what?

Trust me.

He turned his cigarette around, staring at the end consuming itself on its own. I'm going to smoke outside, the queen mother doesn't like to smell cigarettes in the house. That was the second time I'd heard him talk about the old lady like that. I thought there was no better way to put it.

She won't be back any time soon, and I could open a window so she doesn't smell anything when she gets in.

He looked up at me, and you'd have thought a Reinette apple had left marks in the clay at the corners of his eyes. I'd rather, he said.

I felt that same yearning for him to come closer and squeeze me in his arms. I didn't know if he could see it, but I would have so liked him to see it. He hesitated to leave. He must have been fighting in his head to know whether he was going to do what he said, or something else that I was expecting from him and that he must have understood that I was expecting. But no, he was the kind of man to wait. I would have done anything for him not to leave.

Do you still want me to go? He looked pained that I'd ask him that.

You're an odd girl, you don't look like someone who comes from where you come from.

I didn't see why he made that remark in that moment, except to defend himself by attacking me. First of all, what do you know about where I'm from?

He smiled, but this time, there was nothing mocking in his smile. I tried to convince myself that it wasn't the real me standing in front of him, but the girl that came after. I failed, of course, seeing as you can't imagine what you represent to others, especially when you've never thought about it before, when you've never had the chance.

I was giving you a compliment, he said.

A compliment from you?

That's right.

You think I'm kind of pretty? I asked. The words came out all at once without me thinking. I was ready to do anything so that he wouldn't leave me. My question troubled him. You're not answering.

Yes, for Christ's sake, of course I think you're pretty, he stuttered.

Kind of or more than kind of?

Well, you have everything you need, I'm going, he said, lowering his eyes as far he could.

I didn't get my answer, I suppose it embarrasses you that I asked that.

No, not at all.

Well?

Well, yes, more than kind of.

A second compliment, that's a lot for a girl like me, who comes where she comes from, don't you think?

He looked up at me. Clever, aren't you? The edges of his mouth came closer together. If one day I ask you to follow me without discussion, you'll do it. There was no amusement on his face, only seriousness everywhere when he talked.

Do you want to take me for a stroll in the woods? I teased.

I'm not joking.

I'm not joking either, I replied.

Do you trust me?

How should I know, I never know what to think when you start with your riddles.

The back of his hand flew up, like he was swatting a fly. Maybe you think too much about those moments and not enough about others, he said.

There's not much that belongs to me besides what's in my head, so I suppose it's about time someone decided that as well.

That's when we heard dogs barking in the distance. Edmond slipped the cigarette between his lips and looked out the window. You'd have thought he'd just received an order, and that nothing or no one could hold him back now. He let his hands drop to his sides. I'm going this time, think hard about what I told you, he added before he walked out, not even giving me time to speak.

From the window, I watched him move farther away. He joined the master, who was putting the dogs back in the kennel. They started to talk, but the master visibly didn't feel like it, seeing how he turned away. Then Edmond grabbed his arm to hold him back, and the master pushed him, fingers pointing like he was taking aim with a rifle. The master's lips weren't moving anymore, he didn't need words to make himself understood. Edmond didn't flinch. He waited for the master to stop pointing at him and left. He cast a cold gaze in the direction of the castle. I stepped back from the window, uneasy at what I'd just seen, as if it was me who'd just been humiliated.

There was a great din when the master entered. Right after, I heard the office door close, relieved that he hadn't come through the kitchen. I began to mull over things. What struck me was that nobody ever came to Les Forges. It was like these people didn't really have friends, and no acquaintances either, apart from the doctor, who would often stop by unannounced, sometimes without even taking the time to go see the sick mistress. I wondered what connected them, seeing as how the master and him didn't seem to be real friends.

I'd never seen them joke together, always as serious as popes when they talked.

The old lady returned a little before noon. To think that she could have passed for someone fragile. I really didn't know what she was still capable of at her age. She was playing her cards close in truth.

As soon as he heard her enter, the master came out of his office and invited her in. They locked themselves inside. I waited a bit before quietly going up to the door. The wood was awful thick. Even when I stuck my ear against it, I couldn't make out what they were saying, except the word soon, which came up a lot, and also Marie.

Edmond

For God's sake.

I can still see her standing straight as a pin behind the garden gate.

She looked all tangled up in odd thoughts that were leading her somewhere other than where her feet were set.

I felt a warm wind go inside of me.

I went closer.

Christ, I had to stop myself at the gate.

It was like someone else was there, at the same time as her, someone I knew well, someone who'd never left me and who would never leave me, someone who could travel with the wind too.

I couldn't fight it.

I started talking.

There being two of them, two presences that wanted to be one, it was too much for me.

I wasn't thinking of the girl the way I should have been.

I was thinking of her like she was someone else, like another presence had buried itself in that girlish body, and I wasn't looking at her like I ought to have been doing, not like a child to get away from there, to save.

It was stronger than me.

All the things I thought I could never bring back, the presence that had been frozen inside me until then, were here in this girl.

I felt like a little bit of life was returning to me, though it scared me, as if there was some fresh air chasing the rot that I'd been breathing for so long.

I was scared for me and for her too.

Because I didn't believe in things that weren't there, I didn't dream either.

That was by far the worst of it.

I couldn't get back to work when she left.

I held on to the gate, telling myself that I had to keep going, that I better stay in my place.

I'm not sure I can.

Not become a monster.

Good God.

Not like them.

Who could fault me for splitting my pain in two to try to make life a little better?

It's as if this girl grabbed my hand, while she was holding someone else's, and, with that, she took a little pain from them and a little of mine too, which she filtered to make it into something less painful, like how you filter stagnant water, though not for all that expecting it to become drinkable.

Just that.

This girl, this Rose, is leading me to the other presence, and not the reverse.

She woke something inside me.

Something I couldn't admit before.

And yet I don't really know her.

Except I do.

Good God.

I'm not a monster.

Onésime

He crossed sparse pastures that didn't belong to him, since nothing belonged to him in his own right, apart from his house, a barn, a lean-to, and also the little dignity he had left to protect, heavily eroded as of late. He farmed another man's fields. It was his fate to live on the very surface of himself, to walk the earth but barely touch it. Things could have been otherwise, if only he'd untied the purse strings and bought a few acres, at the price of his daughter's freedom. He'd had to give into a great despair when he forced himself to honor that devil's pact—the exchange of his flesh for earth, in the form of a few coins given him by a man about whom he knew nothing apart from his name.

He went through the forest, taking a shortcut via the Trou du Loup, and entered a patch of thick brush, in the process exposing himself to bramble thorns and the whipping of low branches. Then he headed toward the stream at the bottom of a deep gorge lined with twisted oak trees that looked like cripples waiting for a stretcher on the battlefield. He made his way across the water, hopping onto the stones that broke the surface, then climbed the other bank on his hands and knees, grabbing onto various vegetal or mineral moorings, then plunged deeper into the woods, relying on a few old mossy tree trunks to stay on course. He eventually reached a path beaten and scarred by countless hooves, nails, and wheels, and just barely marked by footprints. He walked quickly, prompting a grand carnival of greenery to stream alongside him, casting thick, moving shadows along the hilly terrain.

Onésime advanced resolutely. He felt the weight of the purse in his pocket and the growing desire to rid himself of it quickly, to erase its profound significance. Despite his decision, doubt was spreading too, doubt that he would be capable of redeeming himself without having to ask forgiveness from a girl of fourteen. And even if he had to utter that word that no father should have to say to his daughter in the course of his life, would that "sorry" come to his lips? Would he be able to whisper it so that she would hear it clear as day? Would he be able to set aside his pride, as he'd promised himself? After all, maybe everything would return to normal, maybe silence would make it so, suffice even, and they would both forget that there might exist a single word powerful enough to lead to redemption. And he hoped that a walk side by side would in itself wash the foulness from their hearts; for Onésime, that of having allowed the abominable act, and for his daughter, of having endured it. Maybe a single glance would birth the illusion of forgetting, and they would each allow themselves to be carried by this illusion beneath a green sky.

Dogs barked in the distance. Onésime froze in place. The barking came closer. Soon after, a boar leapt from an embankment and landed growling thirty yards away. Its front legs gave out, its head scraped the earth, then, unperturbed, it got back up and disappeared into the thickets on the other side of the path. Branches bent, whistled, cracked, dead leaves were being trampled, and soon nothing but barking, very close. A first dog appeared, snout lowered to the ground. It periodically lifted its head to let out a doleful cry, then resumed its mission in the solitary boar's perfectly laid wake, just as indifferent to Onésime's presence. Other dogs soon followed the scout. An entire pack, which Onésime gave up counting. Then, a few minutes later, a man emerged from the brush, sliding down the embankment. Once he reached the path, he turned his head, noticing Onésime, who hadn't moved since the boar and dogs had gone by. They looked at each other for several minutes, not to identify each other, since the recognition was immediate, but to try and steel themselves. Onésime moved toward the blacksmith first. He didn't speak first.

"What the hell are you doing here?"

"I've come to get my daughter."

The man didn't react. Onésime stuck one hand in his pocket and took out the purse.

"I didn't touch your money."

Onésime held the purse out to the man, who didn't make the slightest movement. "It's all there. You can check."

"No need. We signed a paper. Your daughter doesn't leave my service," said the man, raising his voice.

"It wouldn't be so hard to tear it up and sign a new one with someone else."

The man pointed to the path behind Onésime.

"You're going to go back where you came from now, and then maybe I'll forget what just happened."

"Nothing's happened yet."

"You're on my land. That's already plenty."

"Let me see her at least, please, then I'll go."

The man placed his hand on the haft of the knife hanging from his belt.

"If I ever see you around here again, I'll make sure you regret it. That clear enough?"

Onésime didn't take his eyes off the knife.

"I made a mistake. I don't want to pay for it the rest of my life."

"That's not my problem."

"What kind of man are you?"

The blacksmith glanced in the direction the pack had taken before looking back at Onésime.

"One who never lets go of his prey."

An ironic smile stretched across his face.

"You'll just have to replace your daughter with a new one. You seem capable enough."

"My wife will never forgive me if I go back without Rose, she told me so."

"Should have thought of that before."

"I'm sure that deep down you have a little goodness in you. You must have children."

The blacksmith stiffened, still staring at Onésime, like someone preparing to pet a small distraught animal.

"Empty the money into your hand!" he snapped.

Onésime obeyed, without understanding his intent.

"Now give me the purse."

Onésime held out the piece of cloth. The man leaned over the ditch, grabbed a small branch, and slid it inside the empty purse.

"To prove to you that I'm not a bad man, we're going to make a new deal."

The blacksmith swirled the fabric held on the end of the stick in front of him.

"A deal with my dogs. If you ever get the notion to come back, they'll remember you, and they'll be much less patient than me. Now clear off!"

Onésime would have liked to respond somehow, but he was incapable. He couldn't hear a single sound around him, he felt emptied, stripped of the sensation of having some weight on this earth and of the very awareness of his own body. Completely robbed of will and force, he watched the blacksmith disappear into the underbrush after his dogs.

Rose

J'd dreamt of Edmond in my sleep, of him truly, not his damned riddles. As long as he was beside me, I'd known that nothing bad could happen to me, and for that whole night it was a little more than just protection that I demanded from him. I touched his shoulders, I think, and the garden gate was wide open. As soon as I woke, I had a single desire, find a free moment to join him and see what it did to me, if there was a way to prolong the dream, if there was any truth in it.

The master had left for the forge, and the old lady had gone up to her room. It was now or never. I had roughly two free hours ahead of me. I dropped everything and went out hoping that neither of them would change their routine. I told myself that I would buckle down on the housekeeping afterward to make up for my delay.

I started by going to the garden. Edmond wasn't there, so I pushed on to the stable. The door was open. I didn't hesitate. I entered without making any noise, just a few steps, and I stopped in the middle of the aisle. I saw him. What I mean is I could see the top of his body over a low wall, between the railings. Edmond was brushing a horse. I couldn't look away from those gentle movements, the strokes of his brush against the horse's black coat, which revealed bluish glints, like when the sun hits a piece of coal. He turned his head in my direction without seeming surprised to see me, all while continuing with the horse. I felt pulled, like I was allowed to approach the stall door. I didn't open it. I felt fine, not at all embarrassed like at the garden, as if something new had happened in the meantime. The night, surely. The whole time he was looking at me, he didn't stop brushing the horse, always with the same care.

You like horses? he asked.

Looking at them is all that I can do, but I think I like them, from what I know of them, I answered.

Bending down slightly he brushed one hand under the horse's neck. This one's Artemis, she's my favorite.

Oh, she's a mare.

You didn't notice? he said smiling at the horse. I felt a little thick. Isn't she magnificent? he said.

Yes, she's very beautiful.

Do you know who Artemis was?

No, not at all.

Zeus's daughter, queen of the hunt.

She doesn't seem wild, I said to say something.

He made his serious face, which dug new furrows in his forehead. You be careful all the same, she knows her world.

I bet.

You have to take your time with horses, you know.

No danger just standing here.

That's for sure. Would you like to touch her?

I don't think I'm part of her world, Edmond, like you said.

He grabbed a rope hanging on the back wall. Come here, he said, like he hadn't heard me. I hesitated a second. He motioned for me to enter. So I opened the door and went toward him, toward them. He slowly placed the rope around the mare's neck. Then, still holding the rope, he held out his other hand to take mine and guide it to the top of the mare's leg, all the way to her elbow. A detail I learned that day, that you say elbow for horses the same as for people.

Pet her first, she needs to get used to you, he said without letting go of my hand. I started to stroke the mare. I had never felt anything so soft, and at the same time I sensed all the power of her muscles at rest, demanding nothing more than to erupt beneath my fingers. In places, large twisted veins swollen with blood seemed to be trying to escape outward. The mare moved her head up, then down. Edmond's hand still holding the rope followed the movement without resisting. He let go of mine. I took a step back, a little frightened, yet I didn't take away my hand. The mare stopped moving. I went back to stroking her, telling her she was beautiful, that I'd never seen anything so beautiful in my whole life. I went closer again. I thought she was the freest and noblest thing I'd ever seen, even shut up in a stable, and told myself that it was only animals that could attain this kind of dignity.

My attention was on the mare's reactions, and most of all on not rushing her. I think she's adopted you, said Edmond. The word adopted didn't seem quite right to me for what were simple touches accepted by a horse.

I don't think we're there yet, Edmond, I said in all seriousness.

Would you like to get on her back? My hand stopped. I looked at him like you'd look at something that's glowing, without understanding where the glow comes from. But the look in his eyes was calm, reassuring.

It's nice enough just touching her, I said.

You didn't answer my question.

I'm wearing a dress.

All you need is to hike it up a little.

She'll probably throw me onto on the ground. In truth, I kept looking for excuses just so he would push them aside.

Not as long as I'm here, I know her inside and out.

I thought of the master and the old lady. What if someone sees me?

No one can see us here, at this hour, it'll be our secret, he said, slowly lowering his voice. He was a lot less afraid than by the ladder. A chill went through my body as I imagined us sharing a secret, a secret that would then bring us a little closer. I got on my tiptoes and brought my mouth toward the mare's ear not quite reaching it.

Say, Artemis, I'd love to climb on your back, if you'll allow it. The mare blinked one eye, a reflex no doubt, but I wanted to take it that she agreed. I turned toward Edmond. How do I do it?

It's not complicated, I'm going to lift you up a little and you just need to swing your right leg over her rump, he said, motioning with his arm. I won't look, he added.

Promise me she won't be afraid.

He let the rope go and caressed the mare for a moment. Then, without saying anything, he grabbed me around the waist and lifted me up. I felt like his hands went all the way around. I swung my leg, as if I'd done it before, and found myself on the mare's back, nose in her mane, using my hips and thighs to sit up while I pulled my dress over my exposed bottom. Once I was more or less stable, I stopped moving. My body was bubbling with energy. Now that my feet weren't touching the floor anymore, I felt freed of something heavy. I was seeing the world different than it had been on the ground, like I'd found a way to escape it and become part of another one. I didn't think for a single second of the moment I'd have to come back down.

Squeeze your thighs hard, said Edmond. I did my best to do what he asked. Then he took the rope and gently pulled it to lead the mare out of the stall. I was unsure at first but I quick gained confidence. I was awful proud sitting up there, nice and straight, like the mare's muscles were extending all the way to me, with my skin rubbing against hers and my underwear in places. You're doing awful well.

Thank you.

Looks like you're getting a taste for it. Edmond had me do several circles, then he stopped the mare. Better get down, now, he said with regret, because you could see that he would have liked to keep leading me, and that's all I'd have wanted, if only there hadn't been anybody else and my work at the castle.

All right, how do I do it? I asked.

Move your right leg to the front and slide down, I'll catch you.

I leaned back, stretching out the front of my dress with one hand. I swung my right leg over her mane and let myself drop. Edmond caught me by my hips and brought me down. When my face slowly passed by his, I smelled tobacco, and something else I had never smelled before. He looked at me embarrassed, and he set me very gently on the ground, like he was being forced into something he didn't really feel like doing. If he had kept me in the air a little longer, I wouldn't have stopped him.

You're so light, he said in an odd voice.

No more than before, I said to tease him.

No, I think you are.

How's that possible?

You're always lighter, after you get on a horse's back, he said gravely, like it was a truth he believed heart and soul.

So, Edmond, according to you, when you get on a horse, you lose something inside, which makes you lighter.

He smiled. The opposite, I think that we gain in lightness and that we don't lose anything at all.

I didn't really understand what he meant. You've given me a beautiful gift, no one's ever given me anything so beautiful.

You'd make an excellent rider.

And I'd end up weighing nothing at all, no thank you, I said joking. In truth, I didn't feel like joking. The problem with things that make you feel good is that you want to do them again, even and especially when you know you can't. Edmond was staring at me and there was still plenty of serious in his eyes. I felt completely wrapped up in that look. I automatically tilted my head back. I didn't need to explain to him why I was doing it, that it wasn't to put distance between us, but on the contrary, to see him better. I was thinking only of letting myself go.

After that, my memories get tangled up with those from the night before. All I remember is that something released in my body, something I'd never felt before, that I didn't even know existed, something just outside of me but also on the inside, something that had belonged to me before and that no longer belonged to me once I offered it to Edmond. I couldn't say today what really happened, I don't even know how I left the stable.

The rest of the day I was in an odd state. My head kept mulling over what had happened, what I had perhaps imagined, there in the stable, like it was planting the seeds of a dream. My head was doing as it pleased, and I couldn't stop it.

The master and the old lady didn't speak at all during lunch. I sensed there was some great tension between them. In the early afternoon, they shut themselves in the office. I had so much to do that I didn't go listen at the door. When they came out, they seemed much more relaxed. Later, judging from their faces during the evening meal, I figured that everything had been settled. Then, as usual, the old lady went up to bed first, but didn't wish her son good night. I should have found that strange, but my mind was still terribly jumbled from not knowing or wanting to untangle true from untrue.

The master went up next. I washed the dishes and prepared for the next morning, but the work didn't bother me. I was still dreaming. Then I put out all the lamps and I left the kitchen. Walking up the stairs, I knew I'd have a hard time falling asleep. I wanted to stretch the day out as long as I could, fighting the night to clear the way for the thoughts that would come to me.

At the landing, I found the door ajar and I saw light spilling out. The old lady had come back. May as well get it over with, I thought, more peeved than scared. I went in. She was sitting comfortably in the chair, like the first time. A candle was burning next to her, casting shadows on her face, like the first time. She patted the bed to make me sit, like the first time. I obeyed, like the first time. What had changed was that she wasn't looking at me, but at the door that I hadn't shut behind me. She was staring at it in fact, not at all like the first time. So I turned to follow her gaze. Good thing I was sitting otherwise I'd have fallen on my bottom when I saw the master's silhouette.

He shut the door behind him and stepped forward. He leaned over squinting as though he wanted to make sure that it was really me who was on the bed. The old lady lifted one arm in the air and let it fall back on her thigh, like she was giving the start signal. Take off your clothes, said the master harshly. My heart stopped beating. I truly believed it wouldn't start again, and even that it wouldn't have bothered me if it didn't, if I fell asleep right then, so that everything could be done with before it ever happened, so that what was taking place in that room never did. I pretended not to understand. The master took off his jacket and hung it on a bed post. He waited, now looking at the old lady.

Do what we tell you, she said.

I can't do what you're telling me.

And why can't you?

I can't, I repeated.

The master looked back at me. He leaned over again with an odd smile. I'll help you, if you can't do it on your own, he said. I lifted my arms to protect myself. I began to shout that

I didn't want to do what he said, that he didn't have the right. There was a heap of curses sticking in my throat, moving up and down, but not wanting to come out one end or the other.

Quiet, do as you're told, the old lady spat out.

With one leap, I retreated to the other end of the bed, against the wall, head in my hands, and I kept shouting. I don't want to, I don't want to, I don't want to.

You see I do have to help you, said the master.

I felt the mattress yielding under his weight. I pivoted, face against the wall. I was crying and at the same time shouting that he didn't have the right to touch me. Then I closed my eyes and I plugged my ears so as not to hear them, not to hear myself, so that it would stop, so they'd disappear, so I could climb back on the mare and Edmond would take my hand and we'd go far away. For a second, I thought that it had worked. I stopped shouting. I couldn't hear anything anymore. I opened my eyes, uncovered my ears, thinking that they had taken pity, or that I had been dreaming.

Go on, let's be done with it. The old lady's voice cut through me. I was incapable of crying now. I started to pray that Jesus, Mary, and Joseph and all the saints would come to my aid, anybody at all, to make the master and the old lady disappear, or even make me disappear, but not a one lifted a finger, just like every time I'd needed them in the past. That's when I understood that the devil comes without you having to call on him.

The master put his thick hands on me. I tried to escape him by wriggling away. He caught me by one ankle and pulled me toward him. I thought that my leg was going to get ripped from the rest of my body. I began to shout again. It was for sure the devil behind me, who was grabbing me by my hips, lifting me so I'd get onto my hands and knees. Next, he hiked up my dress. He slid his hand between my legs and tore away the fabric blocking him from doing what he wanted to do. Stop fighting, there's no point, otherwise I'll make you wish you hadn't! I looked to the side, beseeching, at the old lady. She didn't bat an eyelash, while the devil in person was sticking his finger inside me. It hurt so bad I shouted even louder. Then he took out his finger. I heard him rooting around behind me. For a second, I thought that he would leave me alone. I tried to move, but he grabbed me by my bottom, straightening me out like a piece of meat on a chopping block. He pressed against me and I felt his thing between the cheeks of my bottom. He pushed to force his way in, so hard that I found myself with my head jammed between the bed railings. I tried to stop him going farther with my hands between my legs, which couldn't even reach him. You're hurting me, I'm begging you, I'm begging you, stop, it hurts, I screamed. He kept pushing, huffing like an ox. He didn't care if I screamed that he was hurting me, I think it excited him even more. The old lady was still in the chair, she was reciting words I didn't understand. That added to the pain, her staying there without doing anything, though she had to have known what I was enduring. Between the pain, disgust, and shame, I didn't know what was causing the most suffering. And then the master was inside me, entirely planted inside me. He stopped moving all of a sudden. I had no voice left. I'd been taken past what I could bear.

You had a good laugh at us, you little slut, he said in a voice full of hate. He pulled my hair back, like he was driving a horse, and started thrusting as fast as he could. I began praying for him to finish quickly, to try to shut myself off from the squeaking of the springs, from the master's breathing, his hammering away, the old lady's voice, the pain in my belly, to push it all outside my head. The mare came out of the night at a gallop. I jumped on her back as she passed, and she carried me far away. While we were galloping, I no longer felt anything bad. I no longer felt my body or the injuries being done to it. That didn't last long. Everything came back, not that the mare put me down on the ground, she simply wasn't beneath me anymore, gone. My head released me, I was back on that cursed mattress being taken by the master. He let out a cry and collapsed onto my back. When he pulled out of me, I felt warm liquid spilling onto my thighs, I knew what it was, and what disgusted me more than anything was that it came from him and that I could never wash myself enough to get rid of it completely. I didn't move. I felt dirty, disgusting, even less than nothing. All I wanted at that moment was for the two of them to go, for them to leave me alone to wipe off what was running between my buttocks and down my thighs, what was burning like acid inside me and on my skin. They spoke to each other quietly, but I didn't catch it. Harlot, the old lady said loudly, so I heard. As if it wasn't enough. I didn't turn around. I heard them leave the room. The old lady repeated the word several times as she went down the stairs.

Once I was alone, I pulled the sheet between my thighs to dry myself. When I opened my eyes I began to cry again. The candle flame leapt out at me. I bent over the edge of the bed to vomit everything I had in my stomach. When I had nothing left to vomit, I put a finger in my mouth so that everything that had entered me, everything I couldn't wipe away, that was clinging to me, would come out, everything I thought I could vomit, that I could still feel inside me. While I was throwing up air, the mare came back. She had almost no skin or flesh left. I could see her muscles and bones in places, and her mouth was just a hideous smile.

That night, I understood that it was truly the devil who had hurt me, and that he would surely return, now that he had gotten a taste of me. I wish I'd thought about what I should have done, but I couldn't gather my thoughts, on constant alert for noises that might announce his return. For it all to start again. I clenched my thighs, panicked at the idea that he would come back to take me. I waited. Time passed, and since there were no more sounds, I stretched out on my back, my stomach was hurting me so. As I slowly turned over, my eyes fell on the stained sheet. I right away rolled it into a ball so as not to see the stains anymore. I had blood in my mouth, dead blood, and I couldn't vomit it up, that dead blood that tasted alive on my tongue. I knew I could never spit hard enough to get rid of it. I wish I'd left the house, that I'd been able, that I'd gone through the woods, found Mama, my sisters, and even my father, the man responsible for my misfortune, but I was incapable of moving. If only I could have budged a little, I would have gone to kill the master and the old lady, even if I didn't know how, I would have tried, with Edmond's knife, maybe my hands even, nothing but my hands. But I couldn't move.

My body relaxed little by little when I understood he wouldn't be coming back that night. I eventually fell asleep from exhaustion. Never will I forget that night and the dream inside. I could see myself dreaming the dream, like I had become the dream itself, an empty dream of a dream, an emptiness preferable to true life on earth, with the hope of finding someone there to come to my rescue by stopping me from leaving them forever. The strangest part was that I knew I was dreaming. I wanted to stay inside the dream, to be the dream, and no longer Rose on earth. When I woke, the worst of all was having to accept that I was no longer the dream, but that I remembered being it. This became the most terrible of nightmares, that returning to earth, without having been capable of saving myself by staying in the dream that I had become for a single moment that would perhaps never return.

It was still dark. I fell back asleep, but without dreaming this time. In the early hours, the chirping of sparrows woke me from my sleep. I didn't know what time it was exactly. I didn't care. I didn't get up to prepare breakfast, because I still couldn't move. I heard steps on the stairs. I curled up, and I prayed, prayed, prayed, and prayed again, despite everything.

The closer the steps came, the more I prayed that they wouldn't come, but they got closer all the same. The door opened and I desperately sought the path that would lead me to the dream, with my tearless eyes screaming behind my eyelids, screaming what my mouth could no longer scream. And then there was silence. For a moment, I thought I had entered the dream again.

Get up and get downstairs, you have work to do. The old lady paused. She let out a little yip before continuing. You'll clean up this filth, there's a terrible stench in here. I didn't open my eyes until she was gone. I waited for the door to close. Then I waited again, for a long time, still curled up on the bed, eyes still closed, with the door to the dream getting farther away and that I hadn't even been capable of opening a second time.

Edmond

She came to the stable when I was grooming Artemis.

When I asked her if she wanted to touch the mare, her whole face lit up.

She came closer.

I took her hand and placed it on Artemis's coat.

She let me.

I kept hold of her hand.

Good God.

It was like I was touching the mare myself, like I was feeling what that small hand I could no longer see was feeling.

I suggested she get on Artemis.

She looked at me like I'd spouted nonsense.

When she understood that I hadn't, the gold in her eyes spread.

I helped her straddle the mare.

Oh God.

I saw bits of skin I'd never seen before.

The claws dug in a little deeper.

I turned away but I didn't resist long.

It was beautiful to watch her find her balance, but it hurt at the same time.

She was looking straight ahead, serious as anything.

Her small round bottom curved beneath her dress, and her shoulders leaned to one side and then the other in rhythm.

Every movement she made was as fluid as water flowing around a rock.

From time to time she looked at me, and in that look were all the thank-yous in the world.

I don't know what mine said.

After a while, I checked my watch.

I hated to break the spell, but I didn't want anyone to catch us.

She let herself slide down.

Christ.

Her dress lifted up again.

I didn't look away.

I caught her by the waist.

I didn't want to set her back on the ground.

I didn't even know who was hanging onto whom.

I no longer saw the girl that she was in truth.

I saw a young woman whom I was holding to prove that I could protect her just by keeping her in the air as long as I wanted, without effort.

Good God.

Moss and earth mixed.

Despite myself.

And yet it was the same happiness in my hands, I swear.

Rose.

She loosened a string I had knotted tight after the tragedy.

The earth blossomed.

I don't know how long I kept her in the air.

What I am sure of is that I never could say her name.

I was dying to, but if I had, I would have made her disappear, I'm sure of it.

Dear God.

So I closed my eyes.

She's always there when I close my eyes.

I wish I was blind.

A blind man can't do any harm imagining a thing he can no longer see.

Nothing would move again, if I was truly blind.

She would always be with me.

Rose.

No one can make her less pretty.

Not even them.

When her face stiffens from sadness, her charm remains, making up for the dead smiles hiding just beneath.

Even those who know nothing of beauty can't help but see hers.

Beauty isn't a thing that can be held back. Man invented it, but we never had a choice in the matter, whether our intentions are good or bad.

I only have the best of intentions, I think.

I tried to look elsewhere in the beginning, hiding behind my cigarette smoke, to mask the scent of earth too.

I swear I tried.

Nothing for it.

For all that I go where she's not, she follows me everywhere, not just her, but what she has inside of her, that makes her more than herself, and she doesn't even know it, at least I don't think she truly knows it.

She's a woman.

Their mystery can't be explained, not by us men. All we can do is try to get near it.

I think that all women are born knowing that mystery deep inside them that sends our blood rushing, though roughly at first, like raw cloth they work to make a wedding dress.

All they're waiting for, in the end, is the mixing of our blood, while all we want is to own theirs.

It's possession men want, and women, possibility.

We do nothing for it, and them everything.

So can I, when I'm blind.

Onésime

He listened to the barking slowly fade, abandoned the path for the forest, then sat on a dead tree stump that had the look of a fossilized skull.

He waited a long time, unable to resolve to return home without Rose's hand in his, without even bearing some words from his daughter. He had promised his wife he would come back with her, and he had nothing that could show that his trip hadn't been in vain. He didn't know how to lie. He had promised. Their marriage wouldn't survive this, if in the face of adversity he reneged on that promise made to a wife who had never belonged to him but to whom he knew he had once belonged. The first and perhaps only time he had seduced her, clumsy as it was, had left its mark in the deepest part of him, a seduction that had maddened his heart and made his blood burn.

The blacksmith had taken himself for some kind of god who could decide his daughter's fate, just because he was wellborn and he had paid a price. He had openly threatened Onésime and his entire family. How far could such a man go? Thinking about all the suffering for which he was responsible, Onésime had the certainty that the worst thing wasn't to die, but to lose any reason for dying. He would do as he had promised, whatever it cost him.

He leaned his head back toward the treetops, filled his lungs with fresh air, taking prolonged breaths, as if he needed to stock up for a while, without knowing exactly how long. Then stood up and set out toward the blacksmith's estate. As long as the dogs were in pursuit of the boar, Onésime didn't risk encountering the hunter again.

Reaching the edge of the forest, he jumped over the embankment and found himself back on the path. He began to walk faster, running even, without weakening, despite the ruts battering his joints, his body made malleable through will alone.

Later, he crossed a bridge and came in sight of the property, which was indicated by a sign. He carefully advanced under cover, inspected his surroundings, soon made out an imposing gate topped by a frontispiece of wrought iron. The estate was entirely surrounded by a high wall. He followed it for a while until he discovered a weakness in the stone armor that would allow him to enter without being spotted: an impressive beech tree, large perpendicular branches stretching from its trunk. Onésime climbed the tree and reached a thick offshoot that passed over the wall less than three feet from the top. He gripped the branch tightly with his arms and legs and crawled along it until he could position himself directly above the wall. He slid off, crouched, observing below, then dangled from the edge before dropping to the grass-covered earth.

He cautiously advanced onto the grounds and stationed himself behind a tangle of hedges, to better take in the entire facade of the manor surrounded by smaller buildings. He would wait as long as needed. For the right moment. He wasn't hungry, he was no longer afraid, wasn't thinking about the dogs' sense of smell, the purse steeped in his odor, the man's threats, the man himself who in the end was nothing more than that.

After a period of time he couldn't even measure, and as though he had been granted a request he hadn't even dared to make, fearful of asking too much, a simple wish to see his daughter, he saw her emerge from the house, immediately recognized her silhouette, her walk, in spite of the clothes she had been made to wear and the bonnet that ate up part of her face. He restrained himself from rushing to meet her, for fear of being discovered before they could speak. Wait a little longer. He thought he had lost her when she disappeared behind the house, was relieved to see her reappear shortly thereafter, and head toward what he took to be the entrance to a stable. She paused for a moment before the open door, then went in. Onésime wove in and out of some bushes to get closer. Once he was ten yards away, heart racing, he observed his surroundings again; and not seeing anyone nearby, went back to the wall against which a tall climbing rose wept pink perfumed tears. He advanced slowly, scratched by thorns in the process, before reaching and hiding behind the stable door. He heard nickering, then a man's voice, barely audible, but definitely not his daughter's. His heart burst, as if from the impact of a whip striking a fragile pitcher. The master was already back from the hunt, thought Onésime. He hadn't been quick enough. Hands clinging to the wall, he was trans-fixed, nailed to the stone. He went closer, pressed his ear to the door frame, not daring to look. He heard the voice more distinctly, not the master's, for he would have been able to pick it out among a thousand. Then he heard another, reedy voice, and tears came to his eyes. It was his beloved daugh-ter, whom he had nonetheless shamefully sold to a stranger, believing he was saving them all, her included, as he had thought best to convince himself during that accursed time. What nobody would ever understand, what he would never be able to explain to anyone, not even after years of atone-ment, not even to himself, especially not to himself, pressed to the door, cheek scraping the wood, impervious to the many wounds inflicted by the climbing rose and to the splinter wedged beneath his skin, a small two-edged sword sharpened and buried to the hilt, stopping the blood from flowing, like a cork in a bottleneck. No longer able to hold back from knowing who was with his daughter, Onésime leaned slightly forward, holding his breath, to see inside the stable.

In a stall, halfway between the back of the stable and the door, he saw Rose sitting on a racehorse, smiling at a man whom Onésime could only make out in profile, a man he had never seen in his life. Rose was smiling. A form of pain then pierced the father's body, a pain that he had never imagined he would experience, not this kind. His daughter was happy, it was unmistakable. They let her ride a magnificent animal. That was the reality. And he, Onésime, the most detestable of fathers, the now illegitimate father, for what he had dared to do with no right, who was he to make Rose dismount and return her to the misery of a farm? That farm wasn't her home anymore. What would he have to offer her, besides a past with no better future than what his own past had held? Nothing comparable to what she was living here, in any case. He clearly had nothing to offer, apart from the sadness of a reunion enshrouded in guilt, a pardon that he would perhaps never dare ask from this smiling daughter nobly perched atop a thoroughbred, this daughter who already was no longer his daughter. And for some time he had no longer been her father, had surely never been one in the sense of the mission that a father should fulfill toward his child. What words could have convinced her to follow this traitor who had forever taken the place of the inadequate father? Not any that he could have said. What irreparable disaster had he brought about? The disaster of his daughter's visible happiness, the disaster of having been right to bring her here, only to lose her. And maybe she wouldn't have even seen him or wanted to see him, and been even less willing to answer his plea that he be regarded as the man he had ceased to be. Maybe she would have ignored him, Onésime, henceforth a stranger in Rose's eyes, and she, before the cursed apparition, henceforth disdainful.

He didn't imagine for a single second that she could forgive him. He thought that the only thing she would do would be to send the hateful sight of him to the gates of some hell, from atop her great black horse, a dishonor he couldn't then stomach. The blacksmith was right. You can't go back.

Unable to bear anymore, Onésime slowly regained use of his limbs, retreated along the wall, skinning the backs of his hands on the stones seeping saltpeter, and soon, once again on rose thorns. Tears were falling from his eyes, tears whose deep meaning he would only understand much later, when a pain other than loss would bring forth other tears, that other insurmountable pain that is betrayal. For how would he tell his wife that he had seen his radiant daughter on the back of a great horse bred for racing? How could he speak of the man holding the bridle? What words could he find to describe that scene, without it seeming obscene? What words that she wouldn't, in that moment, distort into a maternal form of abandonment? In any case, she would never believe him, and even if he swore to their God she still wouldn't believe him. But there was nothing else to do but return home, no other choice than try to transform hate into pity.

He kept moving, still glued to the stone enclosure. His gray jacket and his gray pants, camouflaging mended rags, served the way the scales of a wall lizard would. He was resolved to face his wife, anything but the scornful gaze of his daughter. He had no certainties, but he knew at least that one of these women could keep him alive, somehow, while the other would kill him for sure before he was even dead, with a single look, and perhaps worse, with a single word. He had been able to endure the blacksmith's humiliation, but never could he withstand that inflicted by his daughter, a dishonor of blood. Unable to imagine the possible tragedy, able only to think of what was best for her and also for him, without the mercy of another possibility, the possibility he hadn't yet imagined, the one that his daughter, seeing him, would come down from the horse, run toward him, throw herself in his arms, and they would flee together through the woods. An outcome impossible at that moment.

Onésime hid once more behind the hedges, remaining on the grounds a little longer, watching the stable door, as if it would reveal to him a truth other than that of his eternal fall from grace. Then, the sun abruptly rose above the house and struck him in the face. He felt like a great burning finger was pointing at him to tell him it was time to leave, that he had nothing left to do there, that he had never had anything to do there, that his miserable place was elsewhere and that his daughter's was here; that here and elsewhere were now two distinct worlds in which one and the other could not meet.

Rose

They acted like it was nothing, like nothing had happened that night. I did everything not to look at them, but I saw them all the same. I suppose that I was feeling so much disgust that my hatred for myself smothered some of my hatred for them. They had become a them, a kind of two-headed monster that had come inside me, between my legs, into my belly, into my head. I made no difference between them. One wasn't guiltier than the other, less innocent. And there they were, going on with their lives, acting like they hadn't done anything wrong. In the end, I told myself that maybe for them it meant nothing at all to violate a girl of fourteen who said she was sixteen, that I must have done my part too.

I dragged my way through the house, feeling like I wasn't in command of my body. I was sore all over, and waves of nausea sometimes forced me to lean against a piece of furniture so as not to fall. But they saw nothing, or they wanted to see nothing. It didn't matter. They looked like two vultures with their bellies full.

Night came. The darker it got, the more paralyzed I felt. I lit all the lamps and candles that I could find in the dining room and the kitchen. I don't even think they noticed. They ate what I had prepared. The old lady didn't make the slightest remark. Then they went upstairs to bed in the same order as usual. I washed and put everything away, and I sat on a chair. I didn't want to go up to my room after what had happened there. So I let myself drift away. I fell asleep, head on the table.

He arrived immediately in my sleep, he the master, alone, not them together. He was even more violent than in real life, heavier on top of me. He hurt me almost as much as in real life. He didn't have time to see it through, to spit his venom inside me. Not because I was in control of the dream at that moment and could stop him, no, not that time. It was the old lady who stopped him. She surely didn't know, otherwise she would have waited before she spoke. She would have let the master finish, even in a dream, and that's what would have happened, if her voice hadn't pierced through.

What are you still doing here at this hour?

I opened my eyes, tilted my head to the side without lifting it. It took me a moment to understand that I had emerged from one nightmare to fall into another. Go up to bed immediately, she added. I couldn't speak, I looked at her beseeching so she would go, so she would leave me alone, because the worst of nightmares was still better than returning to that room where I had vomited everything I could, and surely not everything I'd have liked.

I will, I finally said.

Right now, she said raising her voice again.

I promise you I'll go up, but let me stay alone just a little longer, please, that's all I ask of you.

Get up immediately, I'm coming with you. She didn't care how I felt, or maybe she did, actually, and it pleased her. Tears began flooding from my eyes. I stood up, again begging her, not that it affected her any more than before. She grabbed my arm and pulled me toward the door. As I went up the stairs, I tried to empty myself, to vomit myself out so that nothing remained but a body that I'd be able to abandon to the master during the time he did his business.

Once upstairs, the old lady pushed me into my room and I shut my eyes. She didn't come in this time. She slammed the door after me, and I instinctively fell back against it. I was terrified, but I couldn't keep my eyes shut any longer. I stood in the darkness, looking for the corner where the master was hiding. In truth, I saw him everywhere as soon as I stared at one spot for too long. I near collapsed a moment later, when

I heard breathing. It took a moment before I understood that it was me, that there was no one else in the room. I was alone.

I thought of Edmond, of what he had hidden from me about the master and his mother. I despised him too. He wasn't any better than them. Everything I had endured was his fault too. He had only advised me to leave without telling me what they were truly capable of. He had to have known what would happen to me if I stayed. He was made from the same wood as them, carved from lies. Everything beautiful that I had experienced, everything that I had felt for him was undone, smothered by pain and hatred.

There was no more room for hesitation. I opened the dresser drawer, took out my things, and stuffed them in my bindle. I quietly opened the door. I waited on the threshold a moment to verify the silence, then I went downstairs carrying my shoes. Once outside, I had no idea what time it was, how long I had slept in the kitchen. I looked at the sky full of stars nearly touching each other. The moon looked like a big even stain with little to do with them. It made me dizzy. I quick pulled myself together, then headed to the open gate. Once past the entrance, I realized I was walking barefoot. I slipped on my shoes and continued down the path with long strides. The farther I got from the castle, the more strength I regained, thinking at the same time about the best way to get away from them. If I left the path for the forest, I'd lose my way for sure. So I told myself that the best thing to do was continue until daybreak, that way, when the sun rose, I'd dash into the forest, and I'd figure it out after that. I still had no idea what time it was. The problem with the moon is that it doesn't move in the sky. But I still thought I had some time ahead of me.

About an hour, that's all I really had left, before the tree line emerged from the brightening sky. I sped up for a few more hundred yards, turning around constantly, and then I entered the forest on the left, seeing as it was the direction that seemed the most logical to me. I hadn't made as much progress as I'd have liked. I raced straight ahead to gain some time. Whenever I ran into underbrush, I would lower my head and dive in not caring about scratches and the branches swinging back in my face, or my bindle getting stuck. I didn't feel fatigue, I didn't feel anything. I walked as fast as my legs could go. I wish I could have flown above the trees and landed anywhere else, as long as it was far from the castle.

And then I heard a muffled voice go in one ear, linger in my head, and come out the other. I thought it was my imagination. I didn't think that for long. The voice came and went, and when it came it was even louder than before, not a human voice, more like howling. Barking. Cold slithered inside me and my legs grew even heavier. The master had already noticed my disappearance and had come after me with his hounds. How could I escape them? I was petrified. I had no chance on foot. I had to find a solution quick. I stopped, I looked around for a tree that I could climb without too much difficulty. I spotted a chestnut that would do the trick. I pulled moss from the ground and rubbed it on my face to cover my scent, hoping it would fool the dogs' noses. I took off my clogs and hung them on the bindle, then I shinnied up the tree, as high as I could climb. Once there, I set my bindle in a fork and I didn't move, hidden in the foliage.

I didn't know if the moss would work. I had heard my father say that certain hunted animals can stop their hearts from beating so as not to spread their smell. I held my breath as long as I could, then I exhaled and did it again. I would have given anything to be the kind of animal that my father had been talking about, but I wasn't one in truth, and the moss didn't help. The hounds arrived, the whole noisy pack. I saw them through the foliage. They began circling the tree in a frenzy, snouts pointed up. I heard the gallop of a horse approaching. I closed my eyes. The galloping stopped. A voice joined the cold in my body. This one was human, the master's, he was thanking his dogs. The dogs calmed down. They were whining like babies. I opened my eyes again and I leaned over to make sure it was really him. I saw him between the leaves and branches, head tilted back, and it felt to me, on the inside, as if I belonged to him, that I was just another animal, but not the kind I'd have liked to be. What surprised me is that he didn't appear angry, more amused, it looked like. He lowered his head.

Where did you think you were going like that? he said, as though he were talking to the tree. I didn't answer. I don't know what I was hoping for by staying quiet. His calm voice chilled me even more than the rage I'd been expecting. Even though I couldn't imagine worse than what he'd already done to me, I had no idea just what horrors he was capable of. I asked you a question, he continued.

Don't hurt me, I'm begging you, I said trembling.

He lifted his head in my direction pretending not to understand what I was saying. But I never wanted to hurt you, child, what are you on about? The dogs had stopped whining, they were lying near the tree, recovering from their hunt. Get down now, said the master in a chilling voice.

I clung to a large branch. I'm too afraid of the dogs, I said. He looked at them, patting the empty air in front of him, like he wanted to apologize on my behalf.

You did get them all worked up.

You see, I can't come down.

The master guided his horse right beside the tree, positioning its rump against the trunk. Get down, I'll catch you, you have nothing to fear from the dogs.

I didn't move. I was still holding on to the branches. I didn't feel the cold anymore, and my hands and arms were heavy as lead. I was scared of letting go, not of breaking my neck in a fall, but of finding myself in the master's clutches again.

I don't like repeating myself, you know that, you're not going to make me come up and get you, are you, or get you down some other way. There was no amusement at all left in his voice. He leaned a little to the side, like he was about to get off his horse. He stroked the butt of the rifle I hadn't noticed before, that was sticking out of a leather scabbard attached to the saddle. I didn't doubt for a second that he was capable of using it. I didn't want to end that way, so I did as he asked. My heart in my throat, I grabbed the bindle, I slid it over my arm, and I went down holding onto the branches on the way, as slow as I could. The descent was fine, until my foot slid on the moss. I landed on the horse, which straightaway began to kick. I immediately felt two arms close around my waist like a noose and pull me backward. Shh, said the master to calm his horse, not letting me go, then he brought his fat face to my ear. You're safe now, he said. I felt his fat belly against my back, his arms encircling me, and I couldn't do anything to stop it. The world was worse than on the ground, not like when Edmond had me get on the mare's back. No, at that moment, the world was very small, and it was closing in on me.

We set off. I watched the dogs silently following us, with their little tongues that dangled like bits of wet rag. What got into you, you're not happy with us? he asked, lies in his voice.

Let me leave, I won't say anything, I swear.

Say what? I don't understand.

You know what.

I breathed out so I didn't have to smell his breath that stank of carrion, that not even the horse's could mask. I couldn't stop thinking of the night he had forced himself on me. You'll see, it'll be different the next time, you'll start to like it, he said, like he was reading my thoughts.

I don't want there to be a second time, I'm begging you, I'd rather die.

He started to laugh. Die, but that's not up to you, you belong to me, I thought you'd understood that once and for all. I struggled. I'd rather have jumped into the pack of dogs to be eaten alive than let it begin again, but he dropped the bridle and held me back, one hand crushing my shoulder. You will always belong to me, he repeated. Worse than the cold, an icy winter wind buried itself inside of me, and it was spring.

I reached into my pocket and took out the knife Edmond had given me, extended the blade with my teeth, and blindly jabbed it backward. It bounced off something hard. The horse kicked. Bitch, yelled the master, grabbing my wrist and twisting it to make me let go of the haft. The knife fell to the ground. There wasn't even blood on the blade. It must not have even gone through his clothes. What were you hoping to do with that needle, he said as he tightened the bridle to calm the horse. Looks like you still need a little lesson, he said as he brought the horse to heel. He thrust hard against my back, and began to laugh. I squeezed my thighs around the horse. My lower belly was burning me but the rest of my body was frozen.

We stopped at the fork. I quick understood that he didn't intend to return to the castle straightaway. I'm going to show you something, he said, before setting off toward the other end of the estate. We went up a steep hill. After several turns, the path came to a dead end. We passed beneath an archway indicating the forge. There was no one around, of course, it was Sunday. We went through a courtyard, then the master got off the horse. He fastened the bridle to a ring affixed to a wall. He came back next to me, his head higher than my hips. He placed his hand at the bottom of my back and I felt his finger push against the cleft of my bottom, rise and then go down. I felt like he was digging into me in a different way than with his thing. He told me not to move, that there'd be no point in me trying to run away again, then he slid his hand down my behind, to the horse's rump, which he started to pat. He waited a little, I think to make sure I had nothing to say. Next, he put the dogs inside a shed, and he came back to help me get down. I turned my head to avoid his fat swollen face, to get away from the stench of his breath. He dragged me by the arm toward a large door set on a rail. He opened a padlock and slid the door in a sound of rolling thunder. We entered, and he shut the door behind him. The thunder was echoing inside. He led me to a workbench covered with bits of irons and odd-looking tools.

Don't move, he said. I had never seen a forge before. Despite the daylight coming through two large windows, inside it was gray and cold. It was as if something was sleeping there, something that wasn't human, or animal, something else that only the master could awaken. He went over to a large stone platform raised a good three feet from the ground and covered with embers. He grabbed several handfuls of the wood shavings piled next to a heap of coal on the ground, scattered them across the embers that were just waiting to be revived. Next, he set to fanning them with a long hand-held bellows, using only the one hand. From time to time, he looked over at me. When the fire began to crackle, the master threw several shovels of coal into the flames, which immediately went down. Despite my situation, I was fascinated by that fire, it seemed alive to me. The coal went from black to yellow, taking on plenty of other pulsating colors. The master went back to working the bellows. When he thought the blaze sufficient, he fetched a long iron rod hanging on one wall, and he pushed it almost halfway into the fire. He kept pumping with the bellows for a while, then he stopped. He turned toward me with a hand motion that didn't tolerate refusal, and his face was pulsating like the coal.

Come here, I'm going to show you something beautiful, he said. I hesitated. Come here, I said, you won't be sorry, he repeated, without annoyance. I went toward him trembling, still fascinated by the flames. The half of the rod immersed in the fire had taken on the same color. The master slipped on a large glove of thick leather. With his other hand, he grabbed me by the arm, and with his gloved hand, he grabbed the rod, taking it out of the fire. It was expanding at the end, like a big coin. Everything after that happened very fast. He forced me to kneel down and lean my head forward. I couldn't fight his grip around my neck. I felt the heat of the blaze on my face, more and more intense, but it was nothing next to the tremendous pain that hit me when he pressed the end of the rod below my right ear. It made the sound of water on embers. In that instant, I thought that the rod had gone through my throat, that it was burning my whole body, that it was burning up my screams too, that all the pain I was feeling had been pushed back into my body in a single great scream that would never come out. The smell was unbearable, the same as when you scald a pig's skin to burn off the bristles.

You belong to me and if you forget it in the future, all you have to do is touch your neck or look in a mirror, he said, now with rage in his voice. The pain was excruciating and I fainted. I woke to the sensation of water flowing beneath the collar of my dress, and dripping even lower. My dress was soaked. I was still kneeling, hands on my thighs so as not to tip over. I heard all manner of noises I couldn't identify. The master tried to make me get up, but I wasn't able to stand straight much less walk. He cursed. He got down, his back to me, grabbed my wrists with a single hand, and lifted me like a bag of grain. He carried me to the horse and set me on top of it. I fell forward, face in its mane, arms dangling on either side of its neck. I heard the dogs snarling, scratching the door, then the steps of the master walking away across the gravel. I reflexively turned my head away from the burned side, not wanting to open my eyes, and I lost consciousness again.

Onésime

He walked at length in the same direction. At one point, too exhausted to go on, he sat down on a bed of moss, his back against an oak tree, waiting for night to fall. It seemed to him that the darkness wasn't coming from above, but was crawling toward him. He let it enter his open eyes, seeing as he couldn't close them. The night had never really brought him joy, but he could think better then, eyes wide open, once the obstacles around his body had disappeared.

What would the tomorrow already jostling in his head bring? If nothing came after night, what was the point of carrying on? What was the point of day? What would that tomorrow serve? If there hadn't been his wife and daughters, whose distinct images kept returning in an echo of his betrayal, he would have hanged himself without hesitation from a tree branch in a remote corner of the forest, so that nobody would find him. But without him, how would they provide for themselves, while he was swinging beneath the leaves, seeping onto the black earth, finally free? He didn't even have that choice, that right to end his existence. Life truly had no meaning.

His stomach began to gurgle. He took the chunk of bread from his pocket, mechanically placed it between his teeth, tore off a bite, and chewed slowly. It wasn't hunger that drove him to this reflexive act, but something else pushing him to build up his strength. The movement of his jaws brought throbbing pain, radiating from inside his mouth, like steel ropes rubbing against his skin. He wanted it to hurt, and so he took his time finishing the piece of bread. By no means serene, he continued chewing, long after he had swallowed the last bite, like a patient ruminant. His teeth gnashed as they scraped against each other, the sound resounded inside his brain, and still he continued.

Later, when his eyes were able to pierce the darkness, as much as was possible, a large animal came near. He could have touched it, just by holding out his arm. A badger no doubt, judging by its sturdy, powerful body. Onésime didn't move. He listened to the animal ferret about, disturbed by his unmoving presence, then move away. Later still, despite his acquiescence to the night, he realized the darkness would never enter him, that it would remain at the threshold of his eyes, that it would offer him no aid, that it was already that terrifying tomorrow. And perhaps it was because of that, or thanks to that, that his head dropped to one shoulder, and he fell asleep the moment the sun rose.

He started awake at the sound of barking. He leapt up, panicked, and set off running frantically, plunging into the forest along the slope. He reached the stream, entered the water, and went against the current so the dogs would lose his trail. The barking faded, masked in part by the noise of his splashing. Soon, drenched, he stopped to see where he was. Scarcely able to hear the dogs' doleful voices, he grasped that they had never been on his trail, or they would have at least come to the spot where he had entered the water. The pack hadn't taken that direction. The barking was clearly heading east. The dogs were on a different scent.

Onésime felt the coolness of the water through his pants, a sign panic was leaving him. He emerged from the stream and gripped roots to climb up the gorge. Once out, he tried to identify exactly where the barking was coming from, but he could no longer hear anything. A light breeze was rustling the leaves, as if the forest was breathing calmly again, and Onésime in harmony with it. Think again. Something the night hadn't been able to whisper to him. What if he had been mistaken, and he had misinterpreted what he had seen in the stable? A fake smile on his daughter's face. If so, this unbearable doubt would continue to grow inside him until it devoured him and took his soul. And if he couldn't even save his soul, he would never find peace in death. He had to give himself the chance of lifting this doubt that shame and cowardice had tried to make him forget.

He broke off a long branch. The feel of the wood seemed to cement his determination, this stick that wouldn't be used to steady himself, but rather as a weapon for combat. And even if he had encountered some mythical animal barring his way, he would have routed it, or beaten it to death with the help of that simple stout stick, or finished it off with his bare hands, if he'd had to.

Onésime found the path again easily. He headed once more in the direction of the blacksmith's manor. At the fork, he heard the distant whinny of a horse coming from the road opposite the one leading to the estate. He tightened the pressure of his hand on the stick, hesitated a moment, and headed down the path strewn with steaming droppings. After walking a hundred yards or so, he spotted the entrance to a forge. Onésime advanced cautiously, passing beneath the archway. What he saw as he entered the courtyard paralyzed him. The blacksmith was emerging from a building, carrying an inert body over one shoulder. A limp body that he hoisted onto his horse's back and that slumped onto the animal's neck, like it no longer contained any life at all. A body that Onésime recognized as his own daughter's. The man began to walk toward a door behind which dogs were excitedly pawing the ground. Onésime raised his stick halfway up and shouted, before the other man could release the pack.

"Stop!"

The blacksmith turned around swiftly, fists clenched. He looked at Onésime, eyes burning with hate.

"I told you not to come back."

"What did you do to my daughter?"

Onésime's gaze went from the man to his daughter. Alerted by the voices, Rose shifted her head to one side, opened her eyes, then immediately closed them. Relieved to see her move, Onésime called to her: "Rose!"

The blacksmith walked toward Onésime. He stopped less than five yards away, towering with all his imposing stature, not at all impressed by the menacing stick.

"Shut your mouth!" he said.

The stick was trembling harder.

"I'm leaving with her," said Onésime.

"You're not going anywhere."

"You don't scare me."

The blacksmith took one step forward and Onésime quickly moved back.

"Doesn't look like it."

"Don't make trouble and we'll leave it at that."

The blacksmith began to laugh, his wide chest and fat stomach shaking, looking like one and the same. "'Don't make trouble and we'll leave it at that.' Now, how about that?!" he said imitating Onésime's voice.

Onésime slowly approached his daughter without taking his eyes off the man. "I'll bring back your horse. You have my word," he said.

"Your word, no less!"

Onésime grabbed the bridle. He moved to unknot it.

"Drop it!" yelled the blacksmith, lunging at him.

Onésime dropped the bridle and brandished his stick with both hands. The horse kicked. Rose's body followed the motion, like a piece of lichen clinging to a wind-jostled branch. The blacksmith grabbed the bridle and pulled it downward to control the animal, which began to snort. "Easy, handsome boy," he said. The horse calmed down. The man slid his hand along the bridle, made a second knot, patted the horse's cheek. He looked at Onésime, a smile on his lips.

"It looks like you and I aren't done yet," he said.

"That all depends on you," replied Onésime in a quaking voice.

"I can't let you leave again, after what just happened."

"Nothing's happened yet."

"You come to challenge me at my home, and you say that nothing's happened…Nobody touches what belongs to me without my permission."

The hounds were near maddened behind the door, the ends of their bloody claws visible. Onésime dug into his pocket and took out some coins.

"I don't want your money anymore. Take it back."

"All right, I'll take it back," said the blacksmith, acting pained.

There was a silent pause, then, without warning, he leapt at Onésime with a flexibility surprising for a man of his corpulence. Onésime didn't have time to shield himself from the attack. He fell backward, losing his grip on his stick, which went flying. He tried to get away from the enormous mass now weighing on him, hitting the blacksmith's sides to little effect. Couldn't reach. His strength left him little by little. Then the blacksmith grabbed the poor man's forearms, pinned them to the ground, and lifted his chest. Large beads of burning sweat were dripping down Onésime's face. "You don't have much grit," said the blacksmith without irony, visibly disappointed by the lack of resistance from his adversary. Immobilized, Onésime was breathing heavily through his mouth, moving his head from right to left as he spat out. The blacksmith watched him twitch, with what could have been taken for compassion. Then he leaned his head back, closed his eyes a moment as if praying, arms tensed, hands still gripping Onésime's forearms. He took a deep breath and smashed his forehead against the face offered to his fury; he did this with inconceivable violence, as if he himself was violence incarnated and not just a man filled by it. Onésime's nose burst on impact. The blacksmith struck again. Other bones cracked, and he struck again and again, with a rage that seemed to feed on all the previous blows. He persisted well after Onésime lost consciousness, and blood began to spill inside his brain, never again to come out.

Rose

I had become nothing. I no longer belonged to myself, the master was right. There were no thoughts in my head and yet I remember everything that happened after the branding, when the ruckus woke me up. I thought I heard my name. I almost fell over when I sat up, because I had forgotten I was on top of a horse. Instead of my neck there was a wave of pain that went all the way up to my eyes hiding behind my eyelids. I figured I had dreamt the voice that was calling me. If only I had resisted the pain a little more in that moment, maybe things would have happened differently, maybe I could have changed something. But I let myself drift. Not very long. Too long.

The voices came back, louder, and then they quieted. There was a strange sound, the same as when my father would crack a walnut between two fingers. The sound came again and again, more and more muffled. I moved my head toward it and I opened my eyes. Two men were on the ground. I immediately recognized the master sitting on a man stretched out under him. It didn't take me long to understand what was making the sound. The master smashed his head into the man's face and then again. All I could see were the man's pants and his shoes that lifted up every time the master hit him. Something familiar that took me a while to comprehend. The heart-shaped inlay on the right pant leg. At first, I thought that my imagination had sewn that piece of fabric just to mock me. My imagination had nothing to do with it. My father had come to find me and bring me home, and he was the one the master was knocking out with great blows of his head.

I found enough energy to slide down the horse's side, holding on to its mane. I almost fell backward when I landed on the ground. My head bumped against something sticking out on one side of the saddle, which proved to be the rifle butt. My legs had trouble holding me up but I stayed on my feet all the same. I gathered all my strength to take the rifle out of its holster. It was the first time I'd held a weapon in my hands. I turned toward the two men, hand on a trigger, my back against the horse. Time's gone by since, but what I saw will haunt me until the end.

I screamed at the master to stop. He didn't hear me, too set on his task. I got closer, wobbly all over, and I kept screaming. I got up right beside them. The master could no longer ignore that I was there, but he kept going anyway. My father didn't have a face anymore, and the master's was covered with red, there were even little pieces of flesh stuck to his forehead. For a second, I thought it wasn't my father, despite the shoes and the inlay, that it couldn't be him. And then I recognized the jacket and vest that went with the shoes and the inlay on the pant leg, the inlay in the shape of a heart. I started to scream even louder, pressing the end of the barrel into the master's back. I told him to stop, that if he didn't stop I would shoot. That's when he paused, stood up, and ran his sleeve over his face to wipe off some blood. He looked at me, then made a point of looking back at the body on the ground that wasn't moving, that had stopped moving. He was staring at it, as if he'd woken up with the surprise of discovering something that he'd done in his sleep, without being truly responsible for what had happened, but not at all displeased to discover it. In truth, he seemed rather proud of himself. Then he turned his head back toward me smiling, and even his smile dripped with blood.

Can't say he wasn't asking for it, he said in a very calm voice.

My eyes were fixed on my father. I wanted him to wake up.

Papa, I called without lowering the barrel.

Papa, repeated the master mocking me with a fake pained air. Poor man, I don't think he's in a state to hear you.

Papa, papa, papa, I began to shout.

What did I tell you, you can see he can't hear you. I pointed the gun at the master's chest, where his heart was. The smile that had never left him widened across his face. Well then, go on, shoot, you won't get a better chance. I didn't hesitate. I pressed on the first trigger, but nothing happened, so I pressed the second one, and again nothing happened. The master made a sad face. He grabbed the barrel and ripped the rifle from my hands. I fell back. He clicked the barrels to check inside. Damn, how dumb of me, I forgot to load it, he said, like he was annoyed with himself.

I was on my knees. I was crying. I began crawling toward my father. There was nothing left on his face that looked like him anymore. All that remained were small patches of skin. Put together, they'd have easily fit in my hand. An air bubble came out of his mouth and burst between his lips. I gingerly lifted his head. I set it on my thighs hoping to see another bubble appear, but no others came. Don't die, I beg of you, don't die, I forgive you for everything, I said cradling his head and still crying. In truth, he was already far away, certainly already dead. The little life that had remained in him had flown away with that bubble. Maybe he didn't even hear me before dying, maybe he died without hearing his daughter scream that she would save him, without hearing me cry as I told him I forgave him. I was no longer thinking of him as the man who had sold me, the man who was responsible for what had come about. I thought I was the only one responsible, that everything had been written the day of my birth. If I hadn't been born, nothing would have happened to him, he'd still be alive, and not me, seeing as I would have never even tasted of this hellish life. I wasn't thinking of my mother or my sisters. I was just thinking of my father and myself, of him dead and me alive, of what should have been, of what wasn't, of what couldn't be changed but that I still couldn't stop myself from picturing, changing it in my head by pushing imaginary air bubbles down his throat to bring him back.

The master tried to lift me by one shoulder, to stand me straight. I fell back onto my father who I was holding in my arms as tight as I could. The master still managed to tear me off his body, then he wrapped a rope around my wrists, he made a knot, and he pulled me to the forge. Once inside, he tied the rope to the foot of a workbench, and then he went out. I tried to get loose, but I couldn't move the bench and the knot was too tight. The master returned not too long after, dragging my father's body by the feet as it dripped blood on the ground. He laid him by the forge. He right away got to reviving the embers with the bellows and feeding the fire with pieces of coal. I pulled even harder on the rope, unable to stop crying, as I had understood what the master wanted to do. He didn't even look at me, concentrated as he was on kindling the fire. When he judged the flames high enough, he grabbed my father and threw him in, like he was nothing but another piece of coal to burn. I closed my eyes, but I couldn't keep them closed very long. I had to watch to the end, though I didn't know why I was inflicting that on myself.

His clothes caught fire first, then a terrible smell reached my nose, not at all like what I had smelled when the master was branding my neck. This smell was much worse, the smell of my father's dead body, all of it, burning, his skin, his flesh, his bones. I was crying and screaming at the master at the same time, that I would turn him in, that he would pay for this with his life. I didn't know how I would do it, but I swore that he would pay one day. I swore, and he couldn't care less about my threats. He was the devil, the same one who had forced himself on me, and who was now pumping the bellows. It could only be the devil, because no man would have been capable of such horror.

After a while, my father's body turned black as coal, shining the same. It shriveled as it burned. The skin and flesh gradually disappeared. I saw the smile of death appear on his face, the same smile that the mare had in my dream. And then there was nothing but bones, they were the same color as coal too. The master stopped pumping. He looked at the remains of my father, who meant nothing at all to him, either living or dead. I felt like his face was aflame too, but without changing his skin. He grabbed a large hammer from behind me, from the worktable, and returned to the fire. He waited for the flames to go out, hammer dangling from his hand, then he lifted it in the air. He held it up for a moment, glancing at me to make sure I didn't miss any of the show, and he began to crush the bones with heavy blows, until they became ashes mixed with coal. I wanted to throw myself into a void, any void, because I couldn't take any more, and I fainted.

Edmond

I heard the dogs barking.

    He had released them without telling me.

That was unusual.

I went up the path as fast as I could.

When I reached the kennel, he was already on Hermes.

It looked like he was floating over the excited pack.

He leaned over to let the dogs sniff something.

The dogs raced toward the gate in a fury.

He set out after them swaying pathetically.

I ran to the house to find out what was about.

The queen mother was alone in the dining room, hands on the back of a chair, as if she were waiting for me.

There was no noise in the kitchen.

I asked her why he was going on a hunt without telling me.

She looked up at the ceiling saying it didn't concern me.

She must have thought her answer would satisfy me and that I would leave, but I insisted on knowing what was happening.

I asked where Rose was.

Her face twisted up.

Her eyes were like two pellets of buckshot set on dirty cotton.

Her hands tensed on the chair and her mouth began to spit out a rant she must have been rehearsing since I was born.

"What is it you think? That I kept quiet, that I closed my eyes to my husband's doings just like that, without getting something out of it? What did you think, you poor fool? That I was going to agree to let you set a single foot in this house out of the kindness of my heart? Of course not, I have no respect for what you are. You mean nothing to me, nothing, you hear me? You're just the role you play, no more, no less. I fought my whole life so that this family would continue…Family…that's what's most important. Preserve the family at all costs, preserve the name we carry, it's the name that lives on. But to understand that, you need to be built on solid foundations, an irrevocable bloodline, not some vulgar construction erected on stilts in the name of who knows what chance misfortune, from an urge quenched on a night of heavy drinking between the thighs of the whore that was your mother. So stick to what we tell you, to what you know how to do. That's your life, and don't think that it will ever be more than the will of the devil carried out before the eyes of God. Everything will end after you, nothing will remain, not your name, not your memory. Nothing, I'm telling you. It's your downfall but certainly also your luck to have nothing lasting to defend, whereas I, I have to fight day after day so that nothing ends, so that everything remains, that essential everything that makes it so that you're nothing and we're everything. You don't have a choice, you never had one and you never will. You'll stay in your place if you don't want her to suffer more because of you. How could you think a half-breed like you could pass down your blood, and that anything but a monstrosity would come out of it one day? You poor fool. Get out, now, you repulse me!"

She pointed at the door.

I was completely stunned.

I couldn't even answer her.

Deep down, I knew that she was right to say that I was nobody.

I should have strangled her and been done with it.

I obeyed, as always, and I left.

I walked to the kennel feeling like there was a large elastic band pulling me from behind.

On the ground was the handkerchief that Charles had let the dogs sniff.

I recognized it right away, with its embroidered *R*.

Good God.

I rushed to the gate.

I heard the echo of barking far off in the forest.

I couldn't make out where the pack was.

So I waited, fear in my belly.

Rose and he returned after noon, both on top of Hermes.

The dogs were scampering around him, they weren't barking.

I set myself in front of them.

I grabbed the horse's bridle to stop it.

Rose's eyes were wide open.

She looked straight ahead, like I wasn't there.

He pulled the bridle toward him, and I let go.

I spoke to Rose.

She turned her head toward me, but I'm sure that she still didn't see me.

That's when I noticed her hair bright red on one side and the mark on her neck.

I grabbed the bridle again, asking why he'd done that to her.

He swung a kick right at my head.

I fell to the ground.

The dogs came over to lick my face.

He told me that I'd be better off not starting up again, that the day he'd have to answer my questions wasn't coming anytime soon.

He headed down the main path with the pack behind him.

I couldn't even see Rose anymore behind his fat body.

I got up and followed them.

When I reached the house, the dogs were running across the grounds and the horse was tied up by the front steps.

I rushed inside.

There was no one downstairs.

I went up the stairs as fast as I could.

I was nearly all the way up when I found myself face to face with him as he was coming down.

He stopped me from passing by placing himself across the width of the step.

He slid one hand beneath his jacket and took out a large knife from its sheath.

He looked at me smiling, then he pointed the tip of the knife at me, ordering me to turn around, saying I really shouldn't tempt him.

He was still smiling.

I obeyed again.

I went down slowly, turning around several times.

He didn't move, the knife in his hand.

With every downward step I took, I swore to myself that this would be the last time he would threaten me, but still I kept retreating.

All my life, all I've done is retreat.

Rose

I awoke in my bed. The old lady was sitting in the chair, right beside me, she was watching me. How do you feel, my dear? she asked. I was all in a haze. You were out for a long time, she added. I wanted to sit up but I felt resistance at my left wrist. Around it was a piece of metal with a lock, attached to a chain fastened to a bed rung. I looked at the old lady to get an explanation without having to ask. She just smiled at me. My free hand instinctively touched my neck, the spot below my right ear. I felt the swelling beneath my fingers and everything came back to me in a muddle: my escape, the hounds, my father, the master and I at the forge, my father's body burning, the unbearable smell, the master crushing the bones with his hammer, and me screaming like a mad-woman, not to stop what I could no longer stop, but to leave this world and enter the empty dream, and stay there for-ever. That damned void and that damned dream that hadn't wanted to open up to me.

The old lady pursed her lips. You have to admit you were asking for it, she said.

But my father didn't do anything, I said crying.

Well, what about your father?

Why did the master kill him, he didn't deserve that. Judg-ing from her surprised face, the master must not have told her yet. Your son killed my father at the forge and burned his body, I said, turning toward her so I wouldn't miss her reaction, thinking that maybe I could get something out of the situation.

She began gently swinging her head from side to side, making an odd noise with her tongue behind her clenched teeth, like when you want to make a child know they've mis-behaved, not to upset them, but more to amuse yourself by observing them feel guilt. Then her face lit up, as if from a revelation, and I looked away, because I wanted nothing to do with that light.

Too bad for him, sounds like your father got the lesson he deserved—that is unless it was your wish that came true, she said, pitching her voice higher and higher as she spoke.

What do you mean? I said.

Maybe it was actually you who wanted to see him dead, in the end, after what he did to you.

I know what I saw, and I've never wanted my father dead, never, I said as I shook with sobs.

Everyone wants someone dead, at one moment or another in their life, she said, the words running together as though gathering momentum, and so that she could get out what seemed to be a fundamental truth in her mind. Selling your own daughter must surely merit such punishment, don't you think? she added in the same tone.

Anger swept away my sobs all at once. You won't get out of this like that, I swear.

She made a pained face. Oh, you swear, but what exactly can you swear on, what in your miserable life has enough value? I lifted my head in the air and since I didn't answer, she kept going. No one cares about you up there, we, on the other hand, welcomed you under our roof, and this is how you thank us, by threatening us. Oh my poor child, you only have yourself to blame for what happened. It's your father's fault and yours as well, even if I can imagine that's hard to admit. I'll let you think about it, if you're capable of such a feat. She rose abruptly. You'd have thought there was someone pulling her from above with a string to make her stand. Watching her leave, I wondered just how wrong she was.

As soon as she'd gone, I tried to slip my wrist through the cuff by twisting it every which way, until I bled. That didn't work, so I pulled on the chain to see if the bed rung would hold. With every yank, a burst of pain would go down my arm and ring through my whole body. Even when I pulled on the chain with two hands, nothing budged, the rung was too solid. There was nothing to be done there. So I stopped pulling. Blood dripped from my battered wrist and stained the sheet. I placed my elbow on the bed so I could slide the cuff as low as possible on my arm, to make space around the wound. It didn't hurt. I licked the blood until it stopped flowing. I didn't move after that. There was utter silence in the house. I turned my apron inside out. I spread it on the bed, then I lay down holding my still-bent elbow above the apron to keep from further staining the sheet. After a while, I felt my hand weighing heavy, dropping, and I fell asleep from exhaustion.

I don't know how long I slept. It was pain that woke me later, not from my wrist or my neck, but a pain worse than any other, the kind that you know you won't be able to bear, without truly knowing where it's coming from, or how far it can push you. The master was in my room. The whole time that he stayed to do what he had to do to me, he didn't even remove the cuff. My wound started gushing blood from the jolting. All I was thinking about was the blood staining the bed and that helped me to bear it. Once he was done, he got dressed, then he took the cuff off. He didn't leave. I wiped between my legs. He watched me do it. His eyes on me gave another pain. They were a look you give someone you've taken everything from, who you're angry at for not having resisted more, hoping there's still a little something left to take.

Then the master took me to the kitchen. It wasn't light out yet. A lamp was burning on the table. He made me sit before he went out. I heard clanking noises in the dining room. He returned carrying a large chain with rings at either end. I watched him do it, completely paralyzed. He placed the rings around my ankles and locked them shut.

You don't have to do that, I won't leave again, I said, my eyes watering.

I don't trust you anymore. After he had locked the irons, he pulled on the chain to test the fasteners. I concentrated on breathing more calmly.

What did you do with my father's remains? I asked. He shook his head, like he didn't understand what I was asking him. I'd like to bury them, I added, thinking that he couldn't refuse me. It seemed evident to me that everyone has the right to end up in a hole that's theirs alone, where people can gather and pray, a right for rich and poor alike, my father as much as anybody. The master was staring at my ankles in the irons.

What exactly do you want to bury?

His ashes, I said, like it was obvious. He looked up at me, again nodding his fat ruddy head, several times in a row.

Ashes, of course, he said like he was reflecting about something important. You'll have to forgive me, but the problem is I couldn't sort them from the coals. Tell yourself he'll help make a beautiful tool come tomorrow. You have to admit that's much better than finding yourself in some common grave. He was pretending to be convinced he had done the right thing.

Hate dried my eyes. They're gonna come looking for him, they'll find his tracks, I said, spitting out the words.

So, what do you think I care?

He surely said where he was going, I insisted.

And yet, apart from you, there's no witness to what happened. A mean smile slid across his face. Here, in memory of your father, he said, holding out an empty purse. Your father spent it all, he wanted more, that's why he came, he wasn't too bothered about you. And if ever anyone else ventures out here, the hounds and I will be delighted to get a little exercise.

I immediately thought of my mother who maybe knew where I was. I felt a fist to my gut imagining that she could end up like my father. My legs started to give way again. The master slapped me, telling me I better get out of the habit of fainting over any little thing. He forced me to walk around the house, satisfied to see that the length of the chain between my ankles just barely allowed me to get around, as I pathetically dragged my feet. I felt like an animal, but I preferred this to the cuff on my wrist, because as long as I had the irons on my feet the master couldn't spread my legs.

The days and nights were all the same, as if time had been replaced by frozen water. Something was dead inside me, and yet I could still breathe, still move. I cooked, I took care of the house, and it was no small matter to go up and down the stairs with the irons and the chain. The old lady found it awful amusing, snickering as she watched me struggle. I had even stopped counting the days that passed, seeing as how all a dead man wants is to escape the living, to rest, to sleep forever, even standing up, not caring where his feet lead him. A dead man is powerless and, I have to think, a dead woman even more so.

It was always the same hell. Every night, the old lady would go to bed after dinner. The master would wait for me to finish my work, smoking his pipe, and then follow me to my room. Once upstairs, he would remove the irons, attach me to the bed by the wrist, and take me. When there was blood flowing between my legs, he would still take me. By the end I felt hardly anything anymore. I had learned to go away during those moments, to feel a little deader each time. At least he did the thing quickly. I had even found a way to make it go quicker still by screaming. After a time I started to believe that I deserved everything that was happening to me, that I had come into the world for this, that it was my fate and there was no point fighting it. The master stopped attaching me to the bed rung. He found it more amusing to release his dogs onto the grounds at night. Amusing, that's the exact word he used to explain what I'd be risking, if I tried to run away again.

And then, one night when I still hadn't fallen asleep, I heard him coming back up the stairs. I figured he hadn't gotten his fill, and the thought did nothing to me either way. I certainly didn't have the power of those hunted animals, but I had learned one that let me split into two what was happening in my head and what my body was being put through. Before he came into the room, I lifted my nightgown and I spread my legs so he would take me quickly. I made out a rectangle of light around the door. When the door opened, I closed my eyes. He came closer. I didn't recognize his breathing. He brought my nightgown back over my legs, pulling it as far down as possible, then he grabbed my ankles to close my thighs. I didn't understand, so I opened my eyes.

It wasn't the master, it was Edmond, a finger over his mouth. He waited a moment, then he sat on the bed staring at the candle in his hand, and never me. I'm sorry, he said. He leaned over to set the candle on the ground, still turned to the side so as not to see me. Next, he placed his hands on the bed. His fingers picked at the top sheet. You'd have thought he was a cat sharpening its claws, like he was expecting something from his hands that he didn't have inside of him, maybe to convince them to find some courage that would belong to them alone, some courage he didn't feel he had the right to claim, but which he would be able to obey without question. It was strange what I felt at that moment. He for sure knew what the master was making me do and he'd never done anything to stop it. I cursed this man in my bedroom, because he hadn't been able to protect me, I cursed him, but at the same time I couldn't make myself hate him completely. This was the same man who let me mount Artemis, the same one who had brought me joy in the stable. I'm sorry, he repeated. Since I still wasn't responding, he stopped moving his fingers. He lifted his head, staring at the wall straight ahead of him, then he slowly turned toward me. His eyes were hollowed, like someone had chiseled out the edges, with two black-currant seeds planted in the middle. You need to know, he said. He stopped talking. He went back to staring at the wall, and then the words came out, the story he could no longer hold back from telling me.

The forge business had never really thrived, and that for some time now. One fine day, about three years ago, Charles went to Paris. All he told me before he left was that he was going to negotiate a big deal that would set things afloat again. During his trip, it was on me to run the forge. He was gone for weeks. He must have been sending news to his mother, and good news, no doubt, since I never saw her worry about the delay. And then he came back. I was there when the buggy entered the grounds. He wasn't alone. There was a woman with him, the big deal in question, I thought. They had gotten married in Paris. She wasn't that pretty, but you could see right away that she had good manners. I learned this later, but she was the daughter of an Empire general, who had died when she was little, and she'd been raised by an aunt, clearly very happy to get rid of her by marrying her off. Her name was Marie. I don't know what the master told her to convince her to follow him, but when she arrived at the estate, she didn't seem to have found whatever he'd offered her in order to seduce her. A big house in the middle of the woods and a forge on the decline never could have drawn someone like her here, of course. He'd always been a good talker. He's awful talented when it comes to hoodwinking people. In any case, it was too late, the trap had already been sprung. The moment Marie set foot here, she belonged to them. She had character. I liked her a lot. She tried to stand up to them at first, but it didn't last long. All they wanted was the dowry to pay the forge debts, and also for Marie to produce an heir. As for feelings, I think he only had them for his dogs. Marie started to waste away. The heir didn't come and Charles treated her like a good-for-nothing, seeing as it could only come from her.

Edmond stopped talking for a moment, he clenched his teeth, then he resumed.

There never was any heir. She isn't really sick.

So it's because she can't have children that they lock her up, I interrupted.

He paused again, and the black-currant seeds seemed to disappear, like they'd been lost in an eddy. Follow me, he said.

Why would I listen to you, and anyway I'm scared they'll see us.

There's no danger, they're sleeping at this hour, I checked before I came up.

I didn't hesitate further. The whole time he'd been talking to me, I'd forgotten to curse him. I had rediscovered the Edmond from the stable and there was nothing for it. In truth, I think that he could have asked me for anything and I would have done it. He blew out the candle, gathered it up, and we left. We went down one floor and walked to the master's wife's bedroom. Edmond took a key from his pocket and he opened the door. He went in first. Seeing as I stayed frozen at the threshold, thinking about the interdiction, he pulled me inside by the hand and gently shut the door. The room smelled of alcohol. Edmond lit the candle again, and light spread around us in a small puddle, like it didn't want to reveal everything right away. Little by little, everything took shape before my eyes. I'll never forget what came next. There was no furniture, apart from a large bed, and in it a body covered by a sheet, the body that I had glimpsed from atop the ladder and that hadn't moved. Edmond went closer holding the candle. He pulled back the sheet covering the head. He lowered the candle. I saw a face, almost black, a little like old waxed wood. For that matter I thought at first it was a statue that had been laid there. It wasn't a statue. And then, Edmond came back toward me, he took my hand and he didn't let it go again. The face grew even blacker in the shadows.

This is Marie, he said with great emotion in his voice.

She's... I couldn't finish my sentence and Edmond didn't say what was obvious either. I couldn't look away from her face. What happened to her? I asked.

He squeezed my hand even tighter, and he continued the story.

One night, I suppose Marie wanted to defy him even more than usual. It sent him into a wild rage. I heard the shouts from outside, so I ran to see what was happening. When I arrived, Marie was lying down in the dining room, face bloody. I bent over her. She was breathing. He had beaten her near to death. The queen mother wasn't there. He wasn't at all panicked about what he'd done. He told me to help him get Marie up to her room and lay her on the bed. Once we did, he looked at her coldly, telling me to stay.

Then he left on horseback to fetch the doctor. That's when the queen mother joined me. She seemed concerned, but not truly upset. Marie wasn't moving. She was still breathing, but barely. We watched over her until the doctor arrived. He asked us to leave the room. The hours went by. We were all waiting silently in the dining room. The doctor came out wiping his hands on a rag. I remember that he wasn't wearing his jacket anymore and that his shirtsleeves were pushed up. He was looking at his hands. He said that she was dead.

Edmond went quiet. He was reliving the scene in his head, you could tell. A single question came to me, to try to understand. How long has she been dead? I asked.

Almost three months. The doctor does what's needed so she doesn't decompose too quickly, nobody knows what truly happened, except those present that night, and now you.

But why do they keep her in that state? I said, trying not to shout at Edmond.

When I asked why they didn't bury her, he told me it was none of my business.

And the doctor, why didn't he say anything?

The doctor's another odd character, he's one of them, they've known each other forever.

I sought logic in what Edmond was telling me, but I didn't find any.

I still can't see what reason they have for pretending she's not dead, they could easily make it seem like an accident, with people like them nobody would go looking for trouble, I said.

He looked at me and I could see clear as anything those same two black-currant seeds buried in the whites of his sad eyes.

They have one thing in mind, make an heir, and for it to be legitimate, it needs to come from Marie. Now you see better what they're thinking.

Edmond's words cut into my gut, I felt like the thing he couldn't say was coming from there and not my mouth.

The heir that he wants me to give him so it becomes theirs, that's what you're telling me?

Once you've given them what they want, the doctor will just have to sign Marie's death certificate, officially dead during childbirth.

Tears started flowing from my eyes. Why didn't you tell me anything?

Edmond got low and put his hands on my shoulders. Look at me, he said, when I told you to leave, I didn't know that was their plan, I suspected they were plotting something, but this, good God, I couldn't imagine, I promise you I didn't know before.

I looked away, at the bed. And you didn't even try to understand why they were keeping her in this room, you dumb fool.

They really are capable of anything, so I told myself it was to buy some time, that maybe they hadn't gotten all of the dowry money yet and to get it, Marie needed to be alive, but you're right, I'm an idiot, if you knew how angry I am at myself for having obeyed them.

It's too late for regrets, you didn't do anything to stop them, that's not going to change now.

You can't think that, he said, slamming his words down.

Well I do, and anyway, why didn't you tell the police everything?

I couldn't, he swore that if I tried anything he would kill you both, I know him well enough to know he wouldn't hesitate for a second.

You both? I said in surprise. Edmond's hands tensed on my shoulders, like he was holding onto something else that wasn't my shoulders. Sounds like you're not telling me everything.

That's not what I meant to say.

Well I don't think it was an accident, I'm listening.

His fingers relaxed. He grabbed my hands.

That won't help. I'm telling you, spit it out.

He sighed, then he took a long pause. My wife, he finally said, dragging the word out, like it was costing him a hell of a lot. What do you mean your wife, what are you talking about, where is she, first of all?

Don't ask me anything else, please, I'll tell you everything soon.

And why not now, while we're at it?

She has nothing to do with you, but her life is at risk too if I don't obey them, he said, worked up this time.

I couldn't take anymore, I wanted to know. Talk, go on, now's the time, after it'll be too late. He looked at me, then he

looked at the dead woman. Her? I asked. I felt lost, I couldn't
see what he was trying to make me understand.

What a ridiculous idea, no, it's not her, I told you the
truth about Marie.

I sensed he'd resisted all he could, that he couldn't retreat
any further.

Charles is my brother, he said.

Your brother?

Yes, my mother was a servant here, long before you,
Charles and I have the same father.

I took my hands out of his. New anger surged inside me.
You're his brother and you consent to being his lackey, you're
an even greater coward than I thought.

You can't even imagine.

So then why, why did you let me mount Artemis, why did
you allow me that brush with beauty?

You seemed so happy that day.

I was, I had decided to trust you.

Shut up, I'm begging you. His eyes were full of madness,
they were rolling like hazelnuts in a too-big shell.

You're no better than them, I said.

Maybe you're right, maybe I'm no better than them, but
after what happened in the stable I didn't want you to leave
anymore.

I don't even want to think about it again, nothing happened.

I couldn't fight back, you understand, he continued without listening to me.

No, I don't understand, and if you care about me so much, why didn't you tell me everything in that moment and open the doors so I could run away? I wouldn't have hesitated for a second.

I couldn't, I thought I could keep you, be strong enough, that's all I was thinking about.

I was waiting for the same thing, for you to be strong enough to protect me. Everything truly good that had happened in the stable was sucked away into a dark corner of my brain. I swore to myself that I would never awaken it again.

I didn't think I had the right, he said.

It's not about that, and you know it.

No, I don't know anything, I don't know anything at all anymore.

And he, he has the right to force himself on me every night, practically in front of you. Do you want me to tell you how it happens? I said raising my voice. I had completely forgotten where I was.

Shut up for God's sake, said Edmond as he put one hand over my mouth.

When I had calmed a little, he took his hand away, but he didn't move it very far from my mouth, in case I started up again. I wanted to curse him more than I had ever cursed him before, but something deep down inside stopped me. I looked at him, planted in front of me. You'd have thought he was a soul struggling to escape from a dying body. After what he had just confessed to me, and since I couldn't make myself curse him, I tried to bring back the man who had put me on the mare, who had brought me down, then who had held me in his arms for a long time, the man with the shoulders I'd watched in the garden, everything that had made up that man from before, who would never again be that man from before, just as I would never again be the girl from after. I tried one last time. I didn't know who he really was, or what he would become, or if I could expect anything from him, but I still wanted to try, one last time. If only he had been a monster, just a monster, like the others, it would have been simpler in my head. I looked at the dead woman and Edmond followed my gaze.

What's to become of me?

I won't let them do it, he answered confidently, as if he'd drawn some determination from the woman's extinguished eyes.

You certainly let them do what they wanted up till now, why would that change? I said, completely emptied. He seemed lost in his thoughts, so I continued, resigned. He'll kill me once he gets what he wants, and you won't stop him.

Edmond turned toward me abruptly, grabbing me by the shoulders again and shaking me like a plum tree. I'll stop him, I promise you.

He killed my father.

Edmond stopped shaking me, but he didn't let me go. Your father, but Charles told me he let him leave.

What are you talking about, when did he tell you that?

Two days ago.

My father came here two days ago?

Yes, Charles told me that you were so angry with him that you hadn't wanted to see him.

And you believed him without asking me if it was true?

I couldn't have known.

You couldn't have known that he would hurt my father, that he would kill him, that he would burn his body in the forge, and yet that's what he did, right in front of me.

Now Edmond was looking at the flame waning at the tip of the candle. His closed lips hung down on either side of his mouth. He looked like the sort of man who's discovered he's guilty of a thing by going back through time to the very moment when he became guilty, someone who doesn't even have the words to help himself, much less anyone else.

I'm sorry, he said without looking up.

And why should I care that you're sorry, does being sorry do anything?

I swear to you.

Stop swearing. A cold anger took hold of me. There still wasn't a monster in front of me, nothing but a scarecrow. You have it in your blood too, better believe it, I said.

I won't let them, he repeated, pretending he hadn't heard me.

It's too late. I moved toward the door.

He hurried after me. Wait, he said. He grabbed my arm. I turned around, ready to spit in his face, but I couldn't. I found him pitiful and very small. You have to trust me, we no longer have a choice.

I don't have a choice, but you, you still do, you always did, now leave me alone, you've done enough harm already.

He dropped my arm and I left the room. Even at my age, I knew what to expect from men, that there were two kinds, those with some power over others, that comes from money or blood, or even both at the same time, and then the cowards. Cowards, like Edmond. Because being a coward doesn't have to mean retreating, it can simply be stepping aside so as not to see something bothersome. It seemed to me that Edmond had always stepped aside, so I had trouble seeing why he'd put himself in the master's path all of a sudden, especially for a girl like me. Despite his little speech and all his regrets, I didn't believe it for a second.

Back before my bedroom door, I looked outside through the dormer in the hallway. The moon was shining like a sun against a black background, a female sun who'd birthed shining dots of light scattered around her, like a vast troop of children watched over by an unmoving mother incapable of love. I didn't hear Edmond go back down the stairs. I saw him leave the house. Two dogs scampered toward him. He knelt to pet them. Seen from above, you'd have thought some strange, very calm beast was bent over on the ground. When he stood up, he brought one hand to his ear to grab a cigarette and lit it. He lifted his head, blowing out smoke at the same time, and he turned toward the manor. He surely couldn't see me in the dark, even with the full moon, and yet his gaze insisted, like he was trying to make me out, like he knew I was watching him. That's when he appeared. I couldn't do anything to stop it. The man from the stable, the garden, the man with the shoulders. I quick entered my room, because I didn't want to give him the chance to come back so easily.

I opened the dresser drawer. I took out the doll that my mother had made for me from dried corn leaves knotted with string, with an ugly piece of fabric on top that she had sewn to look like a dress. My history. Stains on the fabric, little rips, the arm I used to chew on, always the same one, and the other perfect, and then two big eyes made from mismatched buttons, the stitched mouth and the discolored mark where there used to be a nose that I had ripped off with my teeth one day when I was angry. I pushed my face into the doll and smelled it. My whole childhood was contained in that smell, like a map I had always been able to unfold and that allowed me to go to a place I alone knew. Before. Everything that had just given way inside of me. There are lives that are told in great books, and me, I had nothing but that doll I was holding, a kind of book without pages, that nobody but me could ever read. That doll that for the first time couldn't fix anything. And so I put it on the bed. I kneeled on the ground, as if before the Holy Virgin. I didn't pray, I couldn't be bothered to pray in front of what was nothing but a corn doll that smelled bad, a doll that had once belonged to a little girl.

Edmond

Rose is right, I'm no better than them.

She'll never forgive me.

After leaving her I crossed the grounds.

The cricket song felt like needles digging into my skull.

The dogs followed me all the way to the gate.

As I walked away, I heard them whining on the other side of the grating.

I charged headlong into the forest.

It grew darker and darker beneath the trees.

The silence swelled.

A night bird added its voice.

I stopped.

I couldn't hear the crickets anymore.

I could make out a piece of gray sky between the branches.

The coldness got in beneath my skin.

I stamped in place to warm myself up, and leaves broke like glass under my feet.

I looked down, stopped moving.

The sky no longer existed.

I wasn't cold anymore.

I sensed the trees, smelled moss and earth.

I was blind.

Good Lord.

The earth.

It came without me doing anything for it.

The forest helped me.

That girl smelled of the earth.

I had lifted her up one day. If only I had not set her down. If only I had always kept her up in the air, where I could have protected her.

Maybe it wasn't too late.

I had to find a way to save her, so that he would never have his way with her again.

I couldn't think about that anymore.

Concentrate.

I listened to the forest.

I recognized the sounds around me, which left nothing but crumbs of silence.

I knew what was running over the leaves, under the leaves, everywhere.

Dear God.

The solution was here.

Thanks to those small creatures, I knew how everything would end.

Rose would understand, and it would all be over.

Finally.

I wouldn't even have to explain to her what she needed to do.

After, we would go far away.

We would escape.

If she was willing to go with me.

If she was willing to forgive me.

Her

The mother floated, like mold in the pitcher. She began to slowly thicken on the wine's surface, slowly and stubbornly covering up a memory of lips, and also the lips themselves, imprisoned beneath this unstable crust that could have served to make the best of vinegars and that nobody, still, would use for such a purpose.

After ten days, the bitter flower finally bloomed in this pitcher that hadn't left the table, that nobody had dreamt of emptying, or even of looking at with any misplaced insistence, neither the mother nor the daughters, as if they had agreed on this in advance. Onésime had promised not to come back without Rose. He hadn't come back. The more time went by, the more she felt her heart, long burning with anger, extinguish little by little, so all that remained was a cold stone beneath an ancient river of lava. She didn't know where he had gone. He hadn't wanted to say. She didn't even know where to look. And there were her three other girls sitting at the table, each chewing on a piece of the hardened spelt bread baked weeks before, when the family had still been complete. All that remained of the batch was a single partially eaten round loaf that looked like a pale moon reaching its final quarter. A few days before. Centuries even, now that everything had changed. Apart from three young girls eating their chunks of bread, casting about for a quiet spot. Three daughters torn from nothingness, simply because men and women feel compelled to create something more than themselves to escape time, without considering or even imagining for one second the misfortunes to follow and the poisoned gift that a life can become. A gift that could prove far worse than the preceding nothingness, which is merely an absence paid no heed by men, or by any god either. Because taking a small being from the nothingness of before to offer it the nothingness that comes after is an immense responsibility, and to take four, pure madness.

She wasn't hungry. Turned her gaze to the open door, glimpsing a pile of manure seeping into the stones outside. Then she returned to her daughters, watched them tear off bites of bread with their small, still-sound teeth. She, the mother who wasn't eating, who was wondering what would become of them all, was no longer even thinking of the missing man with whom she had conceived this innocent flesh, barely remembered how they had done it, with no true pleasure, like carrying out a mission, leading a flock to the same razed field, incapable of experiencing the joy of birth, capable only of pain for which she today felt solely responsible. A great pain, which Onésime could never again shoulder. Despite the hardships, the mother had never allowed nor would ever allow the slightest feeling of the weakening kind to appear, as if she had always known that you have to be prepared to suffer your fate, that life is a conscious walk toward the nothingness that comes after, that with every childbirth it's not life being given, in the end, but a death sown. All this as the bitter smell of wine rotted beneath her nose. As she watched the remainder of her tribe: three girls, looking like nothing more than a pack of beggars, sitting on benches, not chairs even, heads lowered, bent forward like birds on a perch watching the ground or else some chasm in which to hurl themselves. These three girls were cloistered inside four walls blackened by smoke, trapped in a limp, eternal stream of time flowing with no future. Their only landmarks were useful, arrogant objects of wood or metal, products of irrevocable savoir faire and long tradition, objects that were picked up at times and then set back in their exact places, that were never replaced, that were repaired over and again, and that were handed down from one generation to the next so their owners could believe they were the bearers of some immutable mystery. A tradition that never changes. Like the small, light-colored dresses passed from one daughter to another, mended on countless occasions, fading replicas, like Russian dolls hiding frail bodies dressed in ever-shrinking fabric, and now sitting at the table, eyes hollowed and hair dirtied by all the dust raised by the wind and also themselves alone. She could remember exactly for which daughter she had darned a given spot on a given dress, sewn a given patch, remember as far as the largest dress worn in her time by Rose, which was now covering Rachel, and would soon be passed down to her younger sister, and finally to the littlest one who had complained one day about wearing hand-me-downs. Just the once.

They had asked her about their father's absence, at the very beginning. She replied that he was working elsewhere, to bring in some money. *It'll be a surprise*, she remembered Onésime saying. "Working elsewhere, like Rose," Rachel had said. "That's right," she answered. The girls hadn't asked any further questions, not because they didn't need answers, or because their mother's reply was sufficient in their eyes, but because their silences still carried the hope of seeing the family reunited, even in misery, even in the exhaustion of endless days. The hope the mother drowned in the pitcher, and that it again be filled with cider or else wine.

Rose

I was leaving the kitchen as Edmond came up from the cellar. He acted like he didn't see me and I did the same. I was angry at him. I was angry at myself for still not cursing him. The master had almost finished his omelet.

It should be done soon, said Edmond, at the same time as he set a small glass vial on the table, right beside the master's plate.

The master looked at him with a nasty air, mouth full. Don't leave that filth here, can't you see I'm eating?

Edmond cast me a serious glance, then he grabbed the vial, emphasizing the movement so that I could see what he was doing. I couldn't mistake what was in it. He gave me a longer look, furrowing his brows, to make sure I understood what he was trying to tell me. I lowered my eyes and then raised them.

You going to stand there much longer? said the master, annoyed.

Without a word, Edmond went to a cupboard in the dining room. He opened a door and set the vial on a shelf. This way, I'll have it on hand for the next time, he said loudly. There's enough there to kill every last one of those filthy creatures, he added in a hate-filled tone that surely wasn't meant for the rats. The master didn't react, he dug into the cheese. And then Edmond left. I felt a jab in my stomach, and I nearly fell flat on my face with the irons on my heels. Pain was twisting my insides. I stopped myself from vomiting in the kitchen.

When the old lady arrived a little later, she saw right away I wasn't well. You don't look too good, my child, she said. I didn't like it when she called me my child, I much preferred her my dear. It would appear you're sick, she added in a voice dripping with falseness. I straightened up as best I could, bringing one hand to my stomach. Your stomach hurts, she added.

No, it's more around my heart that it hurts, but it'll pass. That's when the master glanced over. He set to ogling me, like he would have looked at one of his hounds bringing him a piece of game in its mouth. He didn't say anything, he clearly wanted to let the old lady continue.

Do you want us to have the doctor come? she asked.

No, don't bother, I answered more harshly than I intended, but she didn't notice.

Are you sure? You need to take care of your health.

I concentrated on my breathing. It's nothing, I'm already feeling better.

A smile split the old lady's face crooked. I'm happy to hear that, she said.

The master's eyes went from me to her. The old lady's smile finally rent her whole face, and it wasn't pretty to see, a smile on a witch. They got up at the same time, and they shut themselves in the office. They knew what was happening to me, but child that I was, I didn't know anything at all. I thought it was just a stomachache, like when I drank soured milk once, and it had twisted my insides for two days straight. In spite of the pain, I had a single idea in mind. While they were busy talking, I rummaged the cupboard where Edmond had put the vial. The best he could come up with, to help me, was the rat poison he had used to kill the rodents in the cellar. He must not have imagined that I might swallow the contents of the vial, but it was the first idea that came into my mind. And then, I told myself that it would be too easy for them to get away like that, without paying for anything. The way to get rid of them was there, in front of me. I could avenge my father, get my mother out of danger, and also make sure that they would never hurt me, me or anybody else. I shoved the vial in a pocket of my apron, and I went into the kitchen to hide it. I was feverish at the thought that the master or the old lady would discover what I had done.

When they came out of the office, they were merry as anything. The master left for the forge immediately. The old lady stayed in the house dawdling so as to keep an eye on me. Not that I could go far with irons on my feet. I had the answer to my problems within reach. I didn't care much about the consequences. I worked out everything that day, how I would go about it. The idea of spending another night with the master forcing himself on me was unbearable, but I was willing to endure it one last time. All I wanted was for them to die as quickly as possible. When night came, I set to preparing potato galettes with lard, and lots of garlic and parsley, so the taste would cover up the poison. The old lady was still hanging about. I thought for sure I would have to abandon my plan this time around.

The old lady finally went up to her room. As soon as I heard the door slam, I took the vial from its hiding spot. I trembled as I poured the poison in with the galette ingredients. I saved a little, then I placed the vial in my pocket. I began to blend the mixture, very careful not to touch it with my hands. I stuck my nose over it. All I could smell was garlic. Partly reassured, I formed the galettes, each the same size, using two forks. Next, I minced some meat and poured the rest of the rat poison into the mash, to toss to the dogs before I went to bed. It didn't even occur to me that I would certainly be the first one accused. All

I cared about was being able to leave this place once they were dead, and the dogs were dead too. I realized that no one knew that I lived there, apart from the doctor. I couldn't quite believe people would die because of me, seeing as I wasn't even thinking about their deaths. I was only thinking about the evil they had done me, and which was slowly destroying me. I remembered that one day the priest had spoken about the great battles waged against evil in ancient times, even if that evil was surely not the same as mine. In my mind, the only evil to be fought was in that house, and I could put an end to it myself. I never had a doubt about what I needed to do, just about knowing whether I had forgotten anything along the way. I looked at the galettes piled on the plate, almost as if they'd miraculously arrived there, as if I wasn't truly responsible for what was inside, as if the master and the old lady were the monsters, the only ones responsible, like they had forced my hands to do such a thing. This would never make me a murderer in the eyes of the rest of the world, I thought, because not even their deaths would be enough to make up for my father's and Marie's, nor for everything they had put me through.

The master arrived first, still cheerful. He stopped in his office. He came back out almost straightaway and immediately sat down at the table. The old lady came soon after. She entered the kitchen where I was cooking the meal. She looked at me insistently, from top to bottom and bottom to top, pausing in the middle each time. I was afraid she'd find me out, that she'd read my thoughts, even that she was capable of smelling the poison in the galettes frying in the pan. She turned her head toward the stove, wrinkling her nose, and I truly thought I was going to have to confess everything. That's when I thought of the master crushing my father's bones with his hammer, of the ashes he hadn't even wanted me to bury, of his weight on top of me and his stinking breath, of his thing digging inside of me. I would see my plan through to the end, I told myself. The old lady couldn't guess anything, little matter if she was a witch. And yet, she went toward the stove holding her pointy nose, like something was bothering her. I stopped breathing.

What did you make? she asked.

Potato galettes.

That's not what was planned.

I make them as good as my mother, you'll see.

That's beside the point.

I stiffened, thinking that my plan was falling neck and crop. I can prepare something else, if you like, I said, my heart heavy.

She began to look me up and down again. No, it's fine, but don't do it again.

I felt a great release inside my body. You'll see, you won't be disappointed, I thought it wise to add.

I'm telling you that's beside the point. Soon enough I found out the point, which was the thing that had made her forget that I hadn't obeyed her. How do you feel, tonight? she asked.

Fine, I answered.

Your stomachaches went away.

Yes, I said, uneasy.

You'll tell me when they come back.

If they come back, I'll tell you.

They'll come back, my child, believe me, they'll come back. That was the second time in one day that she had called me my child, and this time her words felt like a blade cutting into my belly.

Don't fret for that, I said.

I'm not fretting, but you need to take care of yourself now. The now chilled my blood as much as the my child had. I concentrated on the potato galettes that I couldn't let burn. I turned them over in the pan to occupy my hands, hoping my head would follow. I stared at the drops of oil exploding every which way like liquid embers.

It'll be ready soon, I said.

The old lady rejoined the master in the dining room. I gathered my thoughts, and I carried out the plate of galettes. The master lunged at them, stuffing himself, while the old lady poked at one with her fork, lips pursed. A drop of sweat dripped down my back when she looked up at me. I quick returned to the kitchen so as not to betray myself. I heard them talking in a way they never normally did, and even snicker from time to time. At one point, the conversation turned serious again. The old lady used the word vexed. She must not have been talking about herself, seeing as, when I went to clear, she didn't seem vexed at all, the contrary in fact. There wasn't a single galette left on the plate, no turning back now. Anyhow, I wouldn't have wanted to turn back for anything in the world. I wondered how long it would take for the poison to work. With the dose that I had used, I told myself they surely wouldn't last the night. Since it was Saturday, I would have all Sunday to escape. That was my plan. I didn't know when the bodies would be discovered, or what Edmond intended on doing, if I should go down to warn him before leaving. I hadn't thought about it. I had to think only of myself. I went over everything in my head. The forge workers didn't even know that I existed. As for the doctor, I told myself, me being found served him nothing, seeing as how if the police came into the house they would find the master's wife's body, and he would have a hard time explaining that he hadn't known.

The old lady went upstairs to bed. The master waited for me to finish the dishes, and then came with me to my room. He put his hand on his belly several times as he went up the stairs, he didn't seem too hale. He didn't take his time that night. The poison was well and truly eating away at him. I stayed standing behind the door after he closed it. I waited until I couldn't hear any more noises. I went downstairs barefoot to get the poisoned mash and I threw it to the dogs from the window. They jumped on it like they were starving to death. I quick went upstairs to cram my things into my bindle. Next, I went onto the landing. From the dormer I could see the dogs wolfing down the mash under the fat moon. I didn't know at all how it would go now. The only thing I regretted was that I couldn't be there as they suffered. I so wished I could have watched them die while they watched me. I sat down, I was exhausted. Sleep felled me with one strike. This time, I wasn't outside of the dream, I was poured inside it. Not an image of me that I'd have watched from above without being able to make it move as I liked. Just me, driven by my free will, movements unhindered, completely free inside the dream, and soon, outside of it.

And then I heard noises. It took me a moment to understand that I was awake and the noises were quite real. The racket was coming from the floor below. I looked outside. A dog was dragging itself along the ground like a slug. The others were lying down, not moving. Right after, the master's horse and cart crossed the grounds at a full gallop, and I saw it disappear. It was over, the dose must not have been enough, I thought. I went back to my room and I put the bindle away in a drawer. I was having trouble standing. But though I was trembling so hard from fear that my legs were struggling to hold me up, I had to go downstairs to see what was happening. When I went down, the master's bedroom door was ajar. I approached on my tiptoes. The old lady came out like a fury, closing it behind her. She stood on the landing, distraught. She didn't even pay attention to me at first. With her gray hair unkempt, like little snakes about to bite, she didn't at all look like someone ill the way she should have. What's happened? I asked. It took her a second to realize I was talking to her. Get back to your room immediately, she spit out. I insisted a little more and I truly thought she was going to slap me. And so I returned to my room, leaving the door open. I sat on the bed, wondering what the old lady was doing in the master's bedroom, seeing as he had left in the buggy. It didn't even occur to me to flee at that moment. Everything went silent again downstairs. Later, I heard something like moaning and thrashing. The silence returned, and then the moaning and thrashing again. I couldn't have said how long the horse and cart had been gone when I heard it return. I went out to look through the dormer. The master was back, followed by another buggy. They were parked before the steps. I recognized Edmond, who came out first and the doctor second, no master in sight. They entered the house at a run. That's when I understood that the old lady had sent Edmond to fetch the doctor so he could aid the master.

I'd be lost if I stayed there. I went to grab my bindle thinking that nobody would pay attention to me. When I turned around, the old lady was at my door. I could have shoved her and rushed down the stairs to get away, but that wasn't counting on the way she was looking at me with eyes full of hate, her face ravaged by pain. She didn't say anything, she slammed the door and I heard a key turning in the lock. I threw myself at the door but bounced off. I did it again with a running start, several times, until my shoulder ached. The door was too thick. I was trapped. I sat on the bed, my bindle within reach, and I waited. I didn't hear the thrashing again the rest of the night. I kept my eyes open in the dark. I truly believe that I've never really closed them again since that night, that even when my eyelids are shut I can feel my eyes wide open behind them, never at rest.

The sun was rising when I heard steps on the stairs. I grabbed my bindle, ready to jump at the old lady. The door opened, I leapt, and this time I bounced off the doctor, who sent me flying onto the bed. He came in, the old lady behind him. I looked for Edmond to help me, but he wasn't with them. The old lady had cried so much that tears had dug away the little flesh she had on her bones. I was incapable of getting up. She walked in front of the doctor, came closer to me, and bent over nice and slow. What did you do? she said like she was spitting out venom. I wanted to run from her, but she was everywhere. The thing I saw, the thing I couldn't escape, was her gaze squeezing me in a vise of hate and pain. I didn't answer. You killed him, she added, like she needed to hear it from my mouth. I still couldn't speak. I realized that the master was well and truly dead. I would learn later that the old lady hadn't touched the potato galettes because she couldn't stand the smell of garlic, that she hadn't said anything so as not to vex me in the state I was in. The doctor, who had stood back until then, took a step forward. With the dogs outside, bellies in the air, it hadn't taken him long to conclude that the master had been poisoned, and I was the only possible culprit. He simply held out one hand to me, palm open. Give it, he said. Now the old lady's face was like water boiling in a pot. I took the empty vial from my pocket and I gave it to the doctor. He grabbed it with one hand, and with the other he dealt me a great slap that knocked me to the ground. I saw stars sink into a black hole, and a whistling began to whirl inside my head. Next, he helped me stand up and walk down the stairs. I saw nothing, I felt nothing. My legs did the motions, nothing to do with me.

I heard a door close, and I found myself alone in a room. The smell felt like a noose tightening around my neck. They had locked me in the dead woman's bedroom. Marie's. The idea of seeing her face terrified me. I leapt at the door to try to open it, but couldn't. I sat down in a corner of the room, as far from the bed as possible. A little light came through the shutters. I'd have preferred to shut my eyes, but I couldn't help looking at that corpse that I envied for being rid of life. I stood up then, I went over to the bed, and I took the sheet from her face. I started talking to her, not because I was going mad, the opposite in fact, so I wouldn't be tempted to talk to myself. Thoughts were racing through my head. I was a murderer in the eyes of the law. The old lady was going to tell the police. They would throw me in prison and chop my head off without seeking to understand why I'd done what I'd done. Watch, that's how it'll happen, I said to her, the dead woman. I felt like my fate was already laid out. At least I didn't have irons on my feet and I wasn't chained up. I went to the window, I opened it with the idea of hurling myself out of it, but the shutters were fastened by a large padlock and there wasn't anything in the room to smash them. I tore at them anyway. Nothing doing. I went back and sat on the other side of the bed, facing the window. I didn't talk to the dead woman anymore. I had stopped crying. I was cold. I mechanically stuck my hands in my pockets and I kept them clenched inside.

Time passed. I watched the day go by through the shutters, and then night came, and then another day and another night. Count, that's all I had to do. I didn't have anything left to say to the dead woman and nothing to hope from her. At least she didn't scare me anymore, we'd be the same soon, she and I, I told myself. The door didn't open again until Sunday night, and only partially. I huddled up, not moving. Nobody entered. Someone set down a tray inside, with water, bread, and cured ham. I didn't touch any of it. I just drank a little water on Monday. I began talking to the dead woman again on Tuesday, calling her Marie. Sometimes I thought her lips were moving and she was answering me in a gentle voice. I suspected we had endured the same kind of tortures. I think I must have stayed shut inside there seven days without sleeping. I felt weaker and weaker. I wanted them to leave me alone long enough to die of hunger. To go out quietly, that's all I wished.

On Thursday morning I finally slept, and was still sleeping when the old lady opened the door. The doctor was there too. She began to speak. In my state of exhaustion, I struggled to make the connection between her and the voice. It was as though she wasn't addressing me, or anyone else for that matter, like she was slowly reciting words she had learned ahead of time, to make sure that what she was saying was the same as what she had in her head. The doctor remained silent. He was clearly there for some other reason than to listen. He reminded me of a demon at the gates of hell.

You killed my son, you deserve to die, repeated the old lady several times. I thought she would go on forever, but she stopped talking. The end she was promising me had rung out like a death knell but her threats no longer affected me either way.

Do what you have to, let's be done with it, I answered.

She lifted her arm to silence me. Flames burned in her eyes. It would be too easy to give you over to the hands of the law, you're not going to get off that easily, without thinking about the odious act you committed, believe me. At that moment, she turned toward the doctor, clenching her fists. Believe me, you'll pay, she said again.

The doctor made a small movement with his head that spoke volumes about his obedience. I'd rather die right away, I said watching him. He pinched his lips together to keep himself from answering. Unlike the old lady, nothing was burning in his eyes, not even a little spark in the background. He was the coldest man I'd ever met. He turned around, pushed the door wide open. There were two tall men dressed the same quietly waiting at the door. They looked like statues, all in gray. The doctor motioned at them and they entered. They came toward me. I crossed my arms over my head, but they picked me up like it was nothing. They carried me all the way downstairs without my feet touching the ground. In any case, I couldn't have stood up on my own. When we were outside, the light stunned me like I was a flame whipped from a fire by a gust of air. The men continued to carry me. My eyes quick grew accustomed. I saw a wagon hitched to two horses, coming closer like in a dream. Not mine. I looked around for Edmond in every direction, but he was nowhere.

Next, the men made me get into the wagon, then sit on a bench. One stayed with me, holding me by the shoulders so I didn't fall, and the other locked the door shut. I asked where they were taking me. The man didn't answer, didn't even look at me. Then we set off. Sometimes, through a small window in the back, I saw a little greenness go by against a blue background. The trip didn't take long. The horses stopped. I heard squeaking hinges, a gate that must have been awful heavy to make such a din. The horses set off again at a walk. One or two minutes later, they stopped for good. The man rose, lifting me in the same movement. He waited for the other one to open the door before he sat me down. I looked up. There was a church that made my head swim, even on the ground, with its spire pointed like a needle. I wondered where I was. I had never seen this place. The two men made me go around the wagon. The doctor was there, but not the old lady. He took the lead. We followed him down a gravel path. There were little square houses on one side, all the same, and on the other a large, long building that extended from the church. Strange voices and sometimes even cries emerged from the houses from time to time. We saw a woman dressed as a nun. She walked quickly, looking straight ahead and ignoring our presence. I had time to see her enter one of the houses. The cries inside got louder, then they stopped. I told myself that everything I was hearing and seeing was all in my head, that I was already off the twig, like Marie. That didn't last very long. I would soon realize that the old lady hadn't spared me out of Christian charity, or so I would have time to think about the crime I had committed, it was just because she still needed me.

We stopped in front of one of the square houses. The doctor took a bunch of keys out of his pocket. He opened the door and we entered after him. There was a single room, with a chair, a table, an iron bed attached to the ground and large leather straps dangling from each side. That didn't even shock me at the time. I just wanted to lie down and close my eyes. I couldn't have cared less about what would happen next. The minute that would follow, the hour, the next day, and the days after, they weren't my problem anymore. I still had a body with arms, legs, and a head to think, but in truth I was dead, locked up, firmly resolved to let what was inside my head vanish so that no one could take anything else from me.

The men made me lie down on the bed. I didn't have the strength to resist. In any case, it's what I wanted more than anything, to lie down and go to sleep forever. They fastened my wrists and ankles with the straps. Then everyone left, leaving me alone, arms and legs forming a cross. I heard water dripping from the wall, somewhere behind me. Tears began falling from my eyes again, with no warning. I wasn't sobbing. I wasn't even really crying. The water was coming out of me naturally, nothing but water without anything else inside. I'd have liked for it to never stop flowing, so I could empty myself completely, so I'd dry out like the husk of a forgotten bean, so that everything still alive in me would leave with the water.

I couldn't say how long I stayed stretched out, pinned down like Christ on his cross. At one point, my stomach began to hurt again. I started twisting around. I didn't call out. I clenched my teeth. A little later, the doctor entered, accompanied by a woman, not the same one I'd seen when I arrived. She was dressed almost like a nun too, but in truth it was a nurse's uniform. She was holding an iron box in her hands. The doctor approached. I was covered in sweat.

It hurts? he asked.

I nodded.

Like cramps, yes?

Yes, I finally said.

For how long?

Not long.

When did it start? I mean when did you first feel this kind of pain?

About a week ago, I answered, because I could no longer bear to suffer while restrained. The doctor glanced at the nurse. She set the box on the table, opened it, and took out a syringe. She raised it in front of her face, testing the plunger. Two or three small drops squirted from the end of the needle, then she handed the syringe to the doctor. He pushed up one sleeve of my dress and pressed his thumb against the fold of my elbow. Then he inserted the needle into a vein and injected all the contents of the syringe. They were both on one side of the bed waiting for something to happen. I squinted to see them at the same time, as the pain receded.

You can unfasten her now. Have her eat in a bit, said the doctor to the nurse. She took off the straps. Once I was free, I didn't move. I remained with my arms and legs in the cross. I watched them leave.

A few minutes later, I still hadn't moved. I could no longer hear water dripping and my eyes were dry. I felt myself leave, but I wasn't asleep. It was perfect. Artemis came through the wall. She stopped at the end of the bed, tossing her large head up then down. She was still as beautiful. Her coat shone. I held out one arm. I couldn't touch her, so I asked her to come closer. She did. She leaned her neck toward me, but I still couldn't reach her, as if my hand went right through her head. I had the sensation that it wasn't her who wasn't real, but me. I'd have liked to climb on her back, for her to take me far away, for us to disappear together through the wall, with my fingers clinging to her mane and the wind blowing us toward freedom. Then the mare stepped back. Her hind-quarters entered the wall like it was nothing but a block of butter. She disappeared completely, without me. I wanted to move to follow her, but I was paralyzed, my will gone, surely because of what the doctor had put into my blood. I closed my eyes. At first, I saw lots of faces looking at me, my father, my mother, my sisters, the master, the old lady, the doctor, and also Edmond. They were all looking at me like they were curious, and also like they were getting along. And then they disappeared, sucked through the same place where the mare had disappeared. I hoped she wouldn't cross them on her path. It was that night I understood that sleep doesn't mean anything, that it's just a canter, a few long strides, that the true race that never ends is death.

Her

She told herself the moment had come, that if she waited longer she might lose the courage. She hadn't slept in her bed. Daylight was already peeking into the only window, casting timid shadows throughout the room. She watched her daughters dress in silence. Milk was warming in a pot set on a trivet in the fireplace, and the flat stone serving as a milk guard could be heard cantillating against the tinplate. A porringer in her hand, she approached the fire, ran the tip of one finger across the surface of the milk, immune to the heat; skin spooled around it, like an oily woolen string on a distaff, which she dropped into the porringer. Then she filled three mismatched bowls, identical in size, with milk, back and forth a few times to get equal portions, until the pot was empty. She removed the stone and placed it on the slate, beside the pitcher. She divided the last chunk of bread and leaned the slices against the bowls. Sat at the table. The girls tore up the slices and dipped the pieces in the milk, in silence, then drank, still in silence, a gradation of blond heads with milk making mustaches above their lips. From time to time, they would look at her nervously, taking interminable gulps in this great silence sickened by all the other silences. Once the bowls were emptied, the girls wiped the traces of milk away with the back of their sleeves, almost at the same time, and she echoed this movement in her mind, imagining even their baby skin beneath the flesh on her thumb. Then, she told them that it was time to get going. They cast the same sad and resigned look at their mother. The day before, she had explained to them where she was taking them away for a time. They hadn't protested. And yet they would have hoped and even wanted for her to change her mind, and maybe she would have let herself be convinced, her too, to preserve this semblance of family, if only one of the three at least had pleaded their cause, at that moment. But you can't fervently want something no one ever taught you to desire. Nothing left to do but protect these three small links of a broken chain.

"Leave everything on the table!" she said, when her daughters moved in concert to wash their bowls. "Gather

your things now, and put on your clogs. We need to go."
They obeyed without argument, again in silence, which had
since been multiplied by three, a silence against which their
clogs and the rustling of their clothes and later the breeze in
the foliage would crash. All those sounds would bounce off a
shield forged four times in the same silence. And then, when
all seemed settled, the silence was spoiled by the frailest of
child voices, the most innocent as well. "Why are we going to
grandpa and grandma's house?" There was a pause, and the
silence re-formed in absolute perfection.

She would have liked to stop walking, to turn toward this
fair fresh mirror with cheeks reddened by the morning chill,
to explain to her the reasons for her choice. She did none of
that, for fear of finding in that transparent gaze some reason
to turn back, a reason that could never be sufficient but that
in a bout of weakness she might have thought to be. Knowing that and nothing more than that, she continued walking
without a word. The girls followed her, leaving the question
hanging in the air. A moment later, after thinking for a good
while, she uttered a few words, as if they'd emerged from the
ground; they entered the soles of her feet, rose through her
puny legs and her tense belly, which had carried each of her
daughters, and finally reached her mouth: "You'll be better
off there, for now." Not a one protested, shutting down in the
moment, trying to open back up at the better and the there,
as only a child can do, delegating the question of time to an
adult in whom they have no choice but to place their trust.

Soon she made out the roof covered with browned thatch, then the gray exterior pierced by two arrow slits with cracked lintels, which looked like a petrified face flattened amidst a staggering backdrop of greenery. She placed one hand above her eyes so as to make the sun-bewitched sky disappear. Then she saw her father, sitting on the backless bench with wedge legs meant to compensate as much as possible for dips in the ground, lost in his thoughts; for it was past noon, and at this hour he always sat in this spot for a few minutes of inconsequential rest, and this since he had become old and understood he was old, without ever accepting it.

He lifted his head and watched them approach without moving from the well-worn bench, gathered his thick eyebrows around the vertical furrow extending from the bridge of his nose, then tightened his fist on the smooth knob of his walking stick and placed his other, open hand on top of it, before calmly welcoming this needy, toiling tribe that came from the same world, the same blood, and the same impotence. The mother soon emerged from the house, lurching from the terrible pain in her hips, their cartilage eroded by the strains of a single life. Surprised by the arrivals, the mother paused in the doorway trying to assess the situation, for lack of understanding it, simply knowing the ancestral role she had to play at this exact moment, and nothing more. She extended her arms, as though he hadn't done the same a moment earlier; but her gesture had a maternal pull that drew the girls to her, like a hen spreading its wings to gather its chicks in a safe place; leaving them alone, her and him, daughter and father. Him still seated, scratching the ground with the tip of his stick, an act with no intrinsic meaning, simply intended to get him closer to her without having to look up, without having to speak first.

"Can you keep them for me awhile?" she asked.

"'Course we can."

"Thank you."

"Looks like Rose is missing," he added without taking his eyes off his stick.

She hesitated briefly before answering. "Someone needs to mind the farm."

"And your man?"

"He left to make some money elsewhere. Just for a few days."

"You seem out of sorts."

"All's well, I promise."

He slowly lifted his head. "So how come your eyes say different?"

"My eyes don't say nothing of the kind," she answered nervously.

"That ain't what I see."

A rooster began to crow and she looked in its direction. He moved the tip of the stick forward, pointing to the path.

"You want me to stop by your place tomorrow?"

"You have plenty to do here, especially now that I've brought the girls...don't fret about me."

"You?"

"Don't fret about us, I mean."

He sighed, moved the stick back.

"Is it that hard to say what's really on your mind?" he asked.

She glanced at him, and new lines hardened her face.

"I do like I was taught."

"Sometimes we're not taught right."

"Too late to change that."

He placed his chin on his hands, which were still gripping the stick, his lips sealed because he wasn't in a position to say anything to justify his failings, and also because he didn't want to be the last to speak.

"I'm going," she said.

And with that she left, struggling to free herself from her father's clinging gaze, keen to quickly distance herself from that invisible hold, to no longer feel its weight upon her; for he had at least taught her this—to turn your back on an unmet gaze is far worse than staring it down.

Rose

J had no doubt as to where I'd found myself. A prison for the mad. They only allowed me to leave my room once I had regained enough strength. A male nurse took me outside, supporting me because I didn't have enough force in my legs yet, and also because of the sun, the fresh air, and the medicine they gave me and that I took without a fight. One thing I understood right away was that I shouldn't fight, or else it would be worse, and also, I didn't want to be tied to my bed anymore. We came to a court-yard surrounded by white walls that towered over me. There were three women wearing gray dresses, the same as mine. They each had someone watching them too. Their nurses, all men, were busy in conversation, right beside the gate, as if we were likely to escape. The three women had their hair cut neck-length. Without thinking I touched mine. I hadn't even realized yet that someone had cut it, and that the scar from my burn was clearly visible. Tears welled in my eyes. I tilted back my head so they wouldn't fall.

The nurse walked with me another few feet, holding just my arm, and let me go when he saw that I could stay upright without too much difficulty. He watched me for another minute to be sure I could handle myself, then he joined the other nurses. I felt strange as anything, somewhat ill at ease. I was standing and my head was spinning a bit. One of the women was sitting on a stone bench, legs spread. She was picking up little pebbles and rolling them in the outstretched fabric of her dress. As soon as one dropped to the ground, she would laugh, showing her rotten teeth. Another circled the courtyard without stopping, hugging the walls almost and looking at the sky with her lips puckered. You'd have thought she wanted to swallow it. It didn't take me long to understand that my unease didn't come from those two, who were ignoring me, but from the third woman. She didn't take her eyes off me, straight as a post in the middle of the courtyard. When I felt hale enough to walk, I took the few steps remaining between me and the back wall. The nurses were still talking near the gate without paying us any mind. Once I reached the wall, I leaned against it and I looked up.

That was when I saw the forest stretching above the prison. It gave me quite a shock to see it so close, not even knowing if I could return there one day. Since I couldn't keep myself from looking at the forest, and since it pained me to do so, I let myself slide down slowly to make it disappear. I sat. Bits of trees were still visible above the walls. My head started to spin again. I heard a sound in the background, behind me, a sound I hadn't noticed before. A muffled sound that I would have recognized among a thousand others. A river was flowing just behind the wall I was leaning against. Sensing it there made me feel the same as I had when I saw the forest. You'll pay some other way than death, the old lady had told me. She had kept her word. What I didn't realize yet was that there was something more important to her than knowing I was locked up here.

The nurses were still talking among themselves. They hadn't noticed that the woman who had obediently stood in the center of the courtyard until then was now very quietly approaching me. I was far from reassured, but I didn't want to let anything show. And anyhow, there was nothing mean in her eyes. When her shadow finally got to me, it had a strange effect, like it had entered me, the shadow, and like she, this woman, needed nothing more to make me understand her, like her shadow was the only thing she could give me, even if she didn't know that, because that shadow was the only thing that would never be stolen from her. And when the shadow covered me, I felt a great gentleness, first because I could no longer see the nurses behind the woman, and then because she had naturally offered me the possibility of forgetting the walls. She stopped a few feet away from me. I noticed the thin scar that started at the corner of her right eye and went down to her chin, like the trail of a dried tear.

Eight, she said.

What did you say? I asked.

You've been here eight days, isn't that right?

I don't know.

I'm sure. What's your name?

I looked at her face a long time, thinking that she must have been pretty once, but was now too scraggly for that. Rose, I answered.

Rose, she repeated strangely.

And you? I asked.

She leaned her head to the side, like she hadn't understood my question. You oughtn't to keep that name, she said, more serious now in her eyes and her voice.

I only have the one name, why would I change it?

She lifted her head. Her gaze had hardened, telling me I should shut up and listen to her. A name means nothing here, best get rid of it, and quick, specially that one. She abruptly turned around, then she walked away very quietly, at the same pace she'd approached me, but more labored. I could have sworn her legs were shaking under her dress. Her shadow slid over me as it dragged across the ground like a dark and transparent veil. I could see the nurses again. The woman planted herself in the middle of the courtyard, like before. She didn't look at me again, as if I didn't exist.

Since I arrived, the same nurse, a woman, has taken care of me, except when she's off duty. Even though she doesn't seem mean, I was still distrustful at first. I never was good at judging people. I didn't have much chance to learn how. I sniffed around her for a while. In the end I understood that she was a good person, the only one here I want to speak freely with. She looks kindly on me. I think she feels sorry for me too. I don't know what they told her about me. I never really knew what a friend meant, but, if I was free, I'd want one like her. One day I asked her where I was exactly. She told me the history of the monastery that not long ago had been turned into an asylum, since at a certain point you have to call things by their names. The small square houses are in fact old monk's cells, which were turned into rooms for the sick. A Carthusian monastery, which explained the church and all the priests around. I thanked the nurse when she was done telling me. She smiled, putting one hand on my forehead, not like the doctor checking if I had a fever, no, different than that. A trust developed between us over the weeks, hidden from everyone. She's always there, taking care of me. Her name's Eugénie, but she prefers Génie.

One night, before she left for the day, I asked Génie if she could get me some paper, ink, and a quill so that I could take the time to write everything I'd lived through. I don't know why I thought of it. In truth, the idea had been niggling at me for a long time. All I knew was that if I didn't do it now, I would never do it, and then there would be nothing left of me, that even if my story wasn't much nobody but me could tell it. At first, Génie refused, saying she wasn't allowed, that if she got caught she would lose her job and that her family needed her. I promised her that nobody would find out, that it would be our secret, that words were the only things that could come out free from my fingers. Because I kept insisting, she finally agreed, surprised as anything that a poor girl like me was asking her for such a thing.

The next day, Génie brought me a first notebook, a vial of ink, and a quill stuck to the end of a piece of elder wood. I took her hands and thanked her. Seeing me so happy, she almost did cry. Maybe we would have even cried together, if ever we had let the moment last and if she had had nothing more to do but stay with me. I started to write that very night. Since then I've been telling myself my story, everything that's already happened and everything that's still happening. The words go from my head to my hand with an ease I'd never have thought possible, even the ones I didn't think I knew, words I surely learned in the Landes, or else read in the master's newspaper, and others that I invent. I can't stop myself once I've started. Words make me feel something different, even locked up in this room. They're the only freedom I'm allowed, a freedom no one can take away from me, since no one, except Génie, knows the words exist. It's not so bad here. I don't have to work anymore. I also have someone to talk to from time to time, and words to put down on paper. What more could I ask for now?

It's been weeks now that I've been at the asylum. The days go by all the same. We wake at seven. I'm not given any more treatments, as the doctor calls them. They take me to the refectory for breakfast, then I return to my room. Next there's a walk, from eleven to twelve o'clock, then the noon meal, then I return to my room for a nap, then I can go out between five and six o'clock in the evening, then, once I'm back, the doctor stops by to check on my stomach, to make sure it's all right. He told me everything that's going to happen. My stomach is the only thing that interests him. I let him. I don't care, it's as if whatever's pushing inside my belly doesn't belong to me. Supper is at seven, and then there's Génie.

Here, it's not the madness of the others that scares me, it's that I can't take refuge in it myself. When I'm in the courtyard, I see the woman who counseled me to forget my name. Forget is what she must know how to do best, seeing as now she acts like I don't exist, not even looking at me much less talking to me. It doesn't really bother me. In truth, I want nothing to change, I want my life to freeze forever in one day repeated until I die, the same day with no surprises. Except, something is changing, something inside of me that I rejected as long as I could, and that I can't reject any more.

Last night, when Génie was in my room, I lifted my dress to show her my belly, which is really starting to swell. Do you know many girls in my condition here? I asked her. She didn't answer. She was staring at my belly.

It's because of this that I'm here, not because of something missing in my head. I didn't say because of him or her, but because of this. Hearing myself say that, I felt very sad and completely powerless.

You think you're here because of the child you're carrying? she asked me, like she was just discovering my condition.

The one I'm being made to carry for someone else, I answered. She furrowed her brow, still not looking away from my belly, like it was up to it to answer, or rather up to the thing growing inside. That's when I told her how I'd gotten here. I started talking like it came to me, a little messy. My story shook her hard and I could see she was moved. She couldn't stay long enough for me to tell her everything, maybe it was too much at once for her. So I told her she could read what I had written, if she liked.

At first, she was bent on maintaining a distance she'd been taught to keep, but her intentions didn't last too long and she was soon itching to read me. It's become our nightly ritual. Génie always ends her rounds with me, so she can stay a little longer. She glances outside, locks the door, then I hand her the notebook open to the right page. Next she sits on the bed and reads while I quietly watch for her reactions. She always starts by squinting a bit to concentrate, and then she's off. My story rattles her, that's for sure. More than once I've suspected that she regrets having opened my notebook, when she stops reading and lifts her head to catch her breath and looks away. She never says anything. Maybe she wants to get to the end before talking about it, no doubt she also needs time to let herself believe it all. If I was in her head I'm not sure I'd learn much more about what she thinks in those moments, what with her not knowing what to do with my words. I can tell she'd rather have never met me, rather not have found out about my life, but now that I've saddled her with it, she has no choice but to make do. That's the whole problem with good people, they don't know what to do with the misfortune of others. If they could quietly take a little piece of it, they would, but it doesn't work that way, no one can take on someone else's misfortune, not even a little piece, only imagine the bad things as best they can, that's all. I never held it against Génie for trying. It can't be pleasant to feel guilty for something you didn't do. That's the idea I have of pity, and pity never helped anyone feel better, especially not the one it's for. I got the proof one night that reading my words must have weighed too heavy on her. She started telling me about her life, her husband, and their two young'uns. I quick stopped her. I put both my hands on my bulging belly. I let a long moment go by before I spoke.

You have to get us out of here, I said. She didn't answer. She made like she wanted to go back to reading. Her silence only confirmed what I thought of pity and the lines Génie would never be willing to cross. She's a nice girl, but also and above all a good little soldier who won't break the rules at the risk of losing everything. I don't hold it against her, but it pained me to see her with no reaction, not even a word to say that she was sorry, far too much silence, to show she was powerless. She didn't want to disappoint me. She must have thought that I was in no state to hear her answer, and that guessing it, or thinking of another one, wasn't as bad as receiving the true answer she had in her head, that the doubt hovering over us was a little hope she offered me by staying quiet.

Forget what I just asked you, I said to stop her feeling uncomfortable. She felt obliged to speak. I quick placed one hand on her mouth, smiling. I just want you to do one last thing for me, I said without taking away my hand. I saw her wide eyes dreading what I would say. If something bad happens to me, will you take the notebooks from where I hid them under the mattress, just to get them out of here? After, you do what you judge best, it doesn't matter to me. I wanted her to feel like I wasn't giving her a choice, without pushing her. When she blinked, I knew that she'd do what I asked, that she'd try at least. We won't speak of it again, it's up to her. I moved my hand, her lips were trembling. I shoved my notebook under the mattress and told her to leave me. I wanted to be alone. My belly hurt. I didn't want her to witness my pain.

The doctor decided not to let me out anymore, not even for meals. It's becoming too obvious that I'm with child. He says he doesn't want my condition to trouble his other patients. He tasked Génie with explaining to me the path the delivery will take, a path she's already taken twice without much difficulty, she told me. The whole time she was talking, I couldn't care less about her explanations, seeing as how it wasn't really me she was talking about, but my belly. My belly hasn't belonged to me since the master forced himself on me, but also, more than that, I refuse to accept that he shoved something inside me that still belongs to him, even now that he's dead, something I can't name. Robbing me of my belly was one thing, but that he made this thing grow in there is beyond my understanding, because I'm not capable of conceiving of a child or even the idea of a child. And yet, I'm speaking of it.

My hand trembles as I write. Tonight, the doctor came at the same time as usual, except he wasn't with Génie or another female nurse. It was the old lady who was with him. She looked different from the last time I had seen her, so withered that the skin on her face seemed glued straight to the bone in places and wrinkled in others, like the glue had run out. She gave me a hard look that quickly went to my belly, which wasn't wrinkled at all. The doctor lifted up my dress. He told me to spread my legs. I was used to that normally, but I was uncomfortable that the old lady was there to watch. I still obeyed, closing my eyes. I wanted it to be over as soon as possible. The doctor put his finger between my legs and then pushed it real gentle inside. After a minute, he said the cervix was dilating. I didn't know who he was talking to. I opened my eyes while he was still inspecting me down there, satisfied it seemed. Then he took out his finger. I straightaway pulled down my dress. The old lady started counting slowly on her fingers. She stopped at eight. You didn't have to be too clever to know what she was counting. The doctor went to wash his hands in the basin. Then he dried them with a clean handkerchief he took from his pants pocket and walked back over to me.

Have you had contractions yet? he asked me.

Had what? I said, pretending not to understand. Génie had already used this word she'd explained to me.

Contractions, he repeated, like you're getting kicks inside your stomach, at more or less regular intervals. I watched him, never the old lady.

No, I've never felt anything as strong as that. His eyes were fixed on my face, somewhere other than my eyes.

You must let us know when it happens, it's a question of your health, for both of you. That both of you gnawed at my insides, like they were being scalded with boiling water.

All right, I said, trying to be as convincing as possible to get rid of them. Then they left.

In truth, I've been feeling the kind of pain he spoke of for a few nights, but it's unthinkable that I tell them, or anyone, what's happening inside me. Last night, I thought it was the moment it would come out. I can only accept that the thing in my belly is changing into someone, a little someone that I want to bring into the world on my own, so I can decide after what I'll do with it. Littering is something cows, sheep, any animal can do, why wouldn't I be able to, seeing as how I'm no more than a beast, I think to reassure myself. And if I don't succeed, I'll die, like animals sometimes do. Then everything will stop for me and of course for the someone too. What does it matter? I've been convinced for a long time that nobody controls their own fate, and people with nothing even less than everyone else. My mother used to talk about fate like it was a devil that'd been eating at her table every day. In truth, she didn't know what she was talking about, seeing as how fate isn't something you notice when you're alive, it's nothing but an idea that can't be trusted.

I'VE BEEN PUTTING OFF writing for a while. Until now, I didn't have the strength, or the courage. It came two days after their visit, in the middle of the night. I think I wanted the birth to start so badly that it did. When I felt it was time, I clutched the bed straps and gritted my teeth, and I went along with it. My whole body began to empty out. I was ashamed, even though there was just me there to see it. I don't think I cried out. The idea that the birth might cost me my life didn't occur to me even once, focused as I was on my pain and on trying to contain it. I couldn't say if it lasted long. When you're used to suffering, it's easier to get through it, you know what to do to push it back. And then I felt its head. I barely helped it along with my hands and the whole of it was there, all sticky, covered with the muck it had dragged out, with the cord that still linked us. I had already seen how my father did it with calves and lambs, with his knife. Since I didn't have one, I cut the cord between my teeth, and then I made a knot, so nothing else would drip out. It was like I'd always known what to do, and what order I had to do it in. Next, I put it on my stomach. It started to wriggle like a worm skidding in grease. It wailed two or three times, not very loud. That needed to happen too. I still hadn't quite re-alized that this living thing had come out of my living body. It's when I pulled it higher to place it on my bosom that I realized that it truly existed, far more than I had wanted to believe before it arrived. It started rooting around like it had smelled something it had always known where to find, but without being able to get near that something on its own. I just helped it a little bit. It pushed its head against one of my breasts, mouth pressed there like a cupping glass, and it started to gorge. It hurt, but it was a pain I liked. I stroked it, crying. No pain. There was too much emotion for me to keep it inside anymore. My baby truly existed, and it had come from me. I slipped one hand down to feel between its legs. I found the thing hanging like a little slug. I had made a boy. I had given birth to my son all on my own. He was here drinking from me. When he finished suckling, we stayed wrapped up in the same warmth, and the both of us fell asleep.

Génie came in the morning. We were still sleeping. She thought we were dead. She left in a panic to find the doctor. When they came back, we were awake, and my boy was hungrily pulling at my nipple again. I hadn't cleaned any of the mess. The doctor was wearing a coat. He asked Génie to fetch some hot water. While she was gone, he watched us, touching his scar, visibly not even a little moved by the sight. My baby had finished suckling when Génie came back with the water. The doctor said he needed to do a few tests to check that everything was normal. I made as if to keep him on my stomach. The doctor said it was for his good. I didn't insist. Génie gently took my baby and handed him to the doctor, who straightaway started to poke at him. During this time, he asked me how the birth had gone, if the child had cried. I answered yes, thinking of the wails, that must have sounded like a baby's cry, seeing as I hadn't heard one in a long time. He didn't even ask me how I had gone about cutting the cord. Génie kept her eyes on my baby, who the doctor then handed to her so she could wash him. He took off his coat, dipped his hands in the basin, and shook them over it without drying them. He said he would come back later, that the room needed to be returned to order. He didn't say anything about cleaning, but rather about returning to order.

Génie started to wash my baby. She was talking to him like I didn't exist. I sat up, I moved my legs to the side to try and stand. My head started to spin a little once my feet touched the ground, so I had to stay sitting on the bed watching her do it. He's beautiful, she said still paying me little mind. It was natural, the way she was washing my baby, like he was hers. I felt like crying, from not being able to move closer to take him in my arms and wash him myself, from only being able to watch her do it. Once she was done, she put him back in my arms, and I couldn't stop myself from crying as I rocked him and whispered quiet promises to him.

The doctor returned soon after, his case in hand. He didn't seem happy that I hadn't cleaned myself yet. But he really hadn't been gone very long. He folded back the bedsheet to find a corner with no blood or anything disgusting on it, then he told me to give him the baby, just long enough for a few things necessary to his good health, he said. I finally handed him over, even though I didn't really want to. The doctor took him like he was some commonplace thing,

a simple object, barely looking at him, not even seeing him.
He ordered Génie to help me wash up. While I was cleaning
myself, I didn't take my eyes off my baby. The doctor cut the
cord again cleaner. My baby twisted around making strange
noises with his mouth. I shouted to pay attention, but the
doctor was set on his task, indifferent to my child's look of
pain, and to anything I might say, just busy with disinfecting
and putting a nice bandage over the spot where we had still
been connected a few hours earlier. When the doctor was
done, he didn't even offer to give him back. He handed him
to Génie so she could get him to sleep in her arms. Then he
told me to lie down on the bed. I waited until my baby was
good and calm, and I did as the doctor told me. It was my
turn to be examined, and it was quick. Next, the doctor put
his instruments back in his case as he gave Génie instruc-
tions. Once he had left, Génie helped me get up and sit on the
chair so that I could take my baby, then she set to changing
the sheets. She took her leave reluctantly that night. She had
caressed my little one's head several times before going. Later
still, a nurse came to put a crib next to the bed. Before he
left, he looked at me like I was less than nothing, certainly
not like a mother.

In the days that followed, I thought of nothing but my
baby. Oftentimes, when he had been in my belly, I had imagined ways of getting rid of him, destroying him. Now that he
was here, he represented one single life in which the two of
us were together. Hearing him breathe, watching him sleep,
feeding him, that was all that mattered. I was no longer

thinking of the Rose that came before him, or the one that had carried him, or any other Rose from anywhere else. Now there was a new Rose whose life moved at the rhythm of this little child who had become my baby from one day to the next, and who didn't have a name yet, because I hadn't thought of that either. We could have stayed shut up in that little monk's cell forever, as long as we were together. It would have suited me just fine to live for someone that I loved out of instinct, like I had always had that love inside me, a love like that, that I never could have given to anyone other than him, something as complete as that love without expecting anything back.

Six days. They left me my baby for six days. Six days, he and I. My baby all to myself. It was far from the lifetime I'd wanted with him. Nothing but six short days. The seventh day after the birth, they all entered my room in silence. There was the doctor, two nurses, and the old lady. She went straight to the crib without looking at me. She set her hands on the railing, staring at my little one. She pursed her lips and her narrow chin was trembling. I'd never seen her emotional like that. The doctor told her she could pick him up if she wanted. I was ready to leap if ever she did, but she didn't dare. I don't think she noticed, and that it was more something else bothering her inside that stopped her. The doctor motioned with his head. One of the nurses moved in front of me like a soldier ready for battle. The doctor approached the old lady. He leaned over the crib and he grabbed my little one, who was asleep. I felt my heart trying to get out of my chest. I wanted to jump on the doctor, but the nurse pinned me onto the bed, and the second one started to attach the straps, and I couldn't do anything to stop them. The doctor headed toward the door first, with my baby in his arms. The old lady followed him. As she went by the bed, she stopped, looking at me for the first time. Thank you, is what she said, forcing a smile. I started struggling and screaming like a madwoman. I saw the door shut behind them. I kept on screaming, calling on all the devils to come to my aid, and even when my voice was gone I kept on screaming. I screamed like the madwoman I wanted to become since I couldn't even die. Those screams stayed with me, always, even when my mouth went silent, I'll keep screaming them inside of me until I die. I never saw my baby again.

Her

She remembered that when she was a child, her father had taught her to recognize birds by their song. Her heart began to bleed, as she walked and as they went invisible in the foliage. She couldn't help but identify their distinct songs, which she so wished would fade into a single voice, a powerless, unarmed desire. The winged creatures accompanied her nevertheless, still invisible, for at no moment did she raise her head, or even consider it—too heavy, too unbearably heavy.

She returned to the sad cottage built in its day by Oné-sime to contain a life that, as the seasons passed, had been patched and sealed with the traces of their children's existence in the unspoken aim of convincing themselves they were safe from misfortune. And every stone she saw also revealed the way it had been placed just so; an expertise inherited from men other than Onésime, from ancestors whose hands had tirelessly guided his as he built these solid walls. This house, now empty, which she couldn't force herself to enter.

She pushed the low door, no more than that, remained standing in the entryway, forehead against the lintel, as if she wanted everything to disappear at once, furniture and objects, as on the day the house had been completed, when Onésime had to push her inside, her belly already inhabited by a soon-to-be Rose. That sudden hesitation filling her, as though the act of crossing the threshold equated to her own future dissolving within a greater collective future that would slip away from her sooner or later, that fear that only a woman can have, of being nothing more than a house full of inherited shadows. Onésime, who had offered this home with pride, knew nothing of that in those days. He would never know any of that. Seeing her hesitate, his pride had turned to a kind of shame for not having done more, imagining what disappointment she might feel, since she said nothing and neither did he. Long after, entirely unaware of what she truly wanted, he constructed, with hands rendered immune to blisters and bruises, some furniture, a barn, a pigpen, and other things of little consequence. Hoping for a son. His mother kept saying that a pointed belly meant a girl on the way, and his wife's was round as the full moon. Rose arrived in the spring. This saddened him at the time, but as soon as he took the child in his arms she became his daughter, at least for a while.

"You're disappointed," she said, seeing his worry.

He placed the sleeping child in the crib that he had also made with his hands, then rocked it back and forth with a single finger.

"Don't talk nonsense."

"She's beautiful, isn't she?"

"Couldn't be any other way."

The child stirred, began to mewl. Onésime presented the tip of his pinkie to her lips. He smiled at her.

"I think she's still hungry."

"Give her to me," she said, her tone almost obsequious, as she brought one arm out through the neck of her nightgown to free a heavy, swollen breast, one twisted vein shooting across this milky sky.

He handed her the child, who grabbed the teat which would forever bear the imprint of Rose's lips and the lips of all the others to come.

"She's quite the glutton," he said, moved.

"Next time, we'll make a little boy."

"I'll trust you on that."

Now, in this moment, tangled up in a past disguised as happiness, forehead still pressed to the lintel, she was thinking only of that—the promise she hadn't been able to keep;

for in the end, their misfortunes had sprouted there, in her repeated inability to bring a son into the world. Everything that had led precisely to their loss. If only she had kept her promise, Onésime wouldn't have sold Rose, and they would be reunited in this house, shoulders to the wheel; struggling of course, but filled with hope, without even knowing it. It was entirely her fault, a failing that she thought she had cast onto Onésime. But in truth, she had lied to herself.

She pushed the door wide open, looked at the bowls on the table. A wasp flew from one to the next, taking off more heavily after each stop, then crashed into a window, finally landing on a flaking sash, clumsy insect, moving slowly, like a drunk on a narrow footbridge. She didn't go inside. She left without closing the door, walked around the house, crossed the rear courtyard, stepped over a row of turnips in which an erect hoe handle separated the weeded zone from what remained to be worked. She headed to the lake, not shaking even, not hesitant even; could no longer hear the birds singing around her anymore, and this without trying. When she reached the bank, she took her shoes off, lifted the bottom of her dress with both hands, then entered the cold water. She advanced, first dragging her feet across the sandy bottom, then extricating them from the sludge that deepened the farther she went into the lake. When the water reached her waist, she saw a swallow skim the water, lightly grazing her, and that presence instantly brought her out of her torpor. She dropped the folds of her dress, which spread out on the surface like a poppy flower in bloom, let her palms float on the trembling waves, still advancing, and the nearer her face got to the water, the better she could hear the sound of the small ripples created by her own movement, as if a dressmaker were adjusting a liquid garment on her body as she made her way toward an invisible altar without a cross. Then she froze, immersed up to her chin, waiting for the water to quiet, for the particles of silt to scatter, for the swallow to graze her again.

Rose

All that's keeping me alive now is writing, or rather, if there was some word that meant to both scream and write, that would be better. At least they, the words, don't let me fall. They're what I breathe, the monstrous words and all the others. They're the ones deciding for me. Though I don't really want to be saved.

The doctor no longer stops in to see me now that the old lady has taken away my baby and brought him to the castle. She has what she wanted. I'm of no more value to her. Génie showed me how to get my milk out to ease my pain. Earlier, I begged her to fetch the doctor so I could speak with him. She went right away and, when she returned, I saw from her face that he wouldn't come. I'm not asking for the moon, I just want to hear news of my child. I didn't even have time to give him a name. I didn't even think about it during the six days that he was all mine. I thought of nothing but him. Now, it's like he only ever existed for six days. I can't even christen him. He's gone. It's too late. Not being able to give a name to your own child is pain on top of pain.

It's been nine days since he was born. I can't stop myself from counting. This morning, they gave me permission to return to the courtyard. The tall brown-haired woman was still planted in the same spot. And yet something had changed. She wasn't ignoring me anymore, she followed me with her eyes, like I had become visible again. She turned back toward the nurses, who were deep in conversation, then came closer to me, like she had the first day we met, and she stopped. There was no sun and no shadow either. She began smoothing her hair behind her ears as she stared at me. I was ready for anything. I didn't care what she might do or say.

One hundred seventy-seven, she said. What? I asked. One hundred seventy-seven days, that's how long we haven't seen you in the courtyard. In hours, that makes four thousand two hundred forty-eight, she said next, as if it was critical information.

I guess you have nothing better to do than count the time I've been gone, I said, wanting to get rid of her, seeing as I didn't feel like talking to anyone. She stopped touching her hair, cupped her hands, and started to gently, sadly, swing them from side to side.

They took him from you, right?

It felt like another noose was tightening around my throat. You don't know what you're talking about, I said.

She stopped swinging her hands. The child, they took him from you, that's why you're back with us.

Shut up, I said. I couldn't take any more of her talking about my baby and I couldn't move to get away from her.

I'm not an idiot, you know, is what she said. There was no longer the slightest arrogance in her eyes, or in her voice. She seemed sincere, but I didn't give a damn about her sincerity. I was starting to run out of air.

And so what does it matter, if you're right or not? She came even closer, almost touching me. I lifted my head.

Four thousand three hundred twenty, in days, or one hundred and three thousand six hundred eighty in hours, if you prefer, she said, like she was telling me a secret.

I don't want to play.

No one's asking you to play.

So what, then?

She turned back toward the guards. That's the number of days and hours I've spent here, is what she said, raising her voice a little.

And what's it to me? I felt I was getting dragged into a game whose rules I didn't know.

She leaned toward me. You don't understand what I'm getting at.

No, I don't understand anything, and I don't care how long you've been here.

This can't go on, she said. Sadness took hold of her face. I regretted a little treating her like that.

Everyone thinks that, I suppose, I said, trying to keep my distance from the emotion rising inside me.

Exactly, I'm going to make it so it doesn't go on.

You intend to leave? I said, teasing.

She smiled broadly, all her teeth yellow like a mouse's. No one can stop me, she said.

And you're not afraid I'll tell on you, now that I know what you're planning to do? You don't even know me.

She made a surprised face. Why would you do such a thing after what they've put you through?

You're right, I won't say anything.

It's not my first time escaping, you know, I figured out how.

And yet you're still here as far as I can see.

She smiled again, but the sadness stayed. You want me to tell you how I do it? she said.

Yes, I'm curious to know.

She swallowed a big gulp of air before speaking. Forty-four seconds, that's exactly how long I have to count in my head for it to happen, all I need is to be alone and for there to be no noise around me, forty-four, and I escape, I go home, he hasn't moved, he's exactly where I left him, sleeping in his little wooden bed, there's my man too who's just come back to the house, he always makes the same face when he sees me holding the hammer, he doesn't understand right away, or he doesn't want to understand, he goes to the little bed, he looks inside, and then everything changes after forty-four seconds, at that exact moment the little one is sleeping like an angel, and there's no blood on the hammer that I just used to drive in a nail to hang a braid of garlic from a beam and not for anything else, because now everything happens in this past before the hammer and the blood, because I decide there will never be a forty-fifth second again, because at forty-four, there's only the image of what didn't happen, of what never happened.

She abruptly stopped talking. Her eyes were digging into mine to see if I believed her. I don't know what she read there, but she continued. They said I was mad, but it wasn't any truer at the time than it is now, because my little one was going to die anyway, and we were going to end up dying with him some other way, he was barely breathing, he had a vileness in his body that kept him from moving or talking, he was barely breathing, good God, it's not fair to breathe for nothing, no one could come help him, heal him, no one, except me. She went silent again. She wasn't trying to burrow into my eyes anymore. She simply wanted to make sure I hadn't lost the thread.

Then she resumed. I suppose that not wanting to let someone you love suffer is madness, that it goes against the suffering that God has decided to make us endure. Here, all you have are people stuck on some suffering they never accepted, that's the only truth there is, that's why they take refuge on the other side of that suffering, in time that's moving backward, and so don't you believe that I'm mad, little girl, if ever I was, my boy would still be alive and he would still be breathing, he would be breathing just like before, for nothing, so you see, the hammer, it never left my hand, still feels heavy in it, it will never leave my hand again, except that now it won't be anything but a hammer made to drive in nails and not for something else, at forty-four, it's nothing but that hammer.

She seemed to be waiting for a reaction. I understand, I said. I wasn't lying, in truth I understood her.

She swept her gaze across the courtyard, making a big motion with her hand at the same time. It's when the noise comes back that I begin to doubt and I begin to pretend. I can see that you're not mad either, that you can't decide whether to lose your mind or not, you ought to find a way to escape too, a way that's all yours, because no one will help you here. For me, it's counting that helps.

I thought about Artemis who I had seen come through the wall, and who I hadn't had the power to bring back when I wanted. For me, the moment I got on her back is when time stops, the moment that comes right before everything changed, when I imagined that life might be worth the bother of living.

Seems like you have an idea of how to go about it, or else you're looking for one right this second, she said, watching me.

I was certainly not ready right then. I'd stopped thinking about the mare. I was thinking about my baby they'd stolen from me.

I'll never see him again, I said with a lump in my throat.

You didn't give him a name, at least.

I didn't have time.

That's best.

I can't even call him by his name in my head, I said, feeling the tears rise.

Not having named him can only help you, believe me.

I began to hit at my belly. I should have killed him while he was in here.

Tell yourself that you actually did.

Now tears were streaming from my eyes. Leave me alone, I can't take anymore, I said. She straightened up and started rubbing her hands on her thighs, from top to bottom, faster and faster. I automatically started counting. I'd bet my life she stopped at forty-four. Then she looked at her hands, like someone had just stuck them to the ends of her arms, and now she didn't know what to do with them. I had a good idea of what she wanted to see appear: the hammer she seemed to be looking for. I wanted to convince myself she truly was mad. A first tear fell from each of her large eyes, followed by others. She began to hit at her face with clenched fists, repeating the same word amid her sobs. Her mouth was so chalky that I couldn't make out what she was saying, it sounded like my. The nurses came running, they grabbed her arms so she'd stop hurting herself. It took two of them. She was still shouting when they took her away. Then the silence returned, and I closed my eyes so nobody would see me cry.

That night, when Génie came into my room, she seemed exhausted, preoccupied by something. I didn't want to know. I had a single thing on my mind. I lifted my mattress and took out the two notebooks I had filled and placed them on the bed. I asked her to sit next to me for a moment. She did, even though I could see she didn't really want to. She looked at me sadly, like she was trying to stop me from talking, or stop herself from hearing me. I've almost finished my second notebook, I said.

Her eyes went from me to the notebooks. I'll bring you another one tomorrow, she said.

I forced myself to smile. I don't think I have much left to write that's worth the trouble.

Don't talk nonsense, I'll bring you a new one tomorrow, I promise.

I kept smiling. I didn't intend to rush her. All right, I said. She stood up. Can I ask you one last thing before you leave?

I'm listening, she answered, jittery.

You know the tall brown-haired woman, really thin, with a scar on her cheek?

You mean the Counter? she said, surprised.

You call her that?

Everyone calls her that.

Why is she locked up here?

Génie waited a beat. I'm not sure it's the right time.

Please, I'd like to know.

Why?

Please, don't press me.

She sighed. It's a terrible story, she said.

That's all there is in my life, terrible stories, so what's one more?

She killed her son.

With a hammer, right?

How did you know?

She told me.

Normally she doesn't talk to anyone.

Her child was sick, wasn't he?

What else did she tell you?

That's all.

Génie's voice cracked when she began to talk again. From birth the child suffered from a disease that paralyzed him, she spent her days taking care of him, while her husband worked until late at night, avoiding reality, people said. She claimed she killed her son to free him from his pain, that there was no other solution. She was judged not responsible for her actions, that's how she avoided the death penalty and why she's here. Génie's eyes were all red.

From the way you talk you seem awful moved by her story.

As girls, we were neighbors, always at her house or mine, that creates a bond of course, we lost touch when she married a man from another village, they both worked on some large estate, I never knew more than that. Génie got lost in her thoughts for a moment before continuing. I had the impression it did her good, now that she had started talking. The trial caused quite a stir at the time, there were people defending her and others against, and then it subsided.

Other than the Counter, what's she called? I asked.

It's funny.

What's funny?

Rose, she's called Rose, like you.

Rose, I repeated, as if I was talking about a stranger. Now I better understood her reaction when I had told her my name, and she had said to get rid of it. And her son, what was his name?

What does it matter?

I'm curious, it's not often I have the occasion, you know.

Génie thought for a moment. I don't think he was ever christened, she answered, like she was surprised at her own response. Why are you so interested in her?

I don't know, she seems different to me, not like the others.

Is that all? Génie said.

I didn't want to tell her more. And what became of her husband?

I think he still works on the estate where they were employed, he's never come to see his wife since she was put away, to my knowledge.

I couldn't call the Counter anything different, certainly not Rose, even in my head. Her voice surfaced from my memory, that cry she had let out in the courtyard. I still wonder what it means, if she was calling her dead son, or just anybody to come finish her off with a hammer.

Is something wrong? Génie asked me.

I didn't answer. My mouth was dry. I wanted her to leave as quickly as possible.

Once Génie had gone, I placed my notebooks beneath the mattress and I sat on the floor. I didn't need to close my eyes. It was a dark night, and the darkness was enough to push back the walls. I imagined what great darkness there might have been before my birth, an eternity that ended the moment I came out of my mother's belly, and also the eternity that would begin after my death, except that that one would never end. I was stuck between those two eternities, thinking about what madness it was to take someone from a peaceful eternity to make them aware of the next, all that time spent not understanding why we're in the world, why we cling so tightly to life, always trying to push back the high walls of death, when perhaps it would suffice to climb them, or pass through them, so we'd never have to ask ourselves any more questions. Because living is exactly that, being stuck between two eternities. The first one was never up to us and the second is the work of God, or so they say. But, I thought, if you have the misfortune of not encountering him along the way, it's hard to reconcile with the idea of a nothingness that comes after, with the idea of fate that would make us twigs in a strong current.

Since I hadn't encountered him yet, that damned God, I prayed for the mare to come back. I closed my eyes to the night, calling for her. She didn't come. It was my mother who emerged through the wall, with my sisters, but they didn't even see me. They crossed the room like it was nothing, and they disappeared. Edmond came just after. He stopped in front of me, casting his gaze around the room, not in a hurry to leave, like he was looking for me but didn't see me either. This man who could have saved me but hadn't, who would drag around what he hadn't done until his death, I had no doubt about that. All that my father had set in motion by selling me to the blacksmith was bounded by two things, my meeting Edmond, who set me on top of the mare, and the birth of my baby, two tangled feelings that I had never been given the chance to untangle. I didn't even think about the master's death anymore. I only regretted that he hadn't suffered longer, and that the old lady hadn't died with him. Maybe then Edmond would have come to get me and my child, and we would have left on top of the mare, riding along the river in search of something too far gone. I couldn't help thinking that everything that hadn't happened could have, without suspecting for a single instant that I was wrong about almost all of it.

Her

e looked her over from head to toe for a
while, and the more he looked at her, the
grimmer his face became.

"You're soaked to the bone, now aren't you?"

She only then realized that her clothes
hadn't dried, that she hadn't even taken the time
to change. She felt foolish.

"I slipped in a ditch on the way back," she
said.

"Ditch must have been awful deep."

"Yes, awful deep."

He started tapping one of his shoes with the tip of his stick. "Well, daughter, you managed not to get your clogs wet."

She didn't respond right away, hanging on to that "daughter" that she hadn't heard spoken aloud since she had left the farm on Onésime's arm; that "daughter" that he had intentionally added so she wouldn't consider it a question and most of all so she wouldn't answer him, the way any man of sound mind would do when confronted by the truth of a woman, though not his daughter; which men do sometimes and even often—ask questions with no purpose, whereas women never do anything if they will receive nothing in return, they need to know where they're going, always.

"I came back to get 'em," she said.

He resisted the "why?" so as not to force his daughter to lie. He knew she was prepared for that.

"Already?"

"I don't know what got into me."

"Maybe your head wasn't quite right yesterday."

The girls pelted out of the house, happy to find their mother, as if she had left them weeks ago; not even caring about her soaked dress or her dry shoes; not caring about what might have happened between the moment she left and when she reappeared in her muddy clothes. The grandmother came out in her turn, a few labored steps, before coming to a stop, as if in the middle of nowhere. She saw the little throng pressed around the mother, then looked at her husband, and fear deepened the furrow between her eyes. Her lips were trembling slightly.

"Come inside a moment," said the grandmother, but no one listened to her.

"Why did you come back, Mama?" asked Rachel.

She tousled the mop of hair.

"You're not happy to see me?"

"No I am, I'm really happy."

"I was thinking so hard about you all that I fell flat into a ditch," she said, looking at her mother.

The grandmother shifted her upper body, ready to return to the house. She stayed that way for a moment, holding herself sideways.

"I'm going to give you some food for tonight. You won't have time for anything between now and then."

"Don't bother. We need to leave before nightfall."

"Come inside a minute!" said the grandmother raising her voice.

"All right."

The grandmother pointed her chin at her husband without looking at him. "Stay with the girls."

At no point had the grandmother taken a peremptory tone. Each word seemed steeped in natural authority that would suffer no contradiction. Once inside with her daughter, the grandmother took a clean dish towel from a closet, spread it on the table, near a large slate slab glistening with grease, then went to fetch a cast-iron pot that rested on the trivet in the fireplace and set it on the slate with an "oof!" With the help of a slotted tin ladle, the grandmother struggled to fish out five portions of potatoes grated into a glairy broth, taking care to drain them well before meticulously lining them up on the cloth.

"Will you have enough for five potato pancakes or should I add more?"

"That's more than enough for us. I'll slice a little ham to go with it."

The grandmother folded the towel back up, applying light pressure with her hands, and the cloth soaked up juice in that spot.

"They're fresh-made from yesterday."

"I'll bring back the towel clean next time."

"There's no rush."

The grandmother put the lid back on the pot, placed the ladle upside down on top of it, then gripped the handles, "oof!" and returned it to the trivet. She watched her do this without offering to help. She knew her by heart.

"How'd you go about doing that to yourself?"

"It was dumb. I was rushing."

"Rushing to leave or rushing to come back?"

She said nothing. The grandmother went back to the table, knotted the four ends of the cloth, and held it out to her daughter.

"Though, from what I can recall, you were always quick on your feet."

She took the cloth filled with the potato stuffing. "Just takes a moment."

The grandmother let go of the cloth without moving. "Best to chase away the moments like that."

"I'm going to carve me a nice stick, like Papa."

"Do as you like, but don't slip again, and risk doing something foolish you'll never have the chance to regret."

"It won't happen again…"

"There's one thing I never want to have to do in what remains of my life, a single thing I wouldn't be able to bear…" The grandmother stopped talking, grabbed her daughter's free wrist, squeezed it, shaking it nervously. Her voice didn't tremble. "To one day have to take my daughter to the cemetery, before I get there. That's a thing I could never endure."

"It was just a stupid accident. Everything's fine now…"

"A mother is made to worry. Nothing to be done for it."

Rose

Jthink of the Landes, a place I called home
a long time ago, in another life. Why
shouldn't I want to give in to this damned
eternity beckoning to me? Everything that made
me someone, however insignificant, has been
taken away. What's the point of continuing to
live when there's no hope left in anything, when
you've become a ghost that knows it's a ghost.
My mother and sisters must have accepted
things by now. They've even surely left the farm,
seeing as the work's too hard for women, unless
my mother found another man, though that'd

surprise me from her. I don't think she's capable of such a thing. It pains me to imagine them leaving the Landes, first because it was our home, and also because the last thing that could make them still think of me from time to time is there. A stone where I engraved my initials with a fine-pointed nail. I took my sisters there, one after the other, to engrave their initials with the same nail. We're beside each other for always. An always on a human scale. It's no doubt foolish to engrave letters on a stone that people will sometimes look at in passing, wondering who the people behind the initials were. And maybe they won't even see them, because moss will have covered them up, it's surely already happened. Nothing but a rock covered with moss, that the earth will swallow sooner or later, or that someone will dig up one day and use for a piece of wall. Then there won't be the slightest visible trace of my passage. Because inside the house, there's nothing left of me, not a footprint, not a fingerprint, nothing that can make it so someone remembers. It's terrible to think there's no reminder of me out there, apart from those initials in the stone, next to my sisters'. In truth, I exist for no one. All that really exists is what we share, what we represent to others, even if that's all there is, because a mere memory is worth nothing, it always warps, gets bent in such a way so it can be put away in a corner. Memories, especially the good ones, are nothing but pain that we collect unawares. In the end, I'd have rather never engraved those initials. Knowing they're lying along some path brings me great sadness, the mark of terrible powerlessness. I don't know any stronger words. There must exist at least one, but if I learned it, I wouldn't use it, seeing as I could never give it the meaning and strength I wanted. That's what always happens with new words, you have to tame them before you use them, you need to help them grow, like planting a seed, and you best take care of them afterward too, not abandon them along a path telling yourself they'll get along fine on their own, if you want to harvest what's sprouting inside them.

I can tell I've emptied my bag of words, that I didn't have everything I needed to truly say things the way I felt them the moment I felt them, that sometimes the ones I use don't fit exactly, that I would have needed to know other ones, bigger ones, words with more things inside them. I learned to love all the words, the simple ones, and the complicated ones that I read in the master's newspaper, the ones I don't always understand but that I like all the same, just because they sound good. The music that comes out of them is often enough to transport me somewhere else, quieting whatever they contain in their gut, to make room for something better, dreamlike. I call them magician words: utopia, radiant, jovial, lazaretto, miscellany, miter, meridian, pyracantha, mausoleum, poppycock, iota, ire, paragon, philanderer, Moorish, jurisprudence, confiteor, and so many others that I retained without effort, though I didn't know their meaning. They strike me as lighter to carry than those that are said. They're food for that thing which will fly away from my body when I'm dead, my own music. Perhaps that's what they call a soul. I'd like to take these words all the way to the end, etched into the pages of my notebook, far better than initials on a rock. I will remember these words that create a world just for me, and that are usually enough for me to float far away, far from my memories of the Landes, far from my lost child. Usually.

Now, there's nothing to be done, the words are worthless to me, they're empty, incapable of holding all that I want to place inside them. In truth, words are nothing now. They have no more power, none at all.

I remember my father taking a notebook from the sideboard, which he would do once a week, always on Saturday evening. It was a small notebook with the word expenses written large on it. He couldn't write very well but he knew how to write that, and count too. Usually he didn't drink much either, but those evenings, he would take out the bottle of the hard stuff so as to better swallow the expenses, the earning versus the spending, is how he explained it to me one day. Never anything proud about it, judging from his face when he got to the numbers at the bottom. The only variation being the faster the bottle emptied, the worse the week had been. There was no better barometer to tell the weather in the Landes. When I think back, I never saw the bottle last long. I would watch him sidelong, his eyes receding farther and farther, never disappearing completely, as if the liquor rose to that exact spot and no higher. My father wasn't a violent man. Even when he drank too much, he wasn't. I regret now that there wasn't more violence in him. Maybe then he could have fought harder against the master, and he would still be alive. But what's the point thinking about things you

can't change. A damned sickness. What's the point of counting in a notebook if it's to make subtractions your whole life.

I think about the Counter too. I can't manage calling her
anything else. I think about her advice not to give names
to the people you're meant to love, or, if they already have
a name, to take it away in time. That all you have to do is
watch the scenes from your life before the misfortunes happen, that that's the only way to change things in your head;
you stop time on moments frozen before a thing happens, so
that something else can exist instead. The Counter holding a
hammer in one hand and a nail in the other, or me running
away into the woods with my sisters to make crowns from
chestnut tree leaves, while my father looks for me so he can
bring me to the village and sell me. I don't have the Counter's
experience. I always end up following my father. The only
moment I manage to freeze is when I'm on top of the mare,
and then when I get down and find myself in Edmond's arms.
I don't even remember how he looked at me, or even if he
did truly look at me, when I was still a virgin. If only he had
looked at me for longer, I would have held that gaze to get
him to understand that I was ready to give myself to him,
so that nobody else could ever have me again. Why am I
thinking of that moment? It's all a haze. In truth, I don't even
know what happened anymore. That moment, the moment
time shifted, is like a whirlwind I don't want to enter, that I
never wanted to enter. Because, even after all these years, I'm
certain there was a kind of unmeasurable wanting, a mad
desire in that look Edmond was forcing himself to hold back.

There wasn't the least bit of pity in his eyes. Now, pity is the only thing I inspire in people who feel some kindness toward me. People is an awful big word when I'm only talking about Génie. When you're brought here, it means you're already dead, that you're nothing more than a story that is impossible to change, and not a human person. Inspiring pity in someone means creating some never-lived pain in a heart not prepared to receive it, but that would still like to take a piece of it, without truly being able. Pity is the worst of the feelings you can inspire in others. Pity is the heart's defeat. I never felt pity, not even for my father when he was beaten to death and then burned. All I felt at that moment was hatred for the man who killed him while he let me watch, who wanted me to watch. I don't feel pity for my mother and my sisters either; just sorrow, and it is infinite. I'm no longer part of their world. If I got out of the asylum now, I couldn't return to live with them, I might not even remember the way back to the Landes. If by a miracle I was able to escape this cell where monks once prayed, believing in the salvation of souls, I would go directly to the castle to get my baby, even if it meant I'd have to kill the old lady with my own two hands.

Her

When her father came to see her in the Landes, she couldn't do otherwise than tell him everything. Once she had finished, he remained inside the house for a moment, busy thinking, seated on a corner of the bench. He tried to speak, but nothing came. He stayed quiet for a while longer, still thinking, allowing the time necessary for a few words to rise in his throat, as if along a greased-up rope, not the words he would have liked, but the only ones he was capable of.

"Shouldn't stay here alone anymore."

"I'm not alone. I want to be here when they come back."

"They'll know where to find you."

She looked hard and deep at her father. "I'm not leaving."

He bit his lip. "And if neither of them comes back?"

"It's up to me alone to decide."

"And for the farm?"

"We'll manage."

He nodded, turned to the side to get up, at the same time taking his stick that he had leaned against the table. Once standing, pensive, he nodded again and looked at his daughter, still seated. She returned his gaze, as if it was merely a pretty trifle that she had little use for. Nothing more.

SPRING CAME LATE, the female season, the season of arrivals, the season of subterranean powers graciously offered to the world above; but all of that had been before the collapse. She would never again view it the same way, for this spring, coming after the terrible autumn, was nothing but lies. We awaken in forgetting, but fall asleep in memories.

For a whole year, whether it was sunny or windy or raining or snowing, she would go down the path every night to the first fork; and there she would stand, watching from one side, then the other, still believing a little in Rose's return and not at all in Onésime's, and that for some time. On occasion, for just an instant, she would make out a silhouette that sprung from her memory, seeing it grow and vanish in the heat or the cold, thinking she had frightened it. In the very beginning, she might have run toward the apparition, stopping when she was out of breath, searching for prints on the ground. She found a few, sometimes, never her daughter's. In the beginning. Later, whenever the apparition returned, she no longer ran toward it. Hope had disappeared.

Even after she had tamed her despair, she in no way abandoned her mission, but would return to the same spot, meaning the end of the path where her daughter had disappeared, and later her husband, not expecting Rose anymore, but like someone visiting a grave thinking it to be an easier way to get close to a beloved soul. In this way she patiently built up her suffering, until she decided she would no longer walk the path. The farm then suited her as well as anywhere else, this farm also inhabited by her daughter's hazy silhouette, now folded away on the shelf of her memories and no longer at the front of her mind. She experienced this the first evening that she didn't go up the path, didn't leave the courtyard, didn't even look in the distance, simply staring inside herself at all the walls blackened by imperious shadows that would never fade.

When the year reached its end, feeling herself full of all the shadows she could hold, and not one more, she wrote a note destined for Rose, with a quill made from a blunted duck feather and soaked in a little of her blood. The girls watched her, faces blanketed with the same sorrow, as she placed the letter on the table, against the pitcher. She walked outside and locked the door, abandoning the furniture, over which nothing presided anymore except a few stains devoid of dust. They left the farm together, steering a flock composed of two cows, four goats, a sow, and a boar, with a few hens and rabbits in cages set on the bottom of a cart pulled by one of the cows. The cart also held mattresses, sacks of clothes and linens, all the tableware the family owned, and nothing more. Sitting on the well cover, the sheepdog watched its world leave the farm, then rose sniffing the air. Once it found that everything was in order for the departure, that nobody was missing, it began to trot and joined the sad procession, circling it on the right, without even barking, barely skimming the ground, before returning to its post behind the cart, weaving between the fragile bodies, watching over them with a tender and protective gaze.

She found her father standing near the bench, for it wasn't yet noon. Dew soaked the tips of his clogs, which looked as if they'd been carved from different kinds of wood. Though gnarled in many places and his face hollowed around a white mustache that was lightly stained near his lips, he was still alert at an age that nobody would have dreamt of giving him, leaning on his ever-present stick. This father had also been a child, his childhood stored away in a locked trunk. He straightened up as much as he could as the four shapes approached; in that moment more father than grandfather, forcing himself to show some assurance wrung from the family heritage weighing down on him, that at least; hoping above all that she wouldn't be able to tell the difference between what he was striving to show and what he really had within him; nor the girls. A stubborn man, he had tried his best to avoid asking himself troublesome questions the whole of his existence, for he had always thought that questions force you backward; and if by misfortune he invited one into his head, it had sufficed to turn around and advance some other way, toward something other than what he had planned and that fate had refused him. Walk straight ahead, above all. Never in his life had he seen a bird go backward. It was only terrestrial animals that often chose to do so, as if the mere contact with the earth made them question whether there was any point to tearing themselves away from it between one step and the next. And still, each morning he rekindled the fire that had gone out the night before, all that was expected of a man done, because he knew deep down that men alone are terrestrial animals, and women and children, birds.

Rose

The doctor came back to see me a few weeks after my delivery, maybe months, I don't know anymore. He had me lie down so he could examine me, without saying anything. Génie was there. When he was done, I asked to speak with him one-to-one. He must have read in my eyes that I wouldn't let him leave without a fuss, so he asked Génie to step out. It was just the two of us. He sat down on the bed, at the very end.

How is my child doing?

He stared at the door straight ahead of him. How do you feel? is what he asked the door. Seeing as the door didn't seem like it wanted to answer him, he asked the question again, turning toward me this time. I sat up with my back pressed against the bed railing and I folded up my legs against my chest.

How is my baby? I repeated.

He sighed. You don't need to worry about him, he said.

That's not what I asked you.

That's all you need to know. I could tell he was a little annoyed I wouldn't let up. What do you have to fear from me? His grandmother is taking perfect care of him, that's all I can tell you.

And yet a doctor's supposed to do good for people. He touched the small swelling on his neck that peeked from his collar.

How can you allow a child to be taken from his mother?

You wouldn't be capable of taking care of him properly.

I brought him into the world without anybody's help, and I'm not capable of taking care of him?

The matter is closed, he said coldly.

But that no longer worked on me. It'll never be closed, and you know it.

He placed his two hands flat on his thighs. How do you feel? he asked again.

As if you cared how I feel.

You're my patient.

Stop twisting me around, there's no one here to hear us.

A small, sly smile grew on his face. I have to admit you are particularly hardy.

Hardy? I sneered, that's a word for the outside of the body, and you did what had to be done to empty the inside, guess that's your job, in the end.

He shrugged, then took off his glasses, wiped them with a handkerchief. He rubbed for quite a while. From time to time, he would stop to look through them, and seeming unsatisfied, he would resume, until he placed his glasses back on his nose arranging the arms over his ears. He stared at the door again, then turned toward me, looking me over with those vicious little eyes that revealed what I represented to him, something like an animal with a smashed paw. Perhaps I was just a wounded creature, but I didn't hurt anywhere, and the doctor didn't intimidate me. Nothing mattered to me anymore, especially not him. He brushed one finger right across the scar again.

He branded you too, didn't he? I said. He took away his finger quick. I saw I had touched a sensitive spot, that perhaps I wasn't far from the truth. You're their slave too, like me, I insisted.

His back stiffened, as though he were pushing against a wall that didn't exist. Sometimes there are boundaries you cross without realizing, he said in the way a priest would.

Who are you talking about with your boundaries? Surely not me.

He didn't answer. I was no longer looking at his eyes. All they did was lie. I began to stare at his mouth so as not to miss anything that came out. He changed the subject. My job is to care for people like you, said his mouth.

I slowly turned my head toward the door. There's just us, as you can see, no point spinning yarns, what do you risk?

There's nothing more I can do.

In truth, what bothers you is that I still have my mind, despite everything I've endured, that I fight back, that's what upsets you.

He was very calm. Drop it, he said.

I saw my father die right before my eyes, the master forced himself on me so I'd give him an heir, my child was stolen from me. I'll stop there, you knew all that and you never lifted a finger, doctor though you may be.

Sometimes there are actions we're obliged to take for a greater interest.

An interest greater than that of a mother for her child? I asked to push him a little further.

His gaze returned to the door. You know nothing.

All I'm asking is to know.

For a second I thought he would give in, but he soon thought better. Your child will have a far better future than the one you could have given him, he said smiling oddly at the door.

I began to tremble thinking about my little one who I had carried in my belly for months, who I had brought into the world and kept with me for six days. I loved that child as soon as I saw him dripping and soiled, I will always love him, but I could only show him that for a single week in his entire life.

You're a real bastard, I spat out. What did I have to lose? I lunged at him fists first. The doctor leapt up before I could touch him, and I collapsed on the bed, emptied of strength. I began to cry, and he watched me, adding salt to the wound.

He'll be your son until he dies, but you will never be a mother for him, never again.

A bastard and a monster, that's what you are.

On the contrary, I protected a child from misery.

I allowed the tears that were making it too hard for me to speak fall, then I turned my head toward him. A child without a father, or a true mother, just raised by a mad old woman, there are worse miseries than the one you're talking about, I said.

We acted for the good of that child.

You don't even know what good is, one day you'll be judged for what you did, I said pointing a finger at him.

A nervous tic raised a corner of his mouth, and he touched his scar again. I'm not afraid of being judged by anyone, I'm a man of science.

I have to admit you're awful good at lying, but maybe that won't always be enough, I said nervously.

He didn't respond. He looked at his watch, sighing. He straightened his jacket, then he backed toward the door, still fixing me with small eyes reduced to slits. He stopped midway through opening the door. You may as well die now, there's no more point in you hanging on, he said, like he was asking me a favor.

Die? I repeated automatically. I didn't have time to react. He left right then, and the key turned in the lock. I stayed where I lay. The sounds from outside passed through the walls, unless I imagined them. I heard the weather vane spun around by air currents, like it was anxious at not knowing which direction to point in this valley of misfortune, here where the wind never stops blowing, descending, rising, and disappearing as if by magic. I sat up thinking about the last thing the doctor said. The mark was still there from where he had sat at the end of the bed. I tugged on the sheet to make it disappear, while his words echoed in my head. You may as well die now. He had surely thought he'd finish me off with that.

I think about death often, like the bladder of a fish that grows bigger and bigger until it takes up all the room and finally explodes. And so the doctor's words didn't really hurt me, they barely touched me in truth. I won't give him that pleasure. It will be me alone who decides when to die, and not him. My final power, the only one. The moment for me to let myself go hasn't come yet. I no longer intend to rush things, even if it means breathing longer than I thought I would. When it's time, I'll feel it, I'll stop resisting, I'll let myself gently slip out of my skin. I'll do what's needed, but it won't be him who decides. Never. They say that when you go, something flies away, something not very big and not very heavy, but far more vital than what's destroyed. I hope

I won't be aware of it, I hope that it happens a little like in a dream, that I'll go somewhere else completely, that the light that's extinguished leads to another light that you sink into peacefully. I think I earned that right, that I've paid for it with my blood, with my belly, with my whole body, and also with my heart. But I'm not going to go right away. I promise myself that.

Ever since I decided not to force myself to die, I feel like I've taken my hands off a spring that demands only to gush forth. Something was liberated inside me. Something that I have to write down the way it comes to me. That's flowing right now. All my hand has to do is obey. I don't understand what's happening. I write. Everything that I believed wasn't and which in fact was, everything that I believed to be and which wasn't real. It was there, it had always been there, I'd buried it beneath the misfortune that followed, and also the idea of death. The great whirlwind has finally caught up with me. I let it envelop me. Once inside, everything changes. I should be thinking of my father, my mother, my sisters, but it's not them I'm thinking about in truth, it's Edmond, his shoulders, his hands around my waist, the way he looks at me, which is more than just a look.

The story changes. It flows endlessly. It's not my doing, it spills through my fingers. It's becoming what it always was. The true story, the one I didn't want to believe, never wanted to believe. Everything comes back to me in the whirlwind. It's easy. Inside, we're together, Edmond and me. We can finally say the words that matter and make the gestures that matter, on top of the looks. And in the end, you don't need many words or gestures, just the ones that come effortlessly. I've never felt so alive. If I held on until now, it's surely so I could return to this moment that I stole for myself without knowing it. Edmond's holding me in the air. He says that he can carry me forever. I smile at him. My back pressed to Artemis's side, I tell him this is all I want, that I'm certain of it. And then he brings me down. I don't feel it when I touch the ground. I know that my feet will never touch it the same way, and I owe that to this man leaning his face over mine. I can't even see his eyes. I know what they say. Edmond kisses me, I kiss him and we kiss each other. I've never done that before. It's simple. It feels like I've always known how, and everything that follows too, I've always known how, always wanted. We're pressed against each other, like we wanted to hold our two hearts together until just one remains, and we don't even know when it happens, we don't even think about it it's so obvious. Our mouths joined together for the first time is like the first flight of wild geese in spring before the sky fills with birds heading to a place they've had to go to since always, a place full of sun. And the stable is nothing other than a land like that, beautiful and warm. In truth, you know you've reached that land when mouths are no longer enough. Edmond lays me down on the hay. Artemis is still, I hear her breathing at first, and then I can't hear it anymore. Everything that Edmond does next, I do too, as confident as one of those birds that knows where the journey ends, that golden hay that smells of burning. I don't even feel his weight on me. I can no longer smell him, or feel his hands, his lips, his skin. He's what I feel, him. I've never been so happy, so sure of knowing what I want, what I am, because he's giving me the chance. I think this so hard that I say it to him for real. He answers that he's happy too, or maybe I imagine it, maybe it's nothing but an echo in his breathing. In any case, his eyes and his movements don't lie. He removes the obstacles in his way so we can be even closer, so very close, we don't even know anymore what belongs to the other. It's simple. And then, something tears me gently, something I accept in my body like it was a part of me that was missing, and that I didn't know about before this moment when the girl I was becomes a woman. It doesn't hurt. I trust him. Time is elsewhere. Edmond stops to look at me. I cry from joy. He starts to move again, slowly at first, then faster and faster, then he stiffens like a piece of wood, and relaxes, several times in a row. I know that he's giving me something. I take it, even though I don't know anything about what it really is. I don't even know what to give him in return, apart from the light that's radiating toward him from my wide-open eyes, my way of thanking him for everything that I didn't think to be reality, until I find myself in the whirlwind, until I find him, we find each other, the only reality, yesterday's reality, today's, tomorrow's, the forever reality, the reality of this life and of what comes after.

I don't know why I went back into the whirlwind with Edmond, or what it matters that we are reunited, that I know what's real, but it seems to me that this is the crux of my life.

We're watching the world turn, and not ourselves. Time has stopped in the whirlwind. Time is nothing but the subtraction that begins at birth, like in my father's notebook, and you're not even aware of it as long as you're just a child. A child that tumbles into a woman, that's who I became, again, in the whirlwind, a child watching the woman possess time, a woman who will never again venture farther than the truth of the whirlwind. That moment where everything could have begun, if the moment that followed hadn't. Everything destroyed.

Gabriel

I remained still for several minutes after I finished copying Rose's diary, one finger on the last word written in her hand, "destroyed," my blood frozen in my veins and in my heart, as every time I read it. I began to scratch the page with my nail, for no reason, like removing the scab covering a scar, succeeding only in making the ink bleed. Then I pressed the tip of my finger as hard as I could to erase the word. My flesh whitened from the pressure. It took me a moment to realize I wasn't dreaming. There was an uneven feeling on the paper, a minuscule bump. The sensation eventually disappeared, and when I moved my finger I discovered a pale and straight mark on my skin. Something I hadn't noticed until this final reading. Two pages further, after what I had thought was the last word Rose had written, was a torn-out sheet of paper folded in half and carefully stuck into the notebook. I opened it. It was indeed Rose's handwriting, but it had changed a little, more hesitant, feebler, as if her exhausted hand had abandoned the words on the paper, to let them die in peace. Her true final words.

Rose

Fourteen years I've been shut inside the asylum.

Fourteen years I've promised my-self not to write anymore.

The Counter died during the night, that's what made me change my mind.

Génie told me the news this morning. She had been crying. She didn't want to say more. I didn't ask any questions. She left straightaway. I imagine that she'd been taken back to her child-hood, and that it didn't feel too good.

It had been weeks since I'd seen the Counter in the court-yard. In truth, I sensed that something odd was going on with her, without wanting to think the worst. I felt great sorrow when I heard, but in truth I'm relieved she finally found the way to truly escape. Where she's gone to now, she no longer needs to count, seeing as she's gotten to her final tally. It changes something that she's dead. I don't really know why, but I know what. Maybe because she was called Rose too, because there was a part of me that I recognized in her, on top of her name. I don't know if she decided on her own to leave, if she found a way and the strength to do it. I have no desire to know. She's cleared the path for me. I just want to follow her now. I have nothing left to say, to protect, to hope. There's no point resisting anymore. I hear her in my head.

Fourteen years.

Five thousand one hundred and ten days.

One hundred twenty-two thousand six hundred and forty hours.

Fourteen years I've endured. I wouldn't have thought I'd last so long. There's no denying that the body is a machine that can't be easily stopped, unless you want to risk damning yourself, and me, I never wanted to take that risk. I suffered too much in this life to risk losing everything in the one that comes after, if ever it exists elsewhere and otherwise. You never know.

Still, I held on this whole time without going mad, all by shutting myself inside the whirlwind. That must have thrown the doctor, who thought I would die because he told me to,

just because it suited him. Except here we are, it's only by kill-
ing people that you can choose the moment of their death.
I think that's the only line he didn't dare cross, a boundary
like he said. Kill someone with his own hands, there's a thing
he must never have done, surely a holdover from what he was
taught at those schools for doctors.

Fourteen years.

My little one would be turning fourteen years old today.

He must be turning it somewhere, but I'm not there to
watch him do it.

The time passed quickly. In truth, a day that repeats itself
for no reason doesn't last all that long. I prefer night. When
I haven't had enough, I keep my eyes closed part of the day.
Everything slows in the darkness, seeing as there's nothing
that shows the time if you don't have a clock, and there's not
one in my room, just the bell ringing outside, but I lost count
of that a long time ago. That's why I like the night, because
there's nothing for time to cling to. At night, the door's wide
open to sounds. I always fall asleep to that same continuous
whistling that I took for silence at the beginning but that
isn't sound either. I reckon that what I hear is the breathing
of the soul as it sorts through what's been lived to invent
memories of things that sometimes never even happened, but
that in the end we admit as truths. The body has no say in
those moments. I don't even think it knows the soul exists,
otherwise, after all this time, the body would have found a
way to stop it from breathing so it could feel a little more
alive itself. The soul's not what remains when we're dead,

it's what goes when there's nothing left to be put away. And me, during the fourteen years that have gone by, I tamed my soul. It became my nighttime friend, the unmoving heart of the whirlwind beating slowly, like mine, like my child's fourteen years ago. Sometimes, in the daytime, I can't stop myself from imagining what he looks like today, what he's doing. At night, never. At night, he doesn't change, he's my baby, mine, beside me, still attached to me, covered in me. My child, who came from my belly, fourteen years ago.

Maybe we have powers that we don't realize, if we never think about it, if we don't pay attention to the signs. Last night, I didn't fall asleep with the whistling stuck between my ears. There was nothing but silence, a terrible silence, emptied of sound, emptied of sleep, emptied of my soul that until then had always spared me my child's birthday. If I was meant to go mad, it would have been this night, and for that matter it might have happened if I hadn't started counting the years, the days, the hours, for the first time, for no reason. But I understand the reason now that I've reached the end of my path by the grace of another who's freed me from the days to come. My soul is finally ready to follow that woman whose life I could never make better, but who, in dying, is going to help me leave.

I won't go back on my decision. I won't write another line after tonight. I wouldn't want to blame myself for not knowing to stop in time. It might just be that I'll keep this page for myself, I don't know yet. I have until tonight to decide, because tonight I'm going to give Génie a poisoned chalice.

She never wanted to take my notebooks, but now I'm not going to give her the choice not to. She can do what she likes with them. It will no longer concern me. All that I have to do is return inside the night whirlwind to never emerge again, go find the Counter, and, most importantly, my child.

Edmond

So that's it, you've crossed over to the other side.

 You were never that far in truth.

I don't blame you, you know.

I never even blamed you for what you did.

I didn't have time to tell you before they locked you up.

I never could find the words, couldn't even think them.

I understand why you did it, I think.

I wouldn't say it's courage you had.

Good God, no.

It's something else.

Sometimes, we do what we have to, simply because it's what has to be done so that the boat keeps moving, with fewer people inside.

It's the boat that's important, not the passengers, or so it seems.

Before you died, I didn't dare talk to you, in my head, but I thought of you often.

At first, it was the you with the hammer in your hand, your gaze dark, not a glimmer of light inside.

I remember your big, wide eyes, like it was yesterday, so wide I felt like they weren't eyes, but holes.

All that's in the past.

Now that you're free, she's no longer the woman I see.

The one I talk to now is different, a woman who doesn't have black holes for eyes, and who doesn't have a hammer in her hand either, but who spits fire when she looks at me.

I don't know which of the two pains me more.

But it's the second one I want to keep.

Christ.

You know, I tried everything to see you again, even climbed the walls.

I got caught.

They always stopped me.

I cursed them for that.

They said that they would hurt you, if I kept trying.

I never should have listened to them.

They always made it clear that I was no one.

Nothing worse.

When you're no one, you obey.

For her, I was less than one of her crystal glasses, and for him, less than one of his dogs, just a mistake to hate, in the end.

And good God, I started to believe it.

Even when the girl arrived, I couldn't make myself better.

Though I had the chance.

I stayed the mistake they had invented.

I never had the courage to put an end to it, after.

Even when the girl died, I didn't have the courage.

Now I'm truly alone.

I'm going to have to find the courage.

All my life, I was almost a man.

Gabriel

I didn't sleep at all, trying to decide what I was going to do. I woke the sacristan at dawn, so he could help me prepare the horse and cart. My haste surprised him. He asked me where I wanted him to drive me. I answered that I would indicate the route as we went, not knowing yet which place I would visit first, the Les Forges estate or the asylum.

We left the presbytery in the direction of the forest. After a few minutes, we sank beneath the foliage. I don't know if it was the air whipping my face, the jolts of the buggy, or my own judgment trundling along, but I knew then whom I had to speak to first. When I saw the spire of the old monastery chapel, I easily resisted the temptation to stop. I looked away and we went past the asylum. The time would come. Another seven or eight miles remained before the estate, where, I hoped, Edmond, certainly the man from the cemetery, still lived; for, apart from the doctor, he alone could illuminate the zones of shadow that persisted in Rose's diary.

In the past, I had hardly ever had the occasion to venture so far, having enough to do in my own parish. We soon arrived at the junction near the river, just as Rose had described it. An uphill path extended to the right in the direction of the forge, and another on the left must have led to the manor. With one arm, I indicated the right to Charles. I suppose I still needed to convince myself that all this was real, before encountering Edmond. We took the sloping path that narrowed as it went, then arrived at the forge entrance. There was a gate, its top panel unhinged. The rusted skeleton of a sign had fallen nearby. I asked the sacristan to wait for me there. I got down, then entered a vast courtyard invaded by high grass, bounded by a dilapidated high wall on one end and an L-shaped building on the other. It was all the more sinister as I knew that a man had been killed there in cold blood. The heavy door to the forge was closed. I had to use a rusty iron pipe left lying on the ground to get the door to slide along its rail. There were no longer any tools inside, nothing that could attest to what this place had served for, apart from the broad workbench, the hearth, and the bellows of which nothing remained but twisted metallic pieces, as if someone had picked it clean. The forge had visibly been pillaged. I then asked myself why the thieves had taken care to close the door, unless it had been someone else, later. That question, seemingly irrelevant, gnawed at me all the same. I remained before the hearth for a long time, summoning images of the tragic scene: Rose branded, fastened to the foot of the workbench, while the blacksmith reduced her father's body to dust with blows of his hammer. I imagined a terrible odor floating through the air. My hands trembled, and I rushed out.

I returned to the buggy and climbed up to the seat without a word. Charles gave me a questioning look. I could just motion with my head, and we drove away from that cursed place in the direction of the estate. Once past the open gate and the abandoned grounds, we found an imposing structure with walls covered in ivy and edged with gigantic brambles: the castle. Slate tiles had slid from the roof and crashed onto the exterior stairs. Nobody had lived here in a long time. Everything was faithful to the description Rose had given in her notebook. I imagined her at the mercy of the blacksmith and his mother, wondering as well what had become of the old lady. The oppressive atmosphere seemed to affect even Charles, who fiddled nervously with the reins as he stared at the outbuildings. I climbed down from the buggy, walked toward the manor, then went up the steps leading to the front door. It was locked. I circled around, clearing a passage through the shrubs and brambles in search of an entrance that wasn't closed off. Unlike the manor, the other structures were still in use, judging from the cleared access and trampled grass. A stable, of course. I hesitated a moment before the bolted door, then entered. The smell of horses was still strong. I thought my imagination was playing tricks on me again when I heard a snort, but I wasn't dreaming. There was indeed a horse, majestically watching me from one of the stalls, its hayrack filled with fresh feed. I then had the sensation that time had been done away with, that I was entering the whirlwind with Rose, that I had no other choice but to follow suit, feeling like I was suffocating once inside, like I was violating a past that in no way belonged to me. I don't know how long the catharsis lasted, but, when I returned to myself, I was certain I hadn't erred in coming to the estate. The horse could only belong to one man.

The path wound between the manor gable and the out-buildings, then turned into a simple dirt trail after a few yards. As I walked past a kept garden, I noticed a thread of smoke rising in the sky reddened by the morning sun. I continued downhill. Soon I arrived in sight of a low house with a roof of brown thatch. The man from the cemetery was standing in the doorway. He watched me approach, without moving. As if he had been waiting for me. When I was close enough to see his face, I found more curiosity than annoyance. A hint of a smile froze at the corner of his mouth. I had no doubt as to his identity.

"It would seem you're lost, Vicar."

"Do you really think so?"

"I have other things to do than think."

"You are Edmond, are you not?"

The smile disappeared instantly.

"What do you want from me?"

"I know that it was your wife I buried the other day."

His whole body stiffened. He clenched his fists and jaws to control the rage boiling up.

"I don't wanna hear it."

"I wish you no harm. I'm simply here to talk to you about Rose."

His eyes were full of doubt, but he didn't risk speaking.

"Rose, the young girl who worked for the blacksmith," I added.

The back of his hand whipped through the air.

"Lies. You couldn't have known her."

"It's true, I never met her. But I know her story in part. She wrote it in a diary."

"I don't believe you…"

"You're the half brother of the former blacksmith, to whom Rose fed rat poison. The same Rose whom you put on top of a mare named Artemis, in the stable. You called Charles's mother 'the queen mother.' Should I go on?"

His shoulders slumped, as if he was sinking into the ground.

"The doctor, it must have been he who sent you to drive me mad, huh? Was it him?"

"No, it wasn't him. I'm telling you the truth."

"Christ, enough! What is it you want?"

"I also know about Rose's child... What became of him?"

"The child," he repeated, distressed.

His chest pivoted slightly, but his feet didn't move, as if half of him wanted to go inside the house and the other was unable.

"That's really all you know?"

"Yes. Rose's diary ends once they take her child away."

Edmond hesitated again, then, no doubt sensing that he no longer had to be mistrustful of me, he began to talk. I felt like I was extracting a confession from a coffin.

"It was months after they took Rose to the asylum. One morning, I went up to the manor, as usual. When I entered the kitchen, there was a woman I didn't know. She didn't have time to tell me who she was. I heard voices above my head. I hurried upstairs. The queen mother and the doctor were in Charles's bedroom, beside a crib, and inside it was a baby squirming around and making odd whimpers. Charles's heir, Rose's son, is what they told me. I no longer knew what was happening. I asked how Rose was. The doctor said he would tell me later, but first I had to help put Marie in her coffin."

Edmond abruptly stopped, as if he had just had a revelation.

"Christ! I knew there was something that didn't make sense. You've been lying to me since the beginning, Vicar."

"No, I told you, I'm telling you the truth."

"After Marie was buried, the doctor admitted that Rose hadn't survived the delivery, and you're telling me that her diary stops when they took away the child. How do you explain that?"

"I'm not the one lying to you. Rose didn't die giving birth."

He stepped back. His back bumped against the wall. His entire body was trembling.

"So she's alive," he said.

"I don't know, but it's possible that she's still locked up in the asylum."

He gave me a look full of pain. "We can't just do nothing, Vicar."

"Lucky for us the doctor doesn't suspect a thing."

He straightened up, crushing the emptiness between his fingers. "I'll kill him."

"I'll go to the asylum first to assure myself that Rose is still alive. We'll decide what to do after."

"He'll hoodwink you. He's clever." Edmond lifted his arms, looking at his two clenched fists. "Good God, I'm going to kill him...I'll find a way, but I'm going to kill him."

"Trust me. For now, we don't have a choice."

He didn't protest. He knew I was his only hope of seeing Rose again.

"You still haven't told me what became of the child."

He looked at me, unclenched his fists, and began to talk, as if relieved to finally share something he had never told anyone.

"I was always forbidden to go near him. The queen mother and the wet nurse constantly coddled him. According to the doctor he suffered from a skin disease. Even once he learned to walk, he wasn't allowed to play outside the house alone, always had to be in the shade and covered up like it was the middle of winter. Sometimes I would stay watching him for a while, in secret. It upset me to look at him, because the older he got, the more he looked like Rose. The two women raised him until the accident."

He stopped, swallowed. I felt like a large snake that I hadn't sensed coming was squeezing its coils around my chest.

"What accident? Go on, I beg of you."

"One day, he managed to get away from them. It was the wet nurse who told me everything after, seeing as during that time I was still manning the forge. I can't figure how a sickly little kid could have opened the stable door, but he did. When the old lady heard the row the horses were making, and she couldn't find the boy anywhere in the house, she raced down there. She went in first. The kid was lying in a stall and the horse was near wild. The old lady thought he was badly hurt, so she went to help him without thinking, and the horse sent her flying against the wall with one kick. The wet nurse came to tell me something terrible had happened. I ran all the way to the stable. The old lady was on her stomach, hair sticky with blood. The boy wasn't moving on the hay. I went in quick to calm the horse, and I brought him out and tied him up."

Edmond went silent, shaking his head.

"Continue," I asked, fear in my gut.

"The old lady was already dead, her skull split in two, but the kid was breathing calmly. It looked like he was asleep. His leg was at a funny angle, so I didn't risk moving him.

I told the wet nurse to stay and watch him while I went for help. I galloped all the way to the asylum to fetch the doctor. When we returned, the child was awake, he was grimacing, but without complaint. The wet nurse stepped out of the way. The doctor kneeled to examine the kid. He said that his right leg was certainly broken, that his life wasn't in danger, but that he needed to be taken to the hospital. I helped him make a splint out of battens and string. The whole time we were setting his leg between the pieces of wood, the boy didn't even cry out. I found it strange that he could stand so much pain. Next, it was me who carried him in my arms to the doctor's buggy, and then they left."

As he spoke, Edmond stared at his open hands, as if the child was going to miraculously appear in them, or maybe like he could still feel the weight of that small body.

"What became of him after that?" I asked, now relieved to know that the child had survived.

"The doctor showed up a few days after the accident to tell me he was recovering slowly. I never saw the boy at the manor again, or anywhere else, either. The old lady was dead."

"Do you know where they took him?"

"The doctor had the intention of placing him with another family, since there wasn't any real family left to take care of him. I asked what would become of the estate. He didn't answer, then told me I could stay, in the meantime. When I asked what that meant, in the meantime, he gave me a strange smile. I could sense he was hiding something. I tried to get more out of him but he wouldn't tell me anything else."

"What could he have been hiding from you?"

"I told you. I don't know."

"I don't understand why the doctor obeyed them from the beginning. What did he have to gain?"

"All I know is that Charles apparently saved his life when they were kids. He strangled a wolfhound with his bare hands. I've no trouble believing that Charles was capable of it, even at that age. He used to joke about it in front of the doctor, to remind him of his debt no doubt. But it never made the doctor laugh. He still has the mark on his neck."

Rose had guessed right when, noticing the doctor's scar, she had asked if the blacksmith had branded him too. That was exactly what he had done, in a different way than for her. For all that, I had trouble believing that the doctor's being saved as a child was enough to have made him that family's devoted slave.

Edmond kept his eyes on me, two pale moons hollowed in the center. "You think I'm a coward, Vicar?"

"I don't judge you."

"I imagine others will see to that."

Edmond was distraught, pitiable, battling with his conscience. "I never did a single thing in my life that I can be proud of."

"Why did you stay?"

He hesitated, then, as if he had just found the answer to a question he had never asked himself, he said, "I thought he would come back one day. This place is his home."

I was about to leave when he held out one hand toward me.

"Vicar?"

"Yes."

"So, Rose, she mentions me in her diary?"

I hesitated briefly before answering. "She loved you."

The words came out of my mouth without any true reflection. Now Edmond's eyes looked like gobs of spit on a dirty window, and they were blinking at regular intervals. I couldn't have said whether he was trying to push something out, or if, on the contrary, he wanted to stop that something from escaping as long as I was in front of him. His Adam's apple rose and descended along his throat, then his eyes froze; beseeching.

The Child

eined wood, riddled by thorn scars,
covered with ants swarming in search
of honeydew. Sick leaves, stained with
black, felted in white, the green dissolved. Smell
of the first roses, so rare now. A decade since
anyone has pruned the old climbing rose crack-
ing the stable wall, since the person who could
have gave up.

At first, he remains at a distance from the
small house lost at the end of the path, doesn't
see it, doesn't even guess it's there. Lets himself
be overtaken by the smells and shadows, long

before reaching the manor falling into ruin. He doesn't understand what's happening. He's forgotten nothing of the smells
moving through the air, those smells continuously feeding
the violent current of his memory, with colors too, that turn
up with great fanfare, as when he, the child, confined to the
large house, would see how they all blended together, and
would imagine the smells, before the gaze of the dead father
frozen on canvas, alone, no signs of a mother nobody spoke
to him about, and in whom he had never believed. The child
always bundled up when he was allowed outside, so rarely,
and always accompanied, especially when the sun was out;
and that was, the old lady would say, so as not to burn his
fragile skin. The face of an angel, she would think as she
watched him delight over a fleeing insect. And in thinking
this she lied to herself, seeking a physical resemblance with
her own son, or barring that, some attitude giving the illusion of true filiation, trying also to erase what could never be
erased: the mark of disgrace, if it was ever brought to light.
The face of an angel. The spitting image of his mother.

The ruins are gone. He walks down the path, heads toward the stable. Sees the child, or rather a flimsy projection
expelled from depths he never dared probe, something other
than those of a cold and uninhabited lake. Enters the stable,
where there remains a single horse that seems to be waiting
for him. Opens the stall door, slowly approaches the animal,
then stands facing it and caresses the bridge of its nose for a
time so that the creature takes in his smell, accepts him, rec-
ognizes him. He then moves to grab the halter hanging from

the railing, and places it around the horse's neck. Doesn't move. Standing, lets himself breathe again, holding the bridle, not seeking anything more than what's already in his memory, letting it come forth and take shape. Then he leaves, guiding the horse, who follows him at a walk.

Still firmly holding the bridle, not from fear of letting it go; driven by the simple desire to not be tempted to catch up to the child and stop him in his path, thereby preventing what must be. What is. The child moves farther and farther away, keeps disappearing, keeps being what he always was, that child who enters the stable, whom he recognized without knowing him, that child he's preparing to finally know, amid the spring shadows and smells.

Holding the bridle. Turns around simply, to the manor walls to which a forest of greenery clings, covering even the slatted shutters, some of which, unhinged, permit small glimpses of dry wood that resemble bits of dead skin.

Holding the bridle.

The child senses other people, first the old woman whom he must call grandmother at all times, and also Suzanne, the wet nurse. They haven't noticed his absence yet, for the lady of the house is in the middle of lecturing her servant over a matter of sheets stacked poorly in a wardrobe. It's too late when they discover his disappearance. The worst unfurls beneath the head of ash-colored hair.

Still holding the bridle.

The child is gone. They run, hurtling down the steps outside. The old lady, ahead, shouts the child's name. The child, already lying in the hay, eyes closed, by no means unconscious, masterfully playing the final scene of the last act.

Still holding the bridle. But he's not performing anything right now. Is no longer the child. Hears the shouts come closer. And they're not just ripples. But something else, more violent, more direct, as if the sensations he's perceiving come from re-creating the child who existed before the accident that he can't prevent, wouldn't even dream of it. For you can't change destiny the way you'd change roads, or rather the way you'd stop and choose not to take any road at all, simply not continue. The horse is pawing at the ground next to him. He's lying down, he sees nothing, hears everything: the old lady shouting, the whinnying, the stamping of hooves; he smiles. Until that muffled sound, like a terra-cotta pitcher breaking on hard ground. When the old lady goes quiet, there are other shouts, they fade, then disappear in the distance.

Holding the bridle.

The moment of liberation. Eyes closed, the child silently thanks the horse, not yet conceiving of the death of the old lady that he will no longer have to call otherwise; also thanks heaven and the powers invoked, in a state of blessed ecstasy, promising to devote his earthly existence to them, to willingly serve them, to give them his never-failing and eternal gratitude.

Never again the child.

Holding the bridle.

The noise of a controlled stampede. No shouting, a few words: *easy, easy now.* The sound of hooves receding, then of footsteps coming closer. He opens his eyes. The man leans, kneels, takes off his jacket and places it rolled up beneath the head of the dead child, beneath his own head. Come to life. Almost a man, already. Rays of light leap through the open door, pierce the stable, the stall, dissolving the fabric of the shirt worn by the man, who is not the man with the feverish gaze painted on the canvas; so that the mark on his upper arm becomes transparent, resembling the notched leaf of an American oak. The same mark that fans out on his youthful skin, hidden beneath a thick sweater. From the dead child to the man. Mute. What he thought he had dreamt and which was now surfacing in the stillness of his body attached to the bridle: that mark linking them, the man to the child, the son born of no woman, and not another. All that he becomes. All that he is.

He returns to the buggy, scratches a few words on the slate, then goes to hide behind the stable.

Holding the bridle.

Horse obliging.

Soon he hears Gabriel's insistent calls. Doesn't answer, waits for the buggy to set off, then for it to move far away.

He finally leaves his hiding place.

Holding the bridle.

Gaze steeled in the direction of the invisible hovel set in the dell at the end of the path, where the truth lies, where he must go alone, though not for all that renouncing the holy world; for he knows now that he will have to accept his human destiny, before earning the eternity of a second one.

Gabriel

I caught sight of the buggy, still parked along the path to the manor, but no sign of Charles. I called to him, in vain. The stable door was open. I rushed inside. The horse was gone. I came out, called again. Then I returned to the buggy. The slate was placed visibly on the seat. "Don't wait for me. I'll return alone." So he had left on horseback, for no apparent reason, my sacristan who had never let me down, who had never made the smallest decision without my accord. I had no time to try to guess why; time was running out. He would explain the reason for his sudden departure later.

I spurred the horse onto the path, quickly forgetting Charles's defection. I was thinking only of Rose. I reached the asylum, without even having considered what I would say, what strategy I would employ against the doctor.

The watchman greeted me with surprise.

"Hello, Father."

"Hello. I would like to speak with the director, please."

"No one alerted me."

"It is a case of absolute necessity."

"It's just I can't leave my post."

"I know the way."

The watchman was still blocking me. He hesitated, looked over my shoulder at the horse covered with foam after the mad gallop I had forced him on.

"And if it comes back on me?"

"Don't worry. I'll explain to the doctor…It's a matter of life or death."

The watchman cast another look around.

"If it's really a matter like you say, but be sure and tell the doctor I did my job proper."

"All right."

The watchman unlocked the gate and swung back one of the doors. I thanked him before hurriedly walking through. Each time I found myself within the walls of the old monastery, there was always that same sensation of traveling through time, to a place where men and women hid from it, and despite the unique circumstances, I felt that way again that day. I went down the path, striding past the chapel on the right and the old monk's cells on the left. I saw a nurse. She nodded as I passed. I soon reached the north wing of the building adjacent to the chapel, which served as the infirmary and where the doctor's office was located. Two men were talking on the stairs. I told them I had an appointment. They waved at me and let me by without asking questions. I entered the building and followed the hallway some twenty yards before knocking at the office. I heard the hoarse sound of a voice. I opened the door. The doctor was immersed in a file. He didn't deign to lift his eyes. I closed the door behind me, then moved toward the desk.

"Hello," I said.

He didn't respond, grudgingly looked up from the file, and narrowed his eyes while pointedly observing me. If ever a flash of surprise crossed his face, even for a short instant, I was unable to spot it. The man truly had extraordinary self-control.

"Did someone die without me being notified?" he said with a forced smile.

"A vicar sometimes has things to say to the living."

"You've aroused my curiosity."

He leaned back into the chair and began scratching at the tip of his scar. He seemed to be trying to anticipate my intentions. There was no more room to prevaricate.

"You remember Rose, don't you?"

For a few seconds, his fingers froze on the scar. Then he joined his hands, lifting the index fingers, as if they were crosshairs and I was the target.

"Of course. You were so insistent on getting her tombstone engraved."

"That's not who I'm talking about."

He tried to mask his confusion, pretending to search his memory.

"It's a relatively common name," he said.

"I'm certain that you're not a man to forget anything, or anyone."

He slapped his hands on his desk in a gesture of annoyance.

"I have a lot of work. Would you kindly get to the point?"

"The old blacksmith's maid."

He sank the slightest bit into his chair. He had taken my blow almost without any visible reaction.

"Ah yes, I did see her sometimes, when I would visit the estate."

"How is it that a man so monopolized by his job had the time to visit patients outside the asylum?"

"Charles was my friend, his wife was very sick. A very worrisome case…"

"Carrying a pregnancy to full term in those conditions must have been particularly delicate."

The doctor rose abruptly at that remark, then walked toward the window, gazing outside with his hands behind his back.

"For that matter she didn't survive the delivery…a terrible loss," he said in a lifeless tone.

"At the time, your friend had just died suddenly, from what I've learned, and then her. What a great tragedy indeed," I insisted.

"I must say God wasn't tender with them."

"I thought that the Lord mattered little to you."

He whipped around.

"I'm trying to think as you would," he said.

"No need to defend yourself. All that would be quite enough to shake the foundations of a man of science," I said with a contrite air.

"At least Charles didn't have to watch his wife die."

"She must have loved him very much too."

"Of course..."

"To leave Paris to come here to live, after their wedding. That's quite the proof of love."

"What are you trying to say?"

I let a moment pass, without answering his question.

"Of what exactly did your friend die?"

"A sudden occlusion."

"And his mother who passed away a few years later. How terrible."

"A senseless accident."

"What became of the child after that tragic event?"

The doctor took a long breath before answering me.

"He was placed, given that he didn't have any other family."

"Where?"

"That's not my job."

"I imagine that he'll return one day to inherit the estate, once he's of age."

"Everything was sold a long time ago. All Charles and his mother had left were debts, owing to poor investments."

"So the estate was sold. And yet it appears abandoned."

He marked a beat before continuing: "It was I who bought it at the time, so it wouldn't fall into strangers' hands. I knew there was no profit to be gotten from it. All that is common knowledge. I don't understand why you're so interested in these old stories."

"You're right. I almost forgot the main reason for my visit, that young girl, who was it again? Rose…She was in fact admitted to your establishment, to my understanding?"

He seemed to be trying to summon his memory once again, but in truth, I knew he was weighing each word he was about to say: "It was Charles's mother who alerted me to her case, shortly after her son's death."

"Her case?"

"She was prone to fits of uncontrollable derangement. And so I was forced to take that extreme step. She had become dangerous to those around her as well as to herself."

The show had lasted long enough.

"There's no need to lie anymore."

"Are you casting doubt on my diagnosis?" he said with an offended air.

"It was because of the child she was carrying that Rose was committed."

He couldn't mask his astonishment, or respond to my assertion in any way.

"That child was the product of repeated rapes committed by your friend against his maid, and you covered it up in the name of who knows what sordid link that bonded you together."

"Get out immediately!"

I didn't move an inch, seeking his fleeing gaze, not letting him escape mine.

"It would seem that you have underestimated the pathways of the Lord for too long, Doctor."

He dealt a violent punch to the desk. A few files tumbled.

"Enough. I demand that you leave this instant."

I still didn't move, maintaining my calm. The moment was critical.

"Rose told her story in a diary, which I have in my possession."

"A diary. Rose. How laughable."

I let the silence hover. I had no intention of divulging my sources and thereby pointing the finger at the nurse who had entrusted me with the notebooks.

"How could I know all this?"

"Nothing but fabrications."

"Edmond confirmed everything."

"Him? He never would do such a thing…"

"He has nothing left to lose anymore, now that his wife is dead."

"What do you want?"

"To see Rose."

I saw the lines tighten on his face, while his eyes challenged me, gauged me.

"That's impossible, and even provided that diary truly exists, what are the words of a servant, a mad one at that, against those of an honorable doctor recognized by his peers?"

"What do you have to fear then?"

"You have no right to see her."

I then had the certitude that Rose was still alive.

"Edmond is willing to testify against you, if you persist."

"Testify, are you joking? He has no proof," he said contemptuously.

I knew he was right. I had hoped to lead him toward atonement, or at least awaken some remorse. He was clearly not that kind of man. My only chance was to keep backing him into a corner.

"Why still obey them, now that they're all dead?"

"Shut up!"

"I know that the blacksmith saved you from the claws of a dog. Is that the only reason you remain his lackey?"

"You know nothing," he said, bringing one hand to his scar.

"Unless there's something else you don't dare confess."

"Confessing is for sins and I haven't committed any. I've always worked for the good of this establishment, to care for people, to advance a burgeoning science. Do you think the will of the Holy Spirit is enough for that?"

"Do you mean to say that money is also the reason for your blind attachment?"

A breach seemed to open in his gaze.

"Believe what you want. It matters little to me. This asylum is my whole life," he said.

"To the point of making you complicit in the worst of abjections?"

He didn't react.

"This is the moment to redeem yourself a little. There's still time."

His eyes darkened and I saw the breach close instantly.

"Remorse is the burden of weak men. No one can change the past, no one," he said.

"And that child who will never know his history, does that matter little to you as well?"

"It's no doubt the best thing that could happen to him."

Out of arguments, overcome with anger, that was the first time I regretted being a man of the Church. If that hadn't been the case, I would have brandished a weapon, anything at hand, to threaten him, to force him to take me to Rose. My words had been my sole weapons, and they hadn't been enough.

"I ask that you listen to your conscience, nothing more," I said as a last resort.

"Heaven has never appealed to me. I imagine that one would be bored stiff there."

The doctor rose, walked toward the door, and opened it wide. I turned but didn't move.

"Out. I have work!" he said.

I had lost all hope of seeing Rose. I crossed the room, then the threshold, holding the door to keep him from closing it.

"In the face of death, no lie is more powerful than God," I said coldly, remembering Edmond's words: *I'll kill him.*

He gave a faint, distant smile.

"Are you so sure about that? Coming from a man who's made a profession out of lying, I can't say I'm bothered," he said shutting the door.

The Man

*H*e was somewhere far away, farther than the hands of my watch could reach.

A body carried by the shadows it casts, given life by the smells in the air. He strokes the horse, then begins to walk. Child-man and animal side by side, slowly advancing down the path, without hesitation. His youthful drives haven't yet deserted him entirely, a few buds ready to bloom, surrounded by a thin layer of frost. And spring is finally here.

At the time, I was no longer expecting anything else in my life.

He doesn't know how far he's already come. He advances, without turning around. Finally stops before the small house with the thatched roof. The horse snorts loudly, shakes its head, and then calms.

I'd stopped making up stories long before.

Standing in the house's shadow, the man seems to be seeking some meaning for what he sees, after what the servant of God just revealed to him. He observes the young man, knowing, for some unclear reason, that the words should in no case come from him, or maybe that there won't be any words.

I had given up on ever leaving. Where would I have gone anyway?

The young man releases the bridle, which goes taut as the simple result of gravity. The two ends now hang on either side of the horse's head, like exaggerated fish barbels. The man moves forward, emerging from the shadows, and stops once the boundary has been crossed. His face is a cold furnace, this face that hasn't aged much. And the young man advances a little more too, so the two are only separated by four or five yards, and perhaps still a chasm.

The sun was chasing away the white frost.

The young man stretches out one arm, as if preparing to point to something. Begins to roll his shirtsleeve to the bend in his elbow and higher still, to the spot where a few muscles have developed, that bears a glowing red mark in the shape of a leaf, which, itself, hasn't grown since childhood.

How could I have guessed?

He drops his arm along his body. Doesn't move any farther, gaze set somewhere other than on the man's eyes, set on his face, though: forehead, nose, chin; little matter, as long as it's not his eyes. Then he steps back, stretches the other arm behind him. His hand instinctually finds the bridle. Grabs it. It could finish like this, now, if only he would turn around and go. But it's too late, and they both know it. Now that they're one person, through the shared mark imprinted in their flesh. All the ageless man can see is the mark he had gradually forgotten, by training himself to avoid glancing in mirrors, windows, and puddles. He, they, still don't have the words, not a one, not even that word that burns them, which isn't the same word, and yet means the same thing.

How could I have imagined?

Later, once they've finally entered the house, they still won't be able to say the word, or even write it, not that day; two buds on a rootstock, nourished by the same sap, which spring is preparing to reveal to them. Perhaps they'll even do everything in their power to tell themselves that such a word doesn't exist, for a short while, without believing it for a single second. But try as they might, in the end they'll understand that you don't decide not to know a thing, despite the regrets gathered. Both pairs of hands empty, but each man feeling the mark's considerable weight, knowing that far more time than they could ever have is needed to become that something for the other that they never ceased to be.

Edmond

It was after the vicar's visit.

The birds weren't singing as usual.

I saw him arrive from nowhere, leading Janus by the bridle, haversack over his shoulder.

You'd have thought they'd fallen out of a stormy sky.

The light was amusing itself making them both dance.

He was holding the bridle right near the horse's mouth, in that way that makes it so you can really feel their touch on your hand.

Every time the horse moved its head, his arm followed without resisting.

They were one.

That kind of bond.

He said nothing.

He looked at me as if he didn't really see me, like he could look through me.

He dropped the bridle.

He surely wanted to give me a chance to go down the path alone.

I couldn't move.

He took a few steps toward me, and the horse did the same.

They stopped.

He slowly pushed up his shirtsleeve to his upper arm, and I saw the mark appear on his skin.

Dear Lord.

I felt a burning at the same spot.

I put my hand there, to try to cool it.

I didn't know what to do with it all yet.

My stomach was an anthill.

Good God, it was him.

He reached out to grab the bridle, without even looking.

I was scared he would leave.

He gently turned the horse around and went to attach it to a fence post, beneath the cherry tree, looping over the bridle but not making a knot.

That kind of bond.

He took his time.

My head was a funnel jammed with questions.

I went inside the house.

I knew he would follow me.

My legs were the opposite of heavy, not that they had become light all of a sudden, more like they were floating in some element that negated their weight.

He didn't close the door behind him.

I sat at the table.

He sat across from me and leaned to the side.

He took out a slate, a piece of chalk, and a rag from his sack, and set them on the table.

I understood that I would never hear the sound of his voice.

He stayed like that without doing anything, staring at the objects, fingers curled, but not entirely, as if he was holding a glass in each hand.

His eyes were shining when he looked up.

He was there to learn his true history.

So that's what I did, I told him everything from the beginning, everything I knew, what I had believed, and what the vicar had told me.

I swore to him that I had thought he was Charles's own son, that I had never seen the mark on his arm before that day, that after his accident, I didn't know what had become of him, that I had tried, but that nobody would tell me anything.

I swore so he would believe me.

If only I had known.

If only I hadn't packed so much earth over what happened in the stable with Rose.

If only.

The whole time I was talking, he looked at the chalk in his hand, never me.

When I was done, he turned toward the open door.

The cherry tree branches were swaying against the blue of the sky, and the horse was grazing on a tuft of fescue.

I can't think why I remember that.

He took a deep breath.

Then he started to write.

The chalk broke between his fingers.

I could read the word "*MOTHER*" upside down, with the leg of the *R* dangling like a snake from a branch.

His mother.

Christ.

I told him more about Rose, I invented what I didn't know to make her even more beautiful.

He started to write again.

He told me about the string of chances that led him to find me.

I began believing in chance, that day.

When he was finished, he placed one hand on the other.

I couldn't do otherwise but let myself be trapped by his gaze.

I don't think he wanted to make me pay for anything.

He rubbed his fingers and chalk dust flew away in a little cloud.

I don't think that's all that flew away.
I wanted to believe it.
Good God.
That kind of bond.
Outside, the birds began to sing again.
We didn't know what to do with it all.
So, we waited.

Gabriel

We have nothing to hope from the past. It is man alone who had the audacity to invent time, to make of it partitions for our lives. No one can live long enough to truly seize upon what it means to exist, no one is capable of catching life as it comes. And I am too lucid not to despair that I never did so myself. Only the past courses through us. It always rises to the surface in the end, like a bobbing cork, encumbered by legends born of great passions, great dreams, and immeasurable suffering; all that and nothing more than that. Legends age, they crumble alongside us, and they are rendered anew, endlessly.

I aged too, even more than I could have imagined. To what end? After all these years, all I've learned is that it's futile to combat evil, that wanting to challenge it with your bare hands is already believing yourself the equal of God, a little. So I ask his forgiveness. I tried to pull the cursed sword from the anvil, to undo the spell. Yes, I tried, and I deny nothing.

Of course, I know that faith can do nothing to bend the path of truth, but I console myself with the thought that it can at least better hearts and nourish minds. Changing the course of this story and no other is something I never would have dreamt of before Rose. My prayers had always been intended to guard against misfortune, never to modify the past as it suited me. Yet despite everything, before the first page of this diary written by the poor woman whose secret fell upon me to carry, I find myself doubting God's power to shape our fates without favoring some over others.

O Lord who taketh away the sins of the world, have mercy, keep me from succumbing to the temptation of a spiritual vacuity, which would deliver me from the suffering of another. Deliver me from the doubt that is at this moment weighing upon my own devoted soul. Deliver me from all evil, from its flames, for the rest of my life and forever and always. Amen.

I HAVEN'T SLEPT MUCH in a long time, immune to the night that normally guides men toward rest. Whatever light remains, it's always too dark for my mind to surrender to slumber. Now, I sense the darkest of nights approaching, the final slumber, another reason to cling to my memories. I want to lose nothing of that last flame that will soon flicker out.

Despite the time gone by, I remember them perfectly, sitting at the table in the thatched house after my visit to the asylum, me still not understanding, dwelling on my defeat. The room was swept by waves of emotion, but none of us dreamt of protecting ourselves. I was observing Charles, trying to identify what it was that had clearly changed in him, a gleam of light bouncing around his eyes before finally settling. Edmond rushed to tell me the unbelievable truth. He didn't use the word "son" that day. I hope he's had countless occasions to use it since. When he was done, Edmond asked me what I had learned at the asylum. The doctor would have none of it, I explained, but at least Rose was alive. A long silence followed, during which I wondered how Charles had been placed as a sacristan so close to his home. There looked to be nothing miraculous about it. The doctor had no doubt orchestrated everything, to keep an eye on Charles. He wasn't the sort of man who would have left anything to chance, after buying the manor, certainly for next to nothing, paying a few bribes in the process, so he could continue to fund the asylum. I said none of that. Then Charles, as if some savage determination had possessed him, grabbed the chalk and began drawing shapes on the slate. Edmond and I watched him, incredulous, thinking that his reason was drowning in the flood of revelations. Nothing of the sort. We would soon learn what he had in mind.

TODAY, I hold Rose's story in my hands, though I don't understand why I have been its bearer for forty-four years. It feels to me like I've made a long journey in her company, that I've followed the same paths that closed behind her, like an insurmountable wall was being built at the same time. I still don't know where she came from, but who she was, certainly. I never met her, or even glimpsed her; and yet, not a day goes by that I don't think of her.

WHEN HE LEFT MY EMPLOY, Charles at first refused to take the diary with him. I imagine that he thought, in order to write a new story, he needed to erase the old one, so that no arrears remained, now that he knew who he was. I succeeded in convincing him nonetheless. He thanked me for everything I had done, adding that we would likely never see one another again, that he was happy to have known and served me. I won't say how I answered him. I am keeping that emotion deep inside myself, and the way I showed it in the end.

DAY BREAKS. I look at the altar cross on the shelf, where it presides outside of services. The words of the Gospel according to Saint Mark come back to me: *Jesus began to teach them that the Son of man must suffer many things and be killed, if he wants to rise again.* There's nothing to add. It's time to pay a final homage to Rose, the only one I still can. I bring the diary that I meticulously copied with me. My hands begin to tremble, one of those laws from which an old man cannot escape, as if the final hesitations of the body were nothing but the rattling of the soul on its way. It's time to go.

I'M ALREADY FAR from the village when I hear the seven tolls rung by Victor, my new sacristan, thirty years my junior. Carried by old legs weary from treading these parts countless times, I pass the first lock of the monks' canal, then enter the forest, still following the stone-hemmed waterway constructed centuries ago to supply the monastery, where faith once found itself walled in, and later madness: as if neither could be comprehended by the rest of humanity, or even seen; as if everything that surpasses reason must be hidden from the world, whatever its expression. And I, a mortal servant, am I sufficiently armed to fight off the doubt that still sets my questions afire with human responses? Do I need more time to better arm myself? Or isn't all this doubt merely an illusion, in my poor penitent's hands, which will turn to certainty once I'm in the Lord's? I am far too old to lose everything today.

The canal passes over an abrupt canyon carved by a stream that cuts the forest in half. Its wild waters contrast with the canal's domestic trickle, which ends in a bed of sand where a few fearful crayfish are moving backward; two liquid rhythms, two distinct paths, born from the same source; like two children from the same parents, but whose characters differ greatly. I walk for a time beneath a cover of hornbeam, beech, and oak trees, the sires of great woods; soon reaching a line of ash and elderberry trees bordering a grass-covered prairie trapped in the heart of the forest plunging toward the valley. I think to myself that nature, like humans, can express its own madness, can in a certain way embrace it.

I continue another hundred yards along the canal now almost entirely masked by tall eagle ferns with new shoots in the shape of a bishop's cross. In the distance I see the chapel spire emerging from the canopy, lost amid tendrils of mist like a gigantic dagger, its hilt adorned by a rosette planted in the rotting sky of history. Energy spent, I sit on a flat rock, not far from the now-sealed entrance to the underground tunnel Charles and Edmond cleared to free Rose.

I know they succeeded. Know nothing more. I think of the doctor's astonishment upon discovering her empty room, and begin to smile at the thought. I imagine the three of them, fleeing hand in hand, happy somewhere, perhaps near an ocean, a sea, in the mountains, or anywhere else, far from the suffering of the past. I hope it with all my heart.

News of the escape never left the asylum. I don't know how the doctor handled it. Perhaps an empty coffin was transported out shortly after. In any case, I heard nothing about it and the doctor never again called on me or sought to see me. Though he must have suspected my involvement, a meeting would have confronted him with his own failure, at least that's what I still think. He's been dead a long time and the forest has reclaimed the Forges estate.

I REMAIN STILL, cocooned by happiness, theirs, which I would like to believe is real. My breathing is relaxed as I listen to the sounds coming from the monastery, traveling beneath the surface, as if a pious monk in a habit was speaking to me from the depths of another millennium. Space and time brought together. Will remain joined until the end; that great end that I so fervently desire. But before diving into the abyss, I scratch at the loose layer of undergrowth with my hands, dig a few inches into the earth, then I bury Rose's diary and wipe away the traces. It's now time to join the Lord, in the silence of men.

Epigraph credits

Ralph Waldo Emerson epigraph from "Character," *Essays: Second Series*, 1844.

Franz Kafka epigraph from *The Diaries of Franz Kafka, 1910–1923*, edited by Max Brod, translated by Joseph Kresh. Copyright 1948, 1949 by Schocken Books Inc. Copyright renewed 1975, 1976 by Schocken Books, Inc.

Fyodor Dostoevsky epigraph from *Crime and Punishment*, translated by Richard Pevear and Larissa Volokhonsky. Translation copyright © 1992 by Richard Pevear and Larissa Volokhonsky. Published by Vintage Books, a division of Random House, Inc, New York.